-T

M000032280

"*Creation by Emergence* – Vincenzo Scipioni, I am in awe of this man and his works, as he seems to transcend any form of measurement. His insights into his life, and the world around him is enthralling and has me wanting to drink more of him. My thirst is still not quenched and quite frankly I never want it to be satisfied. It's rare for me to fall in love with such art, but I have...because it is truly beautiful. But what is life without discovery? Go on...I urge you to take a look for yourself." –Oleuanna Twig, Academic & Writer

@oleuanna

"Vincenzo Scipioni is the greatest American writer since Mark Twain, and time will show his legacy of work rivals Mark, Luke, Matthew, and James. This is the best collection of short stories written this century." –Matt Bruno, Educator

"*Silent Pages, Loud Thoughts, Short Stories* is like thirty great books in one! This modern classic is passionate in its language, potent in its emotional effect, and discusses many truths often overlooked in today's society. Anyone who reads this collection of short stories will certainly be moved and never forget them. I just finished reading Volume One, and I hope I don't have to wait too long for Volume Two to come out." –Ryan Brown, Director/Independent Film Maker

VINCENZO SCIPIONI

Silent Pages, Loud Thoughts, Short Stories
Volume I

published in a joint venture with

Wood Press Publications
P.O. Box 700
Saint James, New York 11780

First Edition Book Cover Design, Layout, & Editing by:
Vincenzo Scipioni
@UnSeeingEyes

ISBN-13: 978-0615657561 (Wood Press Publications)

ISBN-10: 0615657567

CONTENTS

"... a living dog is better
than a dead lion."

-Ecclesiastes 9:4

Dedicated to:

My family, teachers, friends, and you the reader.

Reader's Thoughts & Notes Page

Some people go to church; I go to the sea. Not in the wee hours of the morning when you have the athletes jogging before the sun rises above the horizon and it gets too hot; or those nuts walking their dogs, because heaven forbid you bring a dog to the beach when there are people—oh how stupid of me, I forgot that's against the rules. I don't go during the afternoon either because it would be too crowded, and crazy for me, with children running around kicking up sand like little animals, and teenagers blasting music for the entire beach to hear—but that is alright. It's legal to kick sand in someone's face or make a ridiculous ruckus while they're sleeping on a blanket. No, only do I go to the beach when it is black, and the stars and the moon are my only source of light, and my friends silently surround and comfort me.

The beach is wonderful in the night; it is so tranquil and peaceful. Listening to the waves crash, and the wind whipping through the air; I don't have to see to know what is happening around me.

It is a real shame that I must park my Jeep so far away in the trees and sneak onto the beach undetected. The first few times I had to feel my way through the darkness, through the trees and listen for the sea; but now, now I can walk to my favorite beach—my sanctuary, after dusk, when it's illegal to be there, in my sleep. Can you believe that? I am not allowed to enjoy this glorious atmosphere without breaking the law.

So if I break that law so easily, and have done so

nightly ever since I could drive a car, then I surely might as well break another. Part of my nightly ritual is, before going to the beach I make myself a perfect cinnamon hazelnut coffee, with just a touch of half n' half, and a pinch of sugar. By the time I get to my spot, and ascend the lifeguard's chair, my coffee is at a drinkable temperature, and the joint in my pocket is ready for me to smoke.

Yes, in America, for smoking a joint, drinking a coffee, and sitting in the lifeguard's chair after dusk, a police officer can lock me up. It baffles the mind. One time, in fact it was the day my cousin died, I felt the spot light upon my shoulder just as I lit up.

An officer said, "You! You over there! Get over here now! Get down from that chair! What on God's earth are you doing?!" So, I replied back as I descended, "What does it look like I'm doing officer? I am enjoying God's beautiful earth in all of its magnificence, I'm drinking a coffee, pondering my cousin's death, and I'm smoking a joint you stupid bastard—and you, you just ruined my fucking night, and destroyed my peace!"

And after saying that, I took off running through the sand as fast as I could, running in a sort of zigzag like an alligator was chasing me; coffee in one hand, joint in another, I disappeared into the night avoiding that invasive spotlight. I surely wasn't going to leave my friends behind, after all they've been so good to me, and never hurt anyone. When I was safely beyond the reach of capture and punishment, I was happy to have half a joint and half a coffee.

People are being mugged, raped, murdered, and this out of shape bastard has to bust my chops and ruin my beautiful night? Who am I hurting? Who am I bothering? Am I making any noise? Am I destroying anything? That's the kind of asshole I wish would have a heart attack and die.

A normal officer, one with half a brain, would have said, "Are you alright?" I would have replied, "Yes sir I am, just enjoying this beautiful night." And then he would have said, "Enjoy the rest of your night," and I'd reply, "You do the same sir." Now that I think about it, I would have even accepted a good old, "Stay out of trouble." "Get over here now;" who the fuck does he think he is—a man with a badge, fancy uniform, and gun—I am supposed to respect that? Hell, Hitler had a really nice uniform, lots of flashy medallions and a gun as well you know. Where was that officer, or any officer, when I was in Harlem at dusk, surrounded by five men wanting to gut me like a fish, take all my personal belongings, and leave me for dead?

You know if I had a fast car, like a Ferrari or something, and if I were extremely rich, I wouldn't even stop for the police. I would drive to my closest mansion, close the gates, and have my own private army take care of anyone who trespasses and infringes on my autonomy. I would choose not to recognize any of the state and federal laws once on my personal property, and declare myself as living in what I would call "True America."

All governments, all laws conveniently left out the most important part of Kant's philosophy didn't they? And it breaks my heart to know that my government is hardly any better than those around the world. For how intelligent and advanced we are, it's disturbing to me just how ass backwards we've become. We vote for these morons who make the laws and amend our Constitution for the worse. More laws, more constrictions are turning our society into a bunch of mindless bastards who don't think for themselves. We live in a policed state. With every coming year, with each new President, our Constitution is becoming tarnished, weakened, and ultimately will be destroyed. Our civil freedoms and liberties—what is that, what does that mean? Our forefathers—who were they, what were their intentions? How quickly we forgot.

Given any jackass can be a police officer; because after all they are merely pawns obliged to uphold asinine laws, and quote...unquote help people—it's not even worth my time to talk about this. Governments in general; that pig destroying my night; my country's views on explicit sex and violence in popular culture; gays; abortion; marijuana; privacy— those things aren't the point of this story.

Every night, besides that one incident, after finishing my coffee, and smoking my joint, and gazing at the Big Dipper or North Star, or the light Gatsby spoke about, or into the sea thinking about whatever it is that's on my mind; I always throw the roach regardless of its size into the sea, as my offering, as my gift. I don't need to save it, or be selfish and smoke all of it, and I appreciate the sea continuing to work hard every day and bring me peace of mind, so it deserves at the very least a gesture of gratitude.

One night I got to the beach in the early morning—still before the joggers, and the folks with their dogs, but a lot later than I usually do. And I decided to leave my roach up upon the lifeguard's chair, and stick around to see what happens.

Soon, the crazies came and left. And I would say approximately forty-five minutes later, I heard a car in the distance. A beautiful woman arrived. Let me tell you, she could save my life any day. She was 5'8" or 5'9", with long blonde hair, blue eyes, and flawless skin. Definitely movie star material if you ask me.

After taking off her shirt and shorts, I noticed she was wearing the standard one-piece red bathing suit, with white lettering on the front and back saying, "Lifeguard;" and it was creeping up her crack ever so slightly showing her glorious ass. As if the whistle around her neck, her bronzed skin, and her impeccable physique didn't give her away off the bat. Anyway, now she was the only one on the beach, and I was tucked away at a safe viewable distance; just far enough so she couldn't see me.

Mind you there is that old adage that, "the truth is stranger than fiction," and in this case that phrase most definitely holds true. I couldn't make up a story like this if I tried, and it is perfect just the way it is, so I won't embellish in the slightest.

She climbed to her seat, as she probably has so many times before, with a brown paper bag in hand. While arranging her coffee, orange juice, everything bagel, and muffin, she happened to notice the roach. When she noticed it, I saw her take a few glances in every direction, and when she saw not a soul around, she decided to pick it up. With one swift leap she was off the chair, on the sand, roach in hand. She opened her purse, which was placed on a picnic table adjacent to the lifeguard's chair, and pulled out a lighter.

Being sure to cup her hand and block the wind,

13

like a true smoking professional, she started to smoke away. I would say she enjoyed that roach for at least five minutes and got a good number of hits off of it; and why shouldn't she? I know I'm perfectly capable of snapping out of it, and if need be, no intoxicant would stop me from performing a task like driving a car, or saving a child from a burning house.

But perhaps she got more stoned than she could handle; after all I only smoke the best hydro around, and I noticed her gazing out into the sea. More specifically, she was looking at the floating markers defining the parameters people are able to swim within. How large it was she must have thought, because with an Olympians speed, she swam out to the markers, dove deep under the sea, and started to move them. When she was finished what was once the size of more than a football field was reduced to the size of a tennis court—for a singles game mind you.

Upon exiting the water, and toweling herself off, she gazed at what she had just done with a certain sense of accomplishment and satisfaction, for she just made her work day easier by at least ten fold, and it's not like any superiors would be around to check on her. The lifeguard after all is the boss of the beach. Perhaps the person who runs the concession stand would be by later in the morning, and they could both have a good laugh.

Well, it's easy to tell a hot day when it's before 8:00a.m. and you're profusely sweating and those damn cicada bugs won't such the hell up. I knew that day was going to a scorcher and the beach would be packed. Sure enough the families came; the screaming, kicking, shitting little kids, dragging all their beach toys with unenthused parents lugging beach chairs, umbrellas, and coolers; the pasty uninspired and disrespectful teens; the fat bastards wearing socks and sneakers; the book readers trying to find that quiet place — you name it, my beach was packed, and it was unbearably hot.

And where did everyone swim? Yes, people were actually walking fifty, sixty, seventy feet or more, just so they could be in the defined parameters under the lifeguard's supervision. People were next to one another packed like sardines, and couldn't even swim. In the deep water you just had people smiling like mongoloids, bobbing up and down next to one another. Mothers screaming and reprimanding their children for walking along the shoreline even if only one toe was in the water, "It only takes one inch of water for you to drown, now go over by the lifeguard."

I couldn't believe it, not one person questioned a fucking thing! The lifeguard never even had to use her whistle — not even once. Wasn't anyone at the beach the previous day, didn't they notice the difference? Did they think it was a new rule or something?

I don't blame the lifeguard, after all if you can do something like that, and make your minimum wage job easier, and get away with it why not? God forbid someone was to ever drown, you have tremendous responsibilities as a lifeguard; a hell of a lot more than the bitch who sells ice cream sandwiches and makes just as much money as you.

I don't blame her; if a superior was to come, she could have come up with something quick like, "Today I was feeling a bit under the weather, and the safety of all the beach's patrons is my number one priority. In order to perform to the best of my abilities, without endangering another's life, just for today I decided to move the markers in;" and that would have been good enough. I blame the people, or shall I say the cattle, the mindless buffoons. You know, I'm going to go back to the beach during the day; I'm going to confront that girl; tell her I saw what she did — and get her to go out with me! What a set of balls!! Did I mention her physique, and that ass you could bounce a quarter off of?

Sometimes there have been those moments where everything seems to piece together. Lights flickering on the Tiber flow as if part of an ancient voice standing silent for hundreds of silent dreaming years. While sitting on a boat, enjoying an elegant dinner, a few bottles of Chianti, and observing the beautiful landscape of Roma, I thought to myself; this is the one I want to dance with until the end of days; this is the person I'm going to marry. Still the moon is up there, silent, his lighting voice talking only when everybody else is dripping and sipping from their tiny glasses, to learn the sip of truth from the darkest Baccus word.

And what is this sip of truth; is it knowing when you can effortlessly glide through life, or is it when you just know the unknown? HOW CAN YOU KNOW the unknown, I asked myself while trying to concentrate on the dim waves made by our small boat disturbing the quietness of the ancient ruins set there for a reason…to let us know. And when I close my eyes, and listen to this ancient city, listen to the gods, the river, and the moon, and Baccus, without knowing I know everything; I know that I was put here for a reason and that reason was to love Theresa.

And what more love can be given by a lightning bolt thrown out from a chariot, two people sitting there for a moment, having experienced the grandeur of human hope… …the very beginning of human hope… …a new continent, a new nation, celebrated in the silence of the dark night sky.

"Do you want some more of it?"… she asked me as I placed my hand behind her head gently leaning forward giving her a soft but electrifying kiss that seemed to last an eternity. When the kissing became more passionate, and our seats weren't conducive for exploring each other's physical bodies, inspired by a moment of sheer bliss, I swept her up, and laid her on my bed.

We both aren't the kind of people who normally do this, but then again this is the first time we met in this life and the excitement of our past lives, and our finally finding each other was too much to bear.

"Ayuda mi, ayuda mi per favorre," her pants were a labyrinth, and I couldn't wait another second, I needed to taste her sweet nectar; I dared to eat that peach. And with one fluid motion, by her left hand, her belt unbuckled, her pants were open, and I knew paradise, my final resting place was behind a pair of red panties. So there we were, recreating a dream, re-experiencing what we had so many worlds ago, fitting together, exploring what just felt right.

The next morning Theresa was unfortunate enough to have to go to work, work on a Saturday, and at eight in the morning. We had passionately made love for many hours, only sleeping for approximately two, but it was easy to wake up, we need not sleep, we found each other, and were high with love and hope. I proceeded to make her caffé, and while she sipped caffé, I drank a glass of milk, and with rejuvenated eyes we giggled and kissed some more.

Not before long, she was in and out of the shower, and I forcefully made her let me accompany her to work. Why she didn't want me to walk her is beyond me, but once we started walking she was happy to have me by her side. On *di Ponte Santa Angelo* she showed me her favorite angel, and with the Vatican in the background, and the sky almost violet, the view was breathtaking. It was the saddest looking of all the angels; in her face was much lamentation, and I joking said, "She's probably sad because she can't see the grandeur of the Vatican behind her.

You know Theresa works for a tour company at the Vatican, and the Coliseum, and told me, "I know a little something about Roma; I can show you around some time." Finally we arrived at a destination where she demanded I turn around and start my day. She only had to walk a bit further. I gave her a little spin, we kissed for a few moments, and when we finished, she leaned in to give me one last kiss while keeping her eyes locked with mine. Then she walked away into the distance never turning back, but knowing I was there watching her.

I watched her fade into the distance until I could not see her anymore, never expecting it to be the last time I would see or hear from my Theresa. But, who knows how women work; who knows what they think about? Where was all the sadness and indifference behind her eyes stemming from? Why after finally finding each other, knowing we are right, does she question herself rather than floating down the river of romance and life?

I will always remember gazing at pure delight and having wide open eyes for the first time since I was a child; and I will try to view this life, and the next, as a perpetual unwrapping of time, space, and experiences

—always dreaming and hoping that perhaps the next time, there will be more than just those few fleeting moments.

But who knows? Perhaps once again in this life, she will be compelled to find me and dance a little. After all, with her I am completely at peace, so naturally my world stops for her. But I sincerely don't think I will ever see her again. I sincerely don't. And perhaps it's because she is more afraid than I, afraid of what might happen, but I guess I'll never know.

Senza una fine?

I remember perfectly polished brown shoes with three horizontal straps and silver buckles. I remember beautiful dresses with vivid pastel floral patterns. I remember having freshly squeezed glasses of very thick pinkish orange juice and warm silver dollar pancakes drenched in maple syrup. I remember a new white rug that I got chocolate ice cream all over and her saying, "Don't worry, it's only a rug." —but I cannot remember the pitch or tone of her voice.

I remember beautiful soft hands that ran up and down the piano fingerboard, but I cannot hear what was being played. I remember beautiful brown hair, pearl white teeth, and crystal blue eyes, strong shoulders, a slender waist, and strong calf muscles always adorned with nude stockings.

I remember the aroma of her perfume; all the times she beat me at checkers, all the times she helped me win, even her beautiful smile—but the two things I cannot remember are the sound of her voice and her entire face.

Pictures can rekindle some of my memories, but sometimes I just make myself believe that I remember the exact moment in the picture when I really do not. Why is it that I can only remember scattered bits and pieces of moments, fragments of her face, but never the whole moment, the entire face? Do I really remember these images, or were they told and shown to me so many times that I fool myself into believing that I remember them? I really don't know.

The one event that I remember though, I swear it

feels as if it happened yesterday, is a rather sad moment. I can't quite see her face in my head, but I remember the conversation we had word for word, and I see a mouth moving with teeth that didn't seem to fit, but no sound is coming out. When I relive the event in my head, I am the narrator for both characters — her and myself.

I see a sick woman who physically deteriorated faster than it takes chocolate ice cream to melt on the hottest of hot days. I still can't figure out why out of all the people in the world, she was struck with this horrible, fatal cancerous disease. She said to me, "Anthony — can you help me up? I am tired and I really want to take a nap." I said, "Yes, Nana, I can help you!" I was honored that she would even ask me; she usually asked my Aunt Vicki, or my Uncle Paul, or my Mom, or my Dad. She then said to me, "Are you sure you are strong enough?"

I can still feel her hands on my shoulders pushing herself up. I was thinking, what happened to you, Nana? Why are you so thin and frail? You are supposed to be helping me. Why aren't you getting better? Why can't you get better? Just at that instant, her hand slipped off my shoulder and I WAS NOT STRONG ENOUGH. I couldn't catch her. The only image I'm sure wasn't fabricated in my mind is the image of my Nana, the love of my life, hitting the floor — and there was nothing I could do to help her. I just watch her fall like tree in a hurricane.

I ask you this one question — why is it the thing I remember about my Nana frame by frame, the one thing that I want to forget? Why can't I remember all the times we laughed and played outside? Why can't I remember her singing to me? Why can't I remember how her hands felt when she gave me a hug, or how her lips felt on my cheek when she gave me a kiss? The photographs I see of me with her make me cry still to this day, because I really don't remember; I only remember one thing completely, and I know it won't dull or fade with time — I will never forget — my Nana.

-The Painter

Once I was a young man... ...although I vaguely remember; for my art has consumed my life. A few million cigarettes, a couple thousand bottles of wine and vodka, and more women than I can, or care to count, have gotten me to this point; alone with my brushes, my acrylics and oils, my empty canvases, and the same vision I had so many years ago—the one of my youth.

My mother always told me to build to my vision, to my dream, and not to my limitations. She said the only limitations an artist possibly has are those in the confusion and chaos they have created in their mind. My mind has been cluttered with stories, experiences, philosophies, theories, and images—none of which have brought me closer to my vision, to my dream.

I've only wanted to paint, to create one piece— yes, just one picture, the one that has been burned into my mind's eye for countless years now. I remember seeing it, before I even knew what it was as a child; hell who am I kidding, I still don't even know what it is, but I do know it is beautiful. It is so beautiful that I've felt obligated to recreate it; I've spent my entire life trying to replicate it so I can share it with the world.

Sometimes, in fact more times than not, I've viewed it as a plague, and I just wished the damned thing would fade away, but that hasn't been the case. With age it has only gotten more vivid, bolder, and consumed more and more of my mind and my time. Some days I've tried to drink it away, and other days I have feverishly painted for hours upon hours, sleeping only for minutes at a time, because God only knows how much it would kill me if I missed the minute, or the second, when I would possess whatever it is I've been missing up until this point to paint the picture of my mind, the passion of my life.

There are so many tangents I want to go off on now, so I suppose this tangent is as good as any to begin with. Right before my mother's passing, some thirty odd years ago, she told me a story. Perhaps to make me feel better, or maybe because she somehow knew where I would be at this point in my life, at all points in my life; in actuality, I'm not quite sure why she told me the story, nor do I really understand it. I don't remember all the minute details of the story because after all I'm a painter, not a storyteller, and at the same time I don't think my mother ever intended for me to remember what she said verbatim, but the story goes something like this:

There was once this Chinese man whose name was Chuang-tzu. He was an accomplished man with many skills, one of them being a draftsman; he was in fact the very best draftsman of his time. The king of China sent for him, and immediately Chuang-tzu went to see the king. The king wanted Chuang-tzu, this very skilled man to draw for him a crab. The king asked for a picture of a fucking crab! Chuang-tzu of course told the king he would draw a crab for him, but he had some stipulations. He needed a house in the country away from everything, he needed twelve servants, and he also needed five years. The king had no problem with that, and met all of Chuang-tzu's requests.

After five years, not only was the drawing not finished yet, it still hadn't even been begun. Chuang-tzu asked the king for another five years, and this king must have been a very tolerant man, and believed in his abilities because he granted him another five years. After ten years, ten years, Chuang-tzu picked up a brush, and in a split second, with a single stroke, he painted a crab — the most precise, the most beautiful, the most perfect crab anyone has ever seen.

Mom, if you can hear me, what in the hell am I supposed to take from this story?!?! You and your stories,... you and your proverbs! A perfect crab? Was the chink thinking about this fucking crab for ten years, and when he used a single stroke, it was a stroke that had been premeditated and practiced in his mind for ten years?

That's why I never really valued writers, story-tellers, or religious texts because there is always some underlying or "hidden" meaning; or is there really? Maybe that is just what we as humans have come to think. We need closure, or we need to look into things, we need to know "what's correct;" and most of the time I think we see things that the author or storyteller never intended for us to see, or we just draw conclusions that are convenient and comforting for us. Instead of just showing me, or telling me what I need to know, written texts and stories always tend to "beat around the bush" with fancy words and imagery ultimately saying very little or nothing at all — well, at least that's the case for me.

Like take the stories of Adam and Eve, or Abraham and Isaac? From Adam and Eve I suppose I learned that when God tells you not to do something, don't do it? I mean what a stupid story. Women are nice cuts of meat, because they are created from the rib of a man. They are evil temptresses who will ultimately cause your demise. 'Mulier est hominis confusio.' The reason humans live with pain and illness is because of some evil bitch named Eve, and some moron who ate a fucking apple? That makes perfect sense, some jackass eats an apple and all of mankind for eons to come is damned. And besides that, God has never spoken to me, or told me to do or not do anything, so how can I even relate?

Or Abraham, what a stupid bastard that guy was! So God says to him, I want you to take your first born, your only son, the son you have waited your entire life for, and bring him to the top of a mountain, and kill him. Abraham doesn't even blink, doesn't even think, he says "sure!" What should I have learned from this, to blindly follow a higher power that is asking me to conduct a malicious act? That makes a lot of sense.

Or how can I forget my favorite; the drunkard who couldn't even find his way out of a shoe-box building a boat that must have been the size of a continent, and putting two of every known animal aboard. See this is why the world is fucked up, because of stories, philosophies, theories, and religion that people try to make sense of and interpret, and believe they understand.

Aesop and his fables, he's another one—slow and steady wins the race. Wins what race? If you are sprinting 100 meters you better believe that slow won't win even a bronze. The written word, or oral stories, for me at least, have not expanded my mind; they have only cluttered it, and confused the shit out of me. It's not even pleasurable. The only reading I find pleasurable is reading that I can enjoy at face value, like when

27

"Samantha Something's" face and statistics are printed on the back of a milk carton because she has been missing for six months now. Facts, as horrible as they might be, for me are enjoyable to read; I was going to say history, but I know history is told by those with the power, and isn't really factual at all—it's always changing.

On this Wednesday, the children outside were singing a round of "Row, row, row your boat, gently down the stream...merrily, merrily, merrily, merrily, life is but a dream." They obviously aren't thinking about what they are singing, nor should they be because they are children and should be playing and having fun—but in a few years when they do think about that song they loved to sing, what will they, or what are they supposed to take away from that? I sure hope to God they don't come knocking on my door and ask me because I'll be damned if I can give them an answer about that, or about anything for that matter.

When I was a kid, I at least remember singing a good song with my buddies that started off, "There's a place in France where the naked ladies dance, there's a hole in the wall where the boys can see it all;" that's to the point, that song made some sense, that song got us interested in looking at each others' older sisters through the keyhole of the bathroom; and as we got a bit older and bolder, we just swung the doors right open and had ourselves a good hard look. The female body is so fantastic—we learned that young.

Or what about those people who go to the movies, and see films that "really makes you think?" Don't you think all of the God damn time already? Don't you think about what to eat tonight, or the bills you have to pay, or the folks you must telephone, or how taxes are killing you, or when are you going to find time to mow your lawn, trim your bushes, and wash your car, or how your favorite uncle is coming along with his cancer treatment, or when to take a shower and go to the bathroom, or about the dishes pilling up in your sink? I mean we think all of the time. If I were to go to the movies, and I haven't gone in years, but I want to see something fun; something entertaining, I want an escape! Not something that I must ponder because it is a microcosm for life and society or some shit. I'm just not interested in another movie about the travesties that happened in Nazi Germany. I'm sorry for my tirade; I guess that's probably why they say, "different strokes for different folks," and apparently I must be completely insane.

You know when I learned about myself—you know what spoke volumes to me in a number of seconds, I appreciated at face value, and then just stopped speaking; Michelangelo's David, and Sistine Chapel, or Picasso's Blue Period and his surrealist shit—I mean art, visual stimuli I have always felt, I understood, I knew, I experienced, I related to—not some stupid story my mother told me about a man who painted a perfect crab with one stroke. I love the irony, a wonderful storyteller, a lover of language and literature, giving birth to a frustrated and tormented artist who has never created a single painting he was happy with. But, in her defense, and God rest her soul because I love her and everything she did for me—at least she told me stories, and philosophies, and information that she thought was pertinent and would help me—ones that were at least aimed at helping me achieve my dream, and not hers. She never discouraged me from wanting to be an artist, from wanting to create my vision.

Also, I must give some credit to classical music—music that is free and flowing, and not controlled by repetitive phrases and monotonous melodies. I've had many wonderful nights blowing the doors off my car driving to Beethoven, or Mozart, or of course Vivaldi. The highs, the lows, the conquests, the defeats, and on and on and on; I hope classical music and great art never die, but it is very possible as people become more technologically advanced and simpler in their minds that Van Gough, and Bach will just be two names they once heard about in their youth and never experienced.

Well, I can honestly say, at this point in my life I only have one regret. Am I sad that I am alone? Not at all, I chose the life I led and I know this. At any time I could have given up, or stopped being such a perfectionist, settled down and had a family. But, I didn't want that, hence I never attracted those types of women.

The women I've had, or in some instances had me, were just sexual experiences. We just had fun together, we fucked, and when the act was complete, they went their way, and I went back to my painting. Every time except once, I've always woken up in my own bed, or on the floor or in some chair of some random room in my house—and every time except once, no one was around to make me breakfast.

Once I had a wonderful woman, who knew how I was, and knew that I could never love her as much as my work, and it didn't bother her in the slightest. She had an unexplained passion and love for me; I never understood what she saw in me, and why she wanted to be around me. She also had a very interesting name, and she once explained to me that her father was a lover of the dead language Latin, and Latin texts. Her name was Festina Lente Anderson, but she just went by *Festina Lente* because she despised her last name due to its ordinariness. For sure there are many many Andersons', but certainly only one Festina Lente.

I wish I could remember just want her name meant, after all she told me once, and told me that the translation of her name was much like my life, but after I forced her out of my life, I've never found the time or had an interest to research it. I just remember her name being a contradiction of sorts, and never thought much more about it than that. It's probably good I don't know what it means because that would just be another thing for me to think about, another thing to clutter my mind. But, I'm kind of happy I mentioned her, because now in retrospect, I mean I haven't thought about her in twenty-seven years at least, and now I understand that she like her name had something underlining and mysterious about her.

Why did I force her out of my life after having three of the most wonderful months of my life? Even though I could never love her as much as my work, I found myself wanting her, wanting to be around her, and with her. I found myself talking about nonsensical shit, and enjoying it—and I knew if I continued on this path, I would have a child with her, and then my dream, my vision, my passion for creating would have died with the birth of a child. I mean accidents happen, and one of these times she was going to hold me inside of her just long enough to fertilize her womb. The birth of a child for me I guess is like eating "the apple."

I would never be a bad father, because I had no father, and I know the impact that made on my life. I would have to dedicate my life to my child because that is what one should do, and that is an entrapment I almost fell into, but wasn't willing to. She was smart you see, respecting me for me, while at the same time being just elusive enough to entice and excite my interests. Well, enough about Festina Lente because she is no more to me now than a silent move, a collection of stills in my mind that are almost all but gone now.

Am I sad I've destroyed every one of my paintings after painting them, and now only have boxes upon boxes of photographs I've taken of my paintings before tearing and thrashing them into oblivion? I'm not sad at all about that. The truth is, I must destroy my paintings because they aren't quite right, none of them have been the one I am looking for, the one I see in my mind's eye. And if I didn't destroy them, if I didn't get out all that frustration and anger I had pent up inside in a somewhat socially acceptable way, then I don't know what I would do. Imagine having thousands of reminders staring you in the face every day — and where the hell would I have put all of them? After all, I have boxes upon boxes of photos taking up an entire room.

During the course of my life, I've experimented with types of paints, different colors, different textures, different brushes and knives, canvas ranging from the size of a pencil erasure which I had to paint on using a hair and a microscope, to canvas the size of the front of my house. I even painted on glass, on plastic, on wood

—I mean you name it, and I've certainly tried it. I remember once, I couldn't get the red just right, so I decided to slit my palm, make a fist, and squeeze a little warm blood into the paint. It was a beautiful red, but even that wasn't right. I'm just flat out of ideas—I know I have the ability, I also know I have all implements and paints known to man, so what is the problem? My recreations just don't have "it."

Why do I take photos of my paintings before destroying them? Well, everyone knows I'm an artist. That is how I make my livelihood. Believe it or not, my garage is a studio, and I give private lessons to people of all ages. The lesson is for only one hour a pop, I am extremely expensive, and I won't let a person have anymore than ten lessons from me. Why ten? Ten is as good of a number as any, and if I ever bump into a former student of mine on the street, I don't want to recognize them, or anything they've ever painted. I assign them each a number, and give them a card with my signature. Some students have spread their lessons over decades, others have done ten in ten days, but all have respected me, and never tried to have an eleventh. I've always been lucky I suppose, I must say my pupils have been very kind, and passionate, and had great determination. I wish them all the best of luck.

I am the very best teacher I've ever seen. I'm a pupil's dream. I wish as a child I had a teacher like me, or even close to me, although unfortunately I don't think it would have made a difference. I cater to each individual's needs, and help them to explore and develop their own visions, while at the same time never putting any value or tag on their art, or artistic beliefs. I also compare them to no one and nothing, for they are each unique and should be valued as being unique. Who the hell am I to judge? Could I paint the Empire State Building to scale using only my eyes, or could I paint as perfect of a portrait as one could possibly paint after only looking at someone for a second, a portrait of photographic quality, of course so! That is easy. But that was never my dream or vision. If you want to paint landscapes, or buildings, or people, or melting clocks, or bitches with three heads, that's fine with me, and I will teach you—but don't ask me to do that. I'm sensing that you are laughing a bit; why are you laughing? I know my shit my friend, and I don't have to prove anything to anyone other than myself.

My vision goes beyond time and space; I'm trying to paint everything and nothing at the same time. I'm talking about something so beautiful, so wonderful, that at the same time it's actually catastrophic and horrid. I'm talking about a living breathing piece of art that can see through you, and see all of you, and overwhelm you with emotions you didn't even know existed. I'm talking about something I can't possibly explain to you, because I can't explain it to myself nor can I recreate it, nor have I ever seen anything like it before.

I know my clock is ticking, I know my end is near. How long can someone continue to live on a diet of intoxicants, sex, and no sleep? I just want at the very least, when the stench of my decaying body is permeating throughout the neighborhood, and my grass and bushes are long overdue for maintenance, and the owner of the liquor store is curious to know where his best customer is—I want at the very least when they must break down my door to find out what in God's name has happened to me—at the very least I want them to see boxes upon boxes of photographs. My photographs are the only evidence that I have to illustrate that I've worked a lifetime, and didn't just sit around in my house jerking off everyday.

Fuck that, fuck everything, fuck this! You see what has become of me??? I'm destroying my house now. I don't need these paints, I don't need these brushes, these fucking glasses; I don't need anything anymore. Where are those boxes of pictures? Let me slide them over here and take look.

I know; I've never used this room before, now that I think of it I've never ever even been in this fucking room other than the time I set it up! God only knows I'd never had to entertain. Let me just flip my dining room table on its side like this and kick it against the wall; and let me just toss these chairs over here into the adjacent living room like this! Perfect, my dining room floor is a little dirty, but it's empty. Thank God I don't have any carpets in my home, I hate carpets—nothing looks better than hardwood floors.

Now let's spread these pictures out! Let's throw this shit around. Let's get crazy baby! Let's see all my failures spread out on the floor. Do you want to see my failures on the floor? I think you dooo. I think you dooooo. Box number one I'll splash into this corner. Box number two, why don't you go over here! Box number three, here's a spot. Number four; number four, are you ready? Sure you're ready four, I have to shake you out a bit because you have a few more. Numbers five and six; hell I'll throw you both together onto the floor at the same fucking time! Does that sound good to you? Of course it does!

Two more drinks for me, and I think this is going to work out nicely; half the floor is already covered and only six more boxes of pictures to go. They're getting a little bit heavier now. I'll work through the pain, I always have. Number seven, off you go!! Number eight, throw them straight! Number nine will do just fine! Number ten, oh, that throw makes me feel like I'm going to shit a hen. Hell, maybe I do have a gift for language. Eleven, eleven on the floor will seem like heaven, because this box is surely breaking my arm. Twelve, last but not least—I'll spread you over here, and now I'm finished. The entire God damn floor is covered, and all I have left are these thirty-six pictures in my pocket I just got developed today, you can, like your friends, land where you will!

What's happening to me! My arm is numb, and my clothing feels as if I've submerged myself in a pool of sweat. I must sit down. I must sit down. I knew my time has come. I told you the end for me was near.

Oh, this is what…this is what a heart attack feels like? I must sit down, and catch my breath, and focus for a minute on, on my vision, my dream!!! It can't be. It is!!! I've found it; I've got it!!! Un-fucking-believable!!! After all these years I've finally got it!!! I've got it and now I'm going to die!!! Oh, this is good; this is rich. I can't even get off this chair to get my camera to take a picture of all these fucking pictures scattered chaotically all over the God damn floor!! I can't even get to a fucking phone and call an ambulance to save my life!!!

It's the entire dining room floor and it is beautiful! It is everything and nothing; it is just as vivid and wonderful as I imagined it to be all these years. I knew what I was doing and I had no fucking idea. Thank you mom. The fucking crab! The fucking crab!!! What are the odds of this happening? I'll tell you the odds, it's impossible! It's impossible, but it must be possible because I'm looking right at it. Son of a bitch, it's all right here in front of me. I wouldn't change a single thing. I wouldn't change a single thing I tell you!!!

Mom I'll see you in a minute. I just hope when they find me, when they find me cold and dead, I hope they look for a second or two and see everything as one; everything as a whole just as I see it now physically in front of me — just as I've seen it in my mind's eye for as long as I can remember — just as it was meant to be. Please God, please let them look for a second or two before they destroy my vision, my life's work, my creation, by picking all these thousands of individual photos up. Let them see more than just a few thousand photos of paintings scattered around chaotically on the floor. Mom, Mama, I always knew I would see you again. Mama, I did it!!!!!!!!!!!!!!!!

-Hunting The Big Three

I remember hearing about Roberto as a child. He was already a legend in Africa and a legend in my country by the time he was twenty-three. While in his twenties, his thirties, his forties, and his fifties, he was the only man all of the nobles, aristocratic families, politicians, and super rich people wanted to go on a safari with. They would pay, and pay well, to go out on a safari and collect a trophy or two that they would treasure and proudly display; and it would remind them of the experience of a lifetime. You won't believe the amount of money a hunt commands, but once you know what a hunt consists of, you'll sure as hell understand why.

In the 1950's Africa was still beautiful, unknown, and exotic. In fields were just seas of lions, seas of elephants, and seas of rhinos. It was truly an untapped, raw, unadulterated jungle. Africa has always been a very primal country, a country filled with tremendous natural energy, and if you think about it, Africans never had an alphabet, never had any traditions other than that of oral stories, and their oral traditions and ability to manipulate language are the only thing that separates them from pure animals. Let's not confuse the Africans with the Nubians, or Egyptians. There are people with black skin, and there are people with Negro features, and these are two different types of people originating from different geographic locations.

The European world brought what they felt was some sense of order to the chaos for brief periods of time, and they introduced many things, mainly a concept of economics and material wealth. Africans now knew of a life they perceived to be better; and never thought about any consequences concerning their country and people. Africans aren't unified in the slightest, and consciously and unconsciously have been allowing themselves and their country to be raped. They don't see and are not aware of the big picture, but that isn't my point. One factor of many in the raping of Africa was the prestige associated with having ivory piano keys, ivory billiard balls, or ivory carved sculptures in the western world.

Another factor is the rich Arab kings, when their sons were coming of age, they needed a knife handle made from the horn of a rhino. You know the male rhino copulates on top of the female, and copulation takes four to five hours. This is literally tons of weight on a female for hours at a time, and those sick Arabs believe that somehow having a knife with a rhino's horn as a handle will bring them and their sons' power.

The Chinese diplomats with their diplomatic immunity are perhaps the worst of the bunch because they are able to just stroll through airports and customs like the wind, giving the Africans more money than they'd make in twenty years for one rhino horn, just so they can powder it up, make hundreds of thousands of dollars selling grams of this shit, helping all the Chinese men get their little dicks hard. For the wealthy Chinese, the rhino horn is an essential aphrodisiac.

For my entire life I always wanted to be a professional hunter just like Roberto. I had posters and newspaper clippings of him on my walls. Nowadays, if one was to say they hunt elephants, all the red flags go up, but that's just because people are ignorant and don't understand there are hunters, and then there are hunters. There are people who shoot and kill infant elephants, cutting off their ivory tusks and allowing the carcasses to rot; and then there are those who hunt the seventy and eighty year old elephants that are starving to death on their last set of teeth, in their last phase of life.

I always had an affinity and respect for the Native American culture, although there have never been any in my county. They had a wonderful understanding of all nature, and all life, just as the greatest African safari hunters. Native Americans are in a class of their own, and can be compared to no other people living or extinct. Back to hunting, it is a dangerous endeavor; don't think it's easy to kill an elephant, or kill rhino, or lion because they are so big. And hunters for the past hundred years or so have been using guns; it isn't like a gun is a modern invention that makes hunting the big three a joke.

Elephants are extremely smart, and they know when a human is following them; they are also capable of blending in with the jungle. You might have five or six around you at any given time, and not even see them. Don't think that because they are so big, they are easy to spot, easy to shoot. And when you do get a shot, you only get one shot. You must shoot them in a virtual line leading from their eye to their ear—you only have about a six-inch square. If you don't hit that square and put the elephant on its knees with one shot, one kill shot; you're going to have a mountain of muscle and rage coming right towards you and instantly kill you.

Do you have any idea how fast an elephant can

40

run? They can go through hundreds of yards of dense foliage and deep jungle; shit that would be up to your waste, they go through it in a matter of seconds. You must run around the trees, and maneuver through this labyrinth, whereas the elephant just plows through everything in its path. One of the most magnificent, scary, and powerful forces I've ever seen and experienced in my entire life.

Elephants, rhinos, lions surely know the difference between a tourist wanting to take a picture of them, and a poacher, or a hunter. I remember on one hunt, I was tracking an elderly elephant, one who was on his last set of molars, and I noticed three sets of tracks in total.

You see the elderly elephant leaves the pack when he's on his seventh and last set of molars, but two, sometimes three elephants, are sent off with him into the jungle to protect him and allow him to die in peace. Although the elderly male is wasting away and looks like a grey drape hung over a massive skeleton, he can surely kill you and take care of himself. One must realize that if you want to take a shot at this starving infuriated creature, you're going to have two or three elephants come at you from any given direction and there is a better than good chance that you will die.

So, this one time I had "the fever." I mean I had to kill this elephant. I was going to get this one. I had been following and tracking this elderly chap for days. He was taking me 50 or more kilometers a day through the thickest jungle in Africa. He was always so far in front of me, or positioned in such a way that I never could get the shot I needed; and he definitely knew this. I could see him withering away, he was starving to death, and all that remained were these big beautiful tusks—I'd say they weighed about 225-280 pounds or 115 kilograms.

Before long, I realized I was hundreds of kilometers away from my camp, I had blisters the size of pancakes on the souls of my feet, I had no more food or water, and he beat me. He thoroughly exhausted me. I had to give up the hunt. I wasn't going to get him, because if I did—and even if the elephants guarding him didn't kill me, I would have died shortly after capturing my trophy. I didn't have enough energy to kill him, cut his tusks off, and lug them through thick jungle with no food or water. I barely had enough in me to get myself back to camp.

You see, elephants don't regenerate their tusks— once you cut them off, they're gone because they're fixed to bone. Now rhino's on the other hand, you can cut their horn off, and it will grow back because it's connected to loose cartilage.

Nowadays, because the rhino population is so small, I have a rhino farm in Africa and pay two men at all times armed to the teeth to go everywhere my rhinos go. If anyone tries to harm them, these guys are going to kill the culprits. The African government protects the rhino, and helps me protect the rhino, more than it protects its people. There is a big business with rhino horns, they command tens, sometimes hundreds of thousands of dollars, and that's just for one horn.

So, when there horn gets big enough, I shoot them with a tranquilizer gun, chainsaw it off, and when they regain consciousness, although a little groggy and upset, they are still alive and able to produce another horn for me again in the future. The horn is the price they pay for living because without me paying to protect them and their big beautiful horn out in the jungle, they would have been dead long ago and the population would be completely extinct.

Lions are in my opinion the saddest story of the bunch, and after I killed my first one, I vowed never to kill another, unless of course in self-defense. If I have to choose the lion or myself, I choose myself. Lions, just looking at them, you can approximate their age, but I don't care if they are five minutes away from a death by natural causes, I just hate killing an animal solely for a head to hang on my wall, a mane, or for some bitch to wear a fancy lion jacket, or have a really robust rug in her dining room.

So back to Roberto; by the time I was in my twenties, he was in his forties, and I read in the paper that he was going to have a conference in Italy having to do with Safari's in general, but more specifically about the dwindling population of wild rhinos and lions. I knew I just must meet him, at the very least shake his hand and tell him he had been my hero for as long as I could remember.

After his conference, there were hundreds of people, and numerous reporters—all wanting to ask him questions, or have a picture with him, and I felt somewhat defeated. I thought it would be thoroughly impossible for me to meet him. My dream of becoming a professional hunter in Africa was slowly dying in my mind because after all I knew nothing other than his accomplishments. I didn't have the slightest idea about how to legally obtain the necessary licenses, or how to hunt and track these animals for that matter. I mean everything I knew about hunting in Africa I read or heard about; things I've dreamt-up and imagined.

After waiting around for two hours to speak with him, I realized it was going to be impossible, so with much reservation I decided to walk to the train station and travel back to my home. The very next day, I woke up like usual and went to my local coffee bar, and who was standing at the bar enjoying an espresso with a small crowd of folks around him, none other than my hero. Apparently, his mother lives in my very same town, and he was visiting her.

I approached him, and introduced myself, and told him it is my dream to become a professional hunter. He asked me if I was attending a University, and I told him the truth. I attended a University just for the sake of my parents who wanted me to, and I was finished with a degree in Civil Engineering. He was very impressed that I was able to accomplish this difficult task at such a young age. Then he said, "Are you employed now?" And when I told him I wasn't he asked me if I'd like to work with him because he has never seen such an enthusiastic respectful young adult, and he had a gut feeling about me. He told me to meet him at the very same coffee bar tomorrow morning with my identity card, my passport, and we would be in business. We were to leave for Africa in three days.

He wrote for me a list of everything I needed to buy — everything from what type of boots and socks, to what type of watch I should have — he said when we arrived in Africa he would have rifles, knives, and all hunting implements necessary for life on a safari. "When it comes to hunting there is only one type of rifle to use, and I know for a fact at this point in time you can't afford one my boy, so I will provide you with your very own."

Roberto made my dream come true. Here I was going to Africa with the man, the myth, the legend himself; and he is going to take me under his wings because his intuition spoke to him and he had a good gut feeling. Well, I'm sure I don't need to talk about the sheer madness, panic, excitement, and bliss that ensued for those three days. It was a complete whirlwind, a surreal experience. It was my first time going anywhere. My first time leaving my country, my home, everything I know, and I was going to Africa for eight months. Before you know it, poof, I was there and felt like I've always been there.

The first thing I noticed was the heat. It was energizing. I am Italian, I complain when it's too cold, I complain when it's too hot, but I do love the heat; and it was hot. As soon as we got off the plane, Roberto's men picked us in Jeeps. It was a three Jeep parade and I remember feeling comforted. I wasn't taken back by the artillery of weapons; I wasn't taken back by these tall slender blacker than black individuals speaking a language I never heard before, but understood. I felt like one of the team, and I had only gotten off the plane. I took no preconceived notions with me, and realized that I was about to experience, enter, and come to know a completely different world.

Roberto had a sophisticated operation with outposts in urban centers and occasional camps linked together by barely visible paths cut out with machetes. All these paths somehow were linked together leading deep into the heart of the Africa. In the urban centers we met our clients, and deep into the heart of the jungle is where we brought them.

As sophisticated as a system as all this might sound, there is no *pesto*, or fresh bread, or any modern amenity in the jungle. There are creatures I've never seen before, animals that look like plants, plants that look like animals. There are parts of my body that hurt, or are irritated that I didn't even know existed. I was on sensory overload every second of everyday all for the thrill of what Roberto calls the humanitarian hunt. No one gets hurt, and an old warrior rests in peace.

Battling the elements, battling confrontational natives, battling fears, battling inhumane hunters and poachers, feeling lonely — I could go on and on, but all of this is secondary. When you know you're moments away from that kill shot, it's all worth it. You feel nothing at all except anticipation and excitement. And you know you have done many things right, otherwise this opportunity would have never arisen.

Africa is very different today. Africa is also my home. I love the people, I love the country, and I hope it can get back to what it once was, what it should be. And there are no hunters left like Roberto; no hunters left like myself. The entire continent of Africa has changed, and everyone has had to adapt to these climates of confusion. But in short, I wouldn't change a thing, and I am honored to have studied under and know the best of the best.

I see a bright future because I believe the people of Africa are close to uniting. They are closer than ever and have a sense of urgency because if things continue to go the way they do, in the next hundred years, there will be nothing natural or beautiful about this continent. The youth of Africa is determined.

-The Senators' Address

The year is 2084 and by the end of today, with the grace of God, ALL forms of verbal communication should and will be banned under the 163rd Amendment, which states that verbal communication threatens the rights of ALL individuals. Words, clauses, statements, exclamations, jokes, slang, sexually perverse connotations and innuendoes—just by there very nature all constitute harassment and threaten the prosperity of all civilization and our great 120 United States.

Many have wisely applied to government agencies for laryngectomies to prevent any possible legal penalties and repercussions that can and will incur for speaking, uttering, or whispering of inappropriate words, phrases, or clauses stipulated under the General and More Specific Sexual Harassment Act of 2084, SECTIONS I-XXXV, voted on almost unanimously, all with the exception of New York State, and passed today. Whistling, Howling, Lip Smacking, and other deviant behavior, have had recommendations for medical procedures to inhibit and/or control such.

It is my hope that within seven years it will be illegal to have full use of vocal chords and voice boxes, except for special exemptions under proposed Articles XXXVI-L for those recognized for their accomplishments and potential in the performing arts, archaic professions such as "hog and duck callers," military leaders, some teachers, and others of supervisory capabilities.

Furthermore, mandatory amputations of fingers, lips, nerve removals of eye-winking control endings, and other gesture capable parts are under discussion and I support this whole heartedly and urge you the Senate to hop on my ban wagon.

All of the above mandatory amputations are presently being lobbied for an effort to stop once and for all sexual harassment, and harassment of any kind. Silence, and amputations are the only sure solutions to prevent incarcerations from deviant behavior under these laws, which will be strictly enforced to the fullest extent of the law. After the Third World War we have been looking towards 'sure solutions,' and once again this is another brilliant one.

Clinics will open within the next one to two years, and will be available for free and mandatory operations as a public service. It is suggested that you call (721)-338-5678 for an appointment in advance because times are changing and you certainly want to have the necessary operations while appointments are available in abundance and can be scheduled for your convenience. Why be put to death for involuntary winking at an attractive person and highly offending them? Why be put to death for letting the word spelt 'j' 'e' 'r' 'k' slip out of your mouth?

Our record has been a strong and clear one. Look at what happened after the 154th Amendment, which make all physical contact illegal. We stopped the transference and spreading of all highly contagious sexual transmitted diseases. We stopped those archaic sports, sports are unnecessary in our world today, and there is always the chance of some contact as we discovered in tennis. If one must pick up the ball to throw it into the air and serve it, than hit it over the net with a racket, what if that very ball was served into the body of an opponent? Yes, I would say that most certainly constitutes contact.

We now have children growing up healthy and happy in controlled facilities, under the supervision of highly trained government doctors and scientists, only to be delivered to their prospective parents in perfect health, as fine young boys and girls, capable of functioning and contributing to our society in accordance with our fine constitution and their genetic predisposition. Hopefully after today they will undergo these mandatory procedures genetically, as to not infringe on their 'well beings' with semi-invasive mandatory operations and amputations.

Our record has been a clear and strong one. Let's have a look at what started it all. When we outlawed the usage of all stimulants and drugs in 2025, yes our Citizens weren't happy at the time, and it was a radical change, but look at how much we prospered. The average person exists to be now—I believe the average existence expectancy today is 130 year for males, and 155 years for women.

Does anyone today even miss salt, pepper, sugar, caffeine, alcohol, nicotine, marijuana, and other devilish products? Does anyone even think about them other than when you see them in a national museum, or watch an old television show? There aren't many alive who even remember how these wicked intoxicants tasted. Very few of us even have first hand experience as to how they affected and abused our bodies reeking havoc and chaos. Yes, we had a difficult time enforcing this law, but once we destroyed all means for creating these products, and once we genetically altered bodies to die if any of these products were to be ingested, we've weeded out the weak citizens, and look at how prosperous we've all become. We destroyed our last correctional facility in 2027 and wasn't that a glorious and momentous occasion.

Shortly after we made all stimulants illegal, the implementation of GPS tracing devices in all of our citizens, and neural shutdown devices have made it impossible for anyone to be where they should not be, without having their brain temporarily shut down rendering them paralyzed, until they can be contained and scanned. Hasn't that worked wonders? Even take children for example, those who would ask to go to the bathroom, and try to walk outside for a few moments and take in fresh air. Actions like this cannot be tolerated. Boys and girls trying to kiss in the hallways and the transference of salvia; just the thought of such a lude and crude act turns my stomach.

I don't have to prove our record, it has been clear. The record speaks for itself. We haven't made any mistakes in over sixty-four years. The fate of the country, and the individual citizens of the United States of America are in very good hands. If New York continues to act out and cause friction within our beautifully working House and Senate; and if New York citizens, and politicians want to become a country on their own, and live according to the barbaric laws of the 1950's, or even worse yet the 1900's, than so be it. Why not just return to nature and live as the Native Americans so many years ago in wig-wams and teepees? Their abuse of drugs, sickness, and their lack of technology led to their demise.

As far as I'm concerned, and with the grace of God, I hope you the Senate will agree with me when I say New York can float into the great abyss along with the few other uncivilized nations that still exist. It baffles my mind that New York would even consider allowing its citizens to 'sing' potentially offensive songs while 'walking' to work. It baffles my mind that they are upset with these GPS tracking devices, and against having stimulants like caffeine illegal. How could anyone argue that coffee assists in productivity? It's a philosophy of hedonists.

Instead of progressing forward, they seem to want to go backwards to simpler times. Once the center of the world and modern thought and philosophy, New York is now the center of corrupt minds and blasphemers. Perhaps we will never know what went wrong. I suppose all the genetic alterations in the world can't fix the minds of everyone. As long as there is difference, there will always be problems.

New York why don't you let your citizens smoke cigarettes again? I mean really, why not just let your citizens kill themselves? I hope we can all exist in unity and prosper as citizens of America. I hope New York can continue to be a part of this Nation's great history, but Senators, perhaps we would be better off in addition to passing the 163rd Amendment today, passing a 164th Amendment as well stating that the politicians not voting with the vast majority of the general consensus be banned from our glorious, and frictionless government—furthermore loosing all privileges to write books and articles of any kind in our newspapers corrupting the minds of our citizens. If New York leaves the union, we must prevent a tragedy like this from ever happening again. We must also prevent any 'nay sayers' from slowing our process of passing of laws that are for the greater good of all human kind. The greater good of humanity is all we ever had in mind.

Would the distinguished Senator to my left like to say anything?

"Yes, thank you very much Senator. 'The year is 2084 and by the end of today, with the grace of God ALL forms of verbal communication should and will be banned under the 163rd Amendment, which states that verbal communication threatens the rights of ALL individuals.

Words, clauses, statements, exclamations, jokes, slang, sexually perverse connotations and innuendoes —just by there very nature all constitute harassment and threaten the prosperity of all civilization and our great 120 United States...........'"

-Magic Vagina Chocolates

She reads the newspaper every morning while drinking her latte, occasionally licking her index and middle finger, hunting through the pages for interesting articles of no particular importance. One article in today's paper was entitled, "Want To Be More Attractive?" What woman wouldn't be interested in reading that article judging just from the title; I mean it certainly interests me, and it definitely interested Linda because she stopped flipping the pages. Linda spoke to me about the article while reading parts of it aloud. The first line was, "Make sure the folks around you are having a drink or two."

Apparently, Scottish scientists and scholars had a real break through and have found that trace amounts of alcohol in the blood will make the opposite sex, or whatever sex you are attracted to according to your sexual preference more attractive. The quote un quote beer goggles phenomena is true. They had to study 150 straight males and females, and 60 gay folks to figure this out?

Linda laughed and said, "I could have saved them all that the time and work if they just asked me. Four beers, or two glasses of wine increases the perceived attractiveness of members of the sex you're attracted to by approximately 25% — no duh? Imagine how attractive someone looks after five chocolate martinis? Alcohol apparently stimulates a part of the brain called the nucleus accumbens, this I did not know. The nucleus accumbens is linked to our perception of facial attractiveness, now that's interesting.

Why on earth did they write this article? Oh, it says here, the Scottish team conducted this study to see if alcohol consumption could be linked with risky sex. What a bunch of rocket scientists they must have over there."

I love how she laughs, with that cute little snort of hers when her laugh climaxes; and how the lines of her forehead and ridges on her nose become very pronounced. When she laughs very hard, she cries out, "Don't look at me, don't look at me!" ...and her face becomes pumpkin red.

I love the fact we live together, and have lived together for four years now; I know all her subtle mannerisms and nuances. For four years now, we must have giggled and kissed just about every day, but we've never gone further than that. Why not? I know, tell me about it! She's attracted to me, and I'm attracted to her. Perhaps we haven't drunk enough bottles of white wine together at any one given time?

Yes we are both 'gay,' but Linda doesn't want to ruin the relationship that we have by throwing sex into the mix. I used to argue with her all the time, and say if you love me, and I love you, then what is the problem? How could we ruin anything? Making love, having sex, that would just make our relationship all the better. But, she won't hear it. She won't have it. She never said she loves me back. And usually after a discussion like that, we sleep in separate beds for the night, and we don't cuddle or talk while falling into our dream worlds. I suppose that's her way of punishing me.

Lately things have been wonderful, and that's because once again I've laid-off, and stopped pushing the issue. Last time we spoke about this three months ago, she told me, "If you continue to pressure me, if you continue to insist on us becoming a sexual couple, a sexual item, then you and I will have nothing at all, and one day you will come home to an empty apartment! Whatever happens, if I am willing to allow something to happen in the future, then it will just happen. I know how you feel. I know how you think of me! I can see it in your eyes every day. Don't speak too much sweetheart. I know, and I'm sorry for yelling, but I feel that strongly about this matter."

When it gets late, around two, or three in the morning, and she hasn't yet arrived home, I know what's going on. She slips into bed quickly and quietly, before the door to our room even closes. She is sure to keep her hands and mouth under the covers because even though she probably washed them a few times, a trace amount of another woman's pussy I can smell from a block away. Sex has a very distinctive smell. And in the morning after showering, she goes back to her latte and paper, and doesn't say anything other than she had an all right night and didn't do too much of anything.

I don't push her. I don't have to. She knows I know... ...she can see I'm visibly upset, and whether or not she comes out and tells me won't make the slightest difference. She and I are different like that you know. Linda has had numerous sexual escapades over the past four years—I think all one-night-stands. Where I on the other hand have remained a celibate fool waiting, wanting, praying for her to come around and realize that what she really needs, what she really desires is right here under her own noise. I've had opportunities, but I'm really not interested; Linda has my heart.

It is nice of her in a sense to never bring a lover back to our apartment; after all we aren't a sexual item, and that would be her right. I think it is because she has a certain respect for me, and my feelings—it's also because I'd probably break down the door and kill the bitch, and she knows that.

"Listen, I've been flipping through the pages of this newspaper long enough. There is something I must tell you and I'm procrastinating. O.K. are you ready?" 'Yes Linda, I'm ready—I'm listening.' "Yesterday...yesterday I lost my job." 'You lost your job? What are we going to do, how will we pay the rent? You should be looking in the classified section of the paper, and not some article about how alcohol is linked to risky sex!'

"Can you give me a break? Just give me a fucking break. It happened yesterday, the company was cutting back, and it had nothing to do with my performance. I just was one of those 'low men on the totem pole.' I have enough money for my half this month, and for two weeks or so into next month. You see this is why I don't like to tell you anything, you always over-react." 'Oh, now I'm over-reacting. You lost your job, forgive me if I worry about our future; forgive me if I worry about little things like paying for food, water, electricity, and rent!'

Then she told me to shut-up, because 'she has an idea,' 'she isn't worried,' and 'she has everything figured out.' You see Linda, even though she had a clerical job, she really is an amazing sculptor, and quite a pastry chef. Her real passions are cooking wonderful desserts, and creating amazing bronze and ceramic sculptures. Our apartment is full of her work, and you would be hard pressed not to find some sweet dessert of some sort in our apartment at any given time.

"I need you to help me." Linda started to prepare some plaster with lukewarm water; the type of plaster she uses to make her molds. Then to my surprise, she took off all of her clothes. "This is what I need you to do for me sweetheart. I am going to lie down on the table with my legs spread apart, and I want you to make a perfect mold of my vagina. I know it sounds strange, but just do it—I'll help you along."

I was stunned, amazed—I didn't know what was going on, but I knew this was a once in a lifetime opportunity, and I didn't want it to end. This was one mold I was going to take my sweet-ass time making. The lukewarm plaster had the same consistency and texture as thinly sliced prosciutto, and it was very erotic. She said to me, "make sure it's good and wet before you start to smooth it out over my clit." Not only was the plaster good and wet, but so was I—I felt myself dripping with excitement unlike ever before; I had beads of my own juice slowly sliding down the insides of my thigh like warm rain from a sun shower on a windshield.

"Take that sea sponge first, the one over there, and get my vagina wet. I don't want any of this plaster to stick to my sensitive areas when we pull it off sweetheart." I could hardly move, I was moving in slow motion with a sort of trepidation, and I still had no idea why we were making a mold of her vagina, but I didn't question it. I just joked because that's what I do when I'm afraid, and told her this is the best idea she had in four years.

She started snorting a little, and I could see her inner thighs tensing up, her lips squeezing tightly together. "If you continue to make me laugh, we're not going to get a good mold, and we'll have to do this again." So joking I said, 'we wouldn't want that to happen. You know what Linda, you should lose your job more often.' While laughing quite hard this time, and her face starting to blush, instead of saying don't look at me; she motioned for me to move towards her.

"I know this is like a dream for you, and I know you are excited sweetheart. Just as you observe everything, just as you 'know' many things — don't you think I've observed your thighs? Come here, come closer. I'm going to make this dream all you imagined it to be. I am ready sweetheart."

When I came closer she grabbed the back of my neck with one hand, and the small of my back with another, and gave me a kiss. This kiss was deep, it was wet, and unlike any I had ever experienced with her before. She took my hand and moved it down by her clit. She controlled my fingers, first moving them in between her wet lips, back and forth, side to side, round and round; then she curved them a bit, and let me maneuver around inside of her, with her hand on-top of mine.

"You know, you feel so good. You've always been right here sweetheart inside of me, and you never knew it. Oh, you feel so good — go deeper baby, go deeper. Oh, I love you — how I always loved you." It was the first time I heard Linda tell me she loved me, it was the first time I ever felt her pussy, seen her pussy, and it was so delicate, so beautiful, so amazing, so wet, so sweet, so pink. "Take your fingers out of me, I want you to taste me, I want to feel your mouth on my clit."

We made love right there on the table, and it was amazing. She effortlessly managed to take off all of my clothes without me ever knowing, and before long, she was on top of me, with her fingers inside taking me to a higher place than I've ever been before. "Let's cum together baby, I want you to climax with me." While rubbing our clits together, kissing as passionately as I dreamed, we were able to orgasm together and orgasm again together, and once more.

After, we cuddled for what seemed like an eternity on the kitchen table, and I did not know where my being ended and hers began, as abruptly as everything had begun, Linda said, "The party is over, let's get down to business. Make up a fresh batch of plaster with lukewarm water for me sweetheart, we must get this mold finished today, I mean tonight. Would you look at the time; it's already five o'clock!"

Time seemed to stand still for us; while we made love, while we cuddled, but now reality set in, and it was the early evening, the day just flew by. She knew that I would be better able to perform my task of making this delicate mold now that we've experienced each other, now that I tasted her sweet pussy. At least now I could move, I mean I had seen, smelt, touched, and tasted it all.

After smoothing out the thin strips of plaster on all of her intimate parts, blowing on it, and waiting until it was completely dry, I slowly peeled it away, and the mold was complete. It was a perfect replica of her vagina — stubble and all. Then she hopped off the table, and while still naked said, "Now let me show you what we are going to do next."

We proceeded to make another fifteen molds, having sixteen in total. Then out of her Jansport backpack, the one she always carried with her, she pulled out two zip-lock bags. I asked her what the hell was in them. "Well sweetheart, this bag has magic mushrooms in it, and this one is some excellent pepperheads—you know pot." 'What the hell are we going to do with all of these drugs,' I exclaimed. "All of these drugs, I have six more bags of mushrooms, and four more bags of marijuana. You haven't seen anything yet!"

I knew we had just made the most amazing love of my life; I knew that I had helped make molds of her vagina while standing around naked in the kitchen, and didn't question anything—but this—illegal drugs in copious amounts scattered around on the kitchen table like a bunch of groceries—in our apartment—this was something else. I asked her, what in God's name was she going to do with all these drugs? Why did she buy this illegal shit? Why bring this illegal shit into our apartment? We aren't in college anymore—I'm twenty-five, and she's twenty-six.

"Don't worry about it baby." 'What the fuck do you mean don't worry about it? First you lose your job, and on top of that—I'm not stupid, how many thousands of dollars did all of this shit cost?' "Stop over-reacting. Yes, I spent a bit of money, this is true—but it's an investment. Besides that mushrooms and weed, it's not like I bought coke, or some other disgusting drug. You and I both know that they should be legalized; they are both natural, both from the earth. Besides that, there is no way in hell we are going to get caught. Just shut-up and trust me. I figured out a way to solve all of our monetary problems, and you are going to help me, aren't you?"

'Making molds, smoking a joint, or a bong hit or two is one thing—I can even rationalize perhaps a mushroom tea on a rainy Saturday; but selling drugs whether they should be legal, or not is irrelevant; I'm not trying to orchestrate some crusade to legalize shrooms and weed; I don't and won't condone what you're doing. We just can't—the risks greatly outweigh the benefits.' I rather lose the apartment, I rather move back into my parent's house for a little while than see her, see us go to jail. 'Selling drugs, no, I'm not going to help you, I won't be a part of that.'

"We aren't going to sell drugs baby. Would you stop over-reacting and just let me finish. We aren't going to sell drugs. We are going to powder up all of the shrooms, all of the hydro into a very fine dust. Then we are going to measure it out—three grams of shrooms for every one gram of hydro in each chocolate, and we are going to sell 'Magic Vagina Chocolates.' Let me show you what else I have." 'What, what else can you possibly have?' "I have two tickets to Madonna, two tickets to Phish, two tickets to Tori, two tickets to just about every major concert for the rest of this month."

Linda lost her job and she completely lost her fucking mind. She spent her entire savings in this little investment. "Are you coming with me to these shows? Are we going to have a good time?" I explained to her that this was all a lot for me to handle, and I just wanted to go to sleep.

I woke up some hours later smelling the sweetest aroma I've ever smelt, and who was hovering over me with the cutest little smile on her face—Linda with a 'regular vagina chocolate.' "Just eat this sweetheart, and tell me if it's not the creamiest, most wonderful chocolate you've ever had. Come on, eat my virgin chocolate pussy." I couldn't help but laugh a little, and yes, it was the most delicious, and most attractive looking chocolate I've ever had.

A few days went by, and Linda had a few hundred perfectly painted magic vagina chocolates, wrapped in clear cellophane, with pretty little bows. She told me, "each one of these little pussies was going to cost thirty dollars a pop; no discounts whatsoever." That night was the night of the Madonna concert, and of course I went with her, I mean it was Madonna.

She brought only 100 chocolates in her *Jansport*, after all this was her first night selling them, and she didn't know if they would sell. Well they sold, and within the first twenty-five minutes we were at the Garden, before the show even started, Linda was beaming because she had $3,000 dollars in her pocket. She gave me a sensual kiss, grabbed my ass and said, "I told you not to worry; I told you everything would be fine. Let's enjoy the show." The funny thing was that a police officer even stopped her to ask what she was doing, and made her open her bag. She giggled and said, "I'm selling little pieces of chocolate—have a look, aren't they beautiful. I made them special for the concert." The officer blushed and told her to enjoy the concert. Can you believe that?

The days went by, four months went by, we continued to make love nightly, and go to concerts just about every other night; New York always has something good going on. She met me every afternoon during my lunch break, and we would go out to eat at some upscale mid-town spot, drink mimosas, laugh and kiss.

While I was at work during the day, she would slave over the stove making more and more magic vagina chocolates listening to music by the band whose show we were going to see next. The house always smelt sweet, and I almost forgot what she was selling, I mean she was selling chocolate, that's what I started to believe. She was never fucked up, she never ate them, and all who ate them surely loved them. She even started to acquire a small following. "Better they buy from me, and get high quality goods that will not make them sick."

At this point she had 250 vagina molds, 75 molds being my vagina—and was making three to five hundred chocolates a day. The very first month she made the chocolates, she insisted on paying off all of the expenses for both of us, and told me it was the least she could do for all the support I had given her, especially when times got rough. Under our bed was a wine box that I saw her put money into nightly. I asked her how much money she had in the box, and she said, "Not enough yet, but why don't you take a guess?"

I thought maybe at the very most, $10,000—I mean $10,000 is a lot of money to have saved up in four months. How could she have saved more than that with our lavish lifestyle and all of our expenses? We've been going to concerts regularly, bringing our break-fasts in, eating our lunches and dinners out. She said, "You don't have a clue do you? At the last concert alone I made $15,000 profit. People were buying three and four each. They wanted to save a few for a rainy day. Baby, have you taken a look under the bed? I have four wine boxes, and a little over $200,000. That money is for us. That money is for us to start a life; for me to open a studio—perhaps we'll get a little house out on the North Fork of Long Island and leave all of this behind. You can quit your job, and do something else. Maybe we'll open a bed and breakfast, or a little pastry shop." She had a little over $200,000, and that was clean profit, and that was in cash. I was floored; I couldn't believe it!

She took two of the wine boxes out from under the bed, spread all the money out all over, and pushed me on top of it. I thought I was in a movie, I mean we had $100 bills sticking to our bodies while we passionately made love. A few hours later and many orgasms, while smoking a cigarette, I asked her— 'Linda, when are you going to stop? When will enough be enough?'

She explained to me that she wanted a half a million cash so neither one of us would have to worry anymore; and she said it is was going to be difficult for her to stop because this is the easiest money she ever made, the most money she ever made, and she was having a lot of fun going to concerts with me, or walking around Central Park. She said, "Sweetheart, if you want me to stop now, to stop now for you I will, but I think we should wait until the end of the year— by then I am certain we will have $500,000."

I told her I wanted her to stop because she wanted to; isn't enough enough? I mean we had more money than I could fathom. We had more money saved than my parents had saved, and they've each been working for 30 years. I had more than three months salary sticking to my tits and ass after we made love. I just didn't want her to push her luck because we all know 'all good things must come to an end,' and it was just a matter of time before she would sell to an undercover or some shit.

She told me she had thought of this already, and asked me what I thought about her selling the chocolates in quantities of 500 to a few people for $20 a pop. That would mean $10,000 for us a shot, and those people in turn could sell them and make a quick profit of $5,000. She told me she had two people very interested, and they wanted to take 500 each from her every week, but she wanted to discuss it with me first. I liked the idea; that would mean rather than her walking around at the concerts, or the park, now she only had to deal with two people only once a week.

The two people turned to four, the four turned to eight, and she was working day and night trying to make enough of these fucking chocolates to meet the demand. By now every room in the house except our bedroom was full of vagina molds with solidifying chocolate. I can't even tell you how many there were; all I know is the smell was making me sick. All I ever smelt was chocolate, chocolate, chocolate; our apartment was a fucking factory; I lived in Hershey Park. And when she asked me what I thought about quitting my job to help her make them, I exclaimed, 'Have you lost your God damn mind?! Linda, enough is enough. Before you said to me, if I wanted you to stop, you would stop for me. We have boxes and boxes of these chocolates in our fucking living room; we have vagina molds everywhere—so many we can't even walk around in here, except for a few hours on Saturday and Sunday when you unload all of the boxes and collect all of the molds. Will you stop already, stop now!'

I picked up one of the molds and threw it to the ground as hard as I could, then walked into our room and slammed the door. We were spending less and less time together. Some nights, most nights, she wasn't even coming to bed, and when I woke up for work, with an exhausted look on her face, she would still be in the same place I last saw her—behind the stove in the kitchen stirring, grinding, and pouring away.

She was a one-man assembly line. She was losing weight. Her hygiene was going to shit. Black bags adorned her sunken eyes. This was not the Linda I fell in love with. This was not Linda at all. The money was consuming her. All she would do is save it, and save it, and pack it away. By now, under the bed, I don't even know how many wine boxes there were, but I do know we had a newly acquired wine rack, with some of the finest bottles of red and white wine one could purchase. And I had a gut feeling that it was just a matter of time before she got caught, someone ratted her out, or we were fucking robbed.

Now I've known Linda for a number of years, and I know she doesn't like to be pressured. Perhaps me smashing one of her molds wasn't the right thing to do, but how was I going to get through to her. With tears in my eyes, I grabbed her by the hands while she was slaving away, and she told me she couldn't stop now, but I strongly insisted and made her stop for a few moments.

'Linda, you are my everything baby. You are all

I wanted in a life partner, in a lover, in a friend, and infinitely more. I love you more than life itself. I knew we were meant to be from the first moment I saw you, and dreamed about you every night. You told me you would stop when you hit a half million. I'm not an idiot. I know every night I fall asleep above more money than I will ever have in a lifetime. That money is yours. I want no part of it. All I want is you sweetheart. All I want is you. Last week I quit my job, I've tried to tell you, but you were always to busy, or just not around. For the past week, you haven't even noticed me leaving the house much later than usual. And for more weeks than that, every time I said goodbye or tried to talk to you, you haven't even looked at me or acknowledged my existence.

I even told you I quit my job and was looking for another apartment and you said, 'that's nice baby, I'm sorry I must keep working.' We haven't slept together, ate together, or even spoken. Some mornings I find you asleep at the kitchen table, and I put blankets on you. How do you think those blankets got there?

I've been exploring the North Fork. Although I'd love to live out on Orient Point, it's too expensive for just me and I must be realistic. I found a beautiful apartment in Greenport, a beautiful town in the North Fork. I already put down the security deposit, and paid the first and last month's rent. I already got a job with a real estate company, given they're all a bunch of pompous prejudiced bastards, it's a starting point, and they are going to sponsor me so I'll be able to get my real estate license. I hope I will see you there. I will wait for you; we can still make our dreams come true, you have an unimaginable amount of money.

—

Here is my new address, and a key to what I hope will be our apartment. I must go now—I cannot bear to see you like this anymore—just a shell of my beautiful Linda. It has been nine months since I saw that sparkle in your eyes, and nine months is too much. I want you to do what you want, and I will not over-react I will not pressure you. For now I'm saying goodbye my love. Linda, go look at yourself in the mirror! Are you hearing me? Don't you feel anything anymore? I'm not going to get mad, I'm sorry. Goodbye my love, my baby. See you every time I close my eyes.'

I gave her a kiss, and turned away. Before leaving the apartment, before leaving my life in New York City, before closing the door—I glanced at her once more, and instead of seeing the woman I love, instead of seeing someone run after me—she turned the gas back on, started to stir away, saying under her breath, "I knew we shouldn't have become intimate; I knew that would ruin everything." Now I understand the article about risky sex. Perhaps this will be her last batch of Magic Vagina Chocolates. Perhaps she will see the sweetest thing she ever had in her life is gone. But who knows, money sure is a crazy thing.

-Toddler Found Stabbed

No, I'm sorry, but I have given up on watching television news "shows" and reading newspapers. Why should I? I find it all very offensive. The news personalities do nothing other than shout on screen, all discussing the same "news stories," with one of two varying spins depending on what network you are watching; and the newspapers, with their obvious bias and charged language; never sharing anything "pleasant" or "good" other than the weather, are certainly no better. In fact, newspapers just might be worse.

The last article I read was about a toddler found stabbed to death in an elementary school parking lot. And that isn't fiction; that was in the *New York Times*. Such grotesque travesties happening routinely in this day and age is beyond my realm of reality, and staying abreast to all current issues is enough to drive one crazy. For some people, such as the individual who slaughtered this toddler and left them for dead, death is too kind of a punishment, and torture isn't punishment enough.

The UN? When did this turn into a political conversation? Fuck the UN! The United Nations of pussies and idiots! The whole philosophy is perhaps sound, and one day maybe we will have rational, logical thinkers and good people in it, but the UN today???

Five—the five permanent members on the United Nations Security Council are the largest arms dealers in the world. They supply the entire world with weapons. The United States, France, United Kingdom, Russia, and China. Looks like all the big dogs, are still fucking dogs.

The UN is a completely useless committee, and ploy to make humans seem more civilized. It will continue to be ineffectual until humans are all on the same playing field as to the meaning of life, and our purpose on this planet. It's a big jerk-off party. Create problems, solve problems, look bad, look good — just the same cyclical vicious process.

The meaning of life is really quite simple, but as intelligent and sophisticated as we are, we can't seem to implement this harmonious philosophy for living. I know many who know the meaning of life, so I'm not going to say we cannot figure out how to co-exist as a united people. It is just unfortunate that most people throughout the world, including this country have their heads screwed on with ass backward views and amoral philosophies — but nonetheless they know they are completely right.

A friend of mine, one of those people you occasionally bump into once a week when you are around your town at a bar, or supermarket, or 7 Eleven — we started to talk about writing. Little did I know he too considers himself to be a writer. Long story short, he asked me what my approach and philosophy towards writing was, and it turns out that although we have a different approach, our philosophy and what we want to accomplish with our writing is one in the same. I mean we disagree soup to nuts about most issues, we have different dreams and ambitions, but we live life the same, our energies are in sink. We both damn well know what the world could and should be, and he assured me that we are not alone. There is an entire wave of individuals that are just as disgusted as we are, and a change is inevitable. I am sure a change is inevitable, but whether it is for better, or for worse is yet to be seen. I don't know if we'll ever be able to form a collective consciousness?

Anyway, I say fuck looking at the UN as some pristine and holy council of sophisticated intellectuals from around the world, and fuck the news because it is always negative, and sometimes horrific. The real problem is that those who are in charge, and those in the media are so desensitized and out of touch with reality that their views should really be swept under the carpet and ignored.

It is time for us to all start thinking as citizens of the world, it is time for us to try to make our communities and environments better, and in doing so life will become better, and laws concerned with humanity will no longer be necessary because all people will have an inherent sense of right and wrong, and realize that evil, malicious behavior is never right. But how can that be realized when we still worship false malicious gods?

You think the God of the Old Testament wasn't evil killing the first-borns of the Egyptians, creating an apocalyptic flood, and condemning all mankind because some bitch coaxed an idiot into eating a forbidden apple? I don't mean to pick on Christianity because the Christians aren't strapping bombs to themselves, or crashing planes into buildings, or teaching hatred—but when are the Jews, Christians, Muslims, Hindus—when are people in general going to understand that there is only one God, and he is all of us, and we are all of him? The human mind has always looked for psychological crutches when in actuality the only belief one needs to have is the belief in themselves, and the belief that they are a good person, and in doing good they are contributing to the positive energy of this planet.

We should walk with faith in ourselves — never trusting our sight, because the eyes play tricks; never trusting our ears, because we hear what's convenient; and never trusting our religious leaders and holy books, our politicians and government, our logic and rationality.

We are confined to the workings of our minds, and our minds have been corrupted, have been weakened, have been crippled and cluttered with useless information and cannot be trusted. Trust only your gut; trust only your instincts to love, only your instincts to fight, or to flee; you instincts will never lead you astray because they work on an unconscious, on a subconscious level and always lead you in the correct direction.

Don't try to make sense of anything! There is nothing to make sense of! Be comfortable not knowing. Not knowing why you love someone, why you hate someone, why people die, or get sick. Only surround yourself with positive energy, and disassociate yourself from anything negative even if it is difficult.

A toddler found stabbed. A toddler found stabbed. A little baby, found dead in a pool of blood; we did this. Not just one person, but every person. We are a collective whole. This reflects poorly on all humanity, but then again humanity doesn't exist. We are not, nor have we ever been better than any of the animals that occupy this earth. We are animals. We have come so far, but we have gone nowhere, and we will continue to go nowhere until we exude goodness, until we transcend our physical bodies, until we evolve into purely positive energy. Only when we can transcend time and space and the confines of the reality that we have become some complacent in, will we ever exist. Come on, let's go get lunch!

-Who You Gonna Vote For?

What's going on man? Nice to meet you. Nice to meet ya. Was it your father I met? Do you and your father own the company my district just contracted all this work out to? Yea, that's great man. That's just great. Your father is a wonderful guy. I really liked him. I welcome you, your father, and your company. I welcome the help. But I have to ask you a serious question in all honesty. Are you going to do the fucking right thing? Are you gonna do good for us?

I mean first of all, I can't believe the district even contracted a job out to you or anyone for that matter. This school district is a bunch of cheap fucks.

Look at me. Just look at me. I'm the fucking foreman; I'm the general contractor; I'm the electrician; I the handyman; I'm the inspector — and I'm a the head fucking janitor. Look at all I do, and then look at my fucking title and pay check.

Look at me! When you rang the buzzer, and I had to come let you in because I've got all the keys, do you know what I was doing? I was pushing a fucking mop over here. I'm pushing a fucking mop! There are four other guys with me here right now; my guys. And they're fucking good, but you have to stay on top of them and lead by example. You just have to because otherwise nothing would get done around here. I mean they get paid dirt to do what they have to do; to put up with all the shit they have to put up with. You know, you've seen it — you and your father have done other jobs out here.

But if you need help, my guys are good. And

two of them will go anywhere you send them. They'll work day, night, Saturday, Sunday — you just let me know if you need the extra help because they're available. Yea, we go do side jobs all the time. We've got to do something to supplement our shitty income.

Look at this fucking neighborhood. It's a nice neighborhood, but you can't leave a single door open after hours with all the crazy bastards running around. Every door and classroom is actually locked during the day — all except the main entrance of course. Sure, the kids sit in their classrooms with the doors locked, and if they have to go to the bathroom — they knock on the door and a student or the teacher lets them back in.

This place is like a fucking jail. This place was locked down today for about two hours. Nobody in, nobody out — everybody had to stay in the classrooms, or gym, or auditorium, or wherever they were you know.

What happened? What happened was a few kids that got expelled were cracked out, one or two of them had a gun, and they were looking for someone. They got here just before the last bell, and a security guard approached them and was severely beaten. And she's a really nice and really sexy Dominican lady. She only works here because she loves the kids so much. Isabel wound up having to go to the hospital. I sent flowers over there you know. It's the least I could do given the situation. I wish I wasn't working in the boiler room at the time trying to figure out why the school was so fucking cold. When I mean cold, usually we don't let kids wear their jackets, but that day everyone was wearing a winter coat.

You think that's rich? Three days ago, it's

75

Thursday now right; three days ago some guy breaks out of the mental institution over here, and he's running around through the halls violently attacking individuals for no reason. How he got into the fucking school is yet to be known. We've got cameras and shit everywhere you know — it's just a matter of time before they find out. Oh yea, they videotape the shit out of everything. You've got too; some of these kids are fucking animals. You know, you've seen them. You've done other jobs in districts around here. They have cameras on everything now! When we were kids we didn't have any of this shit — the cell phones, GPS devices, digital music players, tablet computers, handheld video games, *iPhones* — you wouldn't believe the thousands of dollars of shit kids have on a regular basis.

And I'll tell you another thing. I like you because I know you're like me. Your work cloths are dirty. Look at your pants; they look like a Jackson Pollack or something. Don't you hate it when someone asks you if you are a painter? What do you reply with? That's a good one. I know some of these guys in their fancy suits, these fucking pencil pushing pricks — and let me tell you something. The worst part about it is they handcuff you — they completely fucking handcuff you from working to the best of your abilities.

I'm sure as you go higher up on the hierarchy scale the same fucking thing happens to all the pencil pushers. They get fucked I'm sure; and they have limited resources and stresses. Some of them are lazy, and some of them work like dogs; but most of them have no conscience, and all of them are greedy fucks. These guys are the worst because they have no idea what really goes on. Once you have real money, you become so detached from reality it is really very sad.

They have no fucking idea about all the miracles we pull off on a regular basis to keep this place going. The rich will claim to remember what it was like, but they don't feel it. They aren't moping up piss day in and day out. Regular people pull off so many fucking miracles that a miracle can't even be called a miracle anymore. We have to perform miracles—it's like mandatory.

This place has got to run and be exactly how they want it to be; and they give us all these demands and tasks, but none of the resources to accomplish anything. These guys just sit in their offices all day, and they don't do dick! They just sit in their office and they don't do dick! Make a few phone calls, slip as many dollars into their pocket as they possibly can, bitch a little, and for the most part just hide in their office all day pretending to be busy or taking their sweet-ass time.

This is a big school? You think this place is big—you think this school is big? You don't know what big is! This place is three hundred thousand square feet my friend. Square feet, none of this—none of this circular nonsense. This place is three hundred thousand square feet and is packed balls to the walls with for the most part a generation of nasty and disrespectful kids. This place is fucking huge! You wouldn't believe with all the normal daily traffic how much garbage there is at the end of the day. The fucking garbage is unbelievable. I always wondered where the hell they really bring all the garbage. If they really bring it all to Virginia the entire state would be like the Staten Island Fresh Kills Landfill back in the day—I mean really. You know besides the Great Wall of China, I'm pretty sure that's the only thing you can see from outer space. In fact, if this was Jeopardy, I'd be right!

Anyway we have got to get things done right. And we are going to have to work efficiently. When do you think your guys are going to be starting the auditorium, and how long is that component of the job going to take? How long are your guys going to be in there—three days or so? Are you going to drop cover everything—I'm going to tell you one thing, don't fuck up any of the lighting on the stage, and don't paint the sound system. Those speakers are new—they just put them in three months ago; three or four months ago max.

Did you know you are doing all the stairwells? There are a few things we've got to talk about and square away; I'm glad you are here. You know you and your father are difficult to get a hold of. Oh, really, how much did that run you? The cell phone companies fuck you in the ass. What a scam. What a complete rip off. Look at my phone—this thing was three hundred some odd dollars and it's a piece of shit.

But what I'm saying is this school—none of the shit would get done and organized if it wasn't for me. I laugh when they get guys like you in here to do work. You see this floor over here, this is still asbestos. They subbed out the asbestos job, but there was a mistake in the fucking paperwork and just the west wing third floor, and center wing first floor were done. Figure that one out right? And who the fuck knows when they are going to finish that job. That's why me and my guys have to keep covering these floors with wax to make sure none of the friable particles come loose.

I'm happy your guys are here, but I'm telling you, don't make my job any harder for me and my guys. I work hard enough and I'll kick you guys off the fucking job if it isn't done right. I know how to do everything, and to not hear my fucking bosses I'll do it on my own nonexistent time for no pay. I'll also create a shit storm in the process. Even though the pencil pushers are morons, I'm getting sick of seeing this school district getting fucked over. I love this school, I've got to look out for it, you know. And it's a sad thing, but a lot of times people only see half their money you know what I'm saying.

I'm sorry if I sound like a teacher, but I want us to be clear. I don't want to see paint all over the fucking floor, the doors, the bulletin boards, the stage, and the fucking speakers. If anything happens in the auditorium I'll never hear the fucking end of it.

All the shit that happens here, none of it is my fault, but who does the whip come down on? Who has to listen to all the bullshit and remedy every God damn situation? It sure as hell isn't the principal, I can tell you that much. I'm supposed to be keeping an eye on everything that's going on so I can report back to the assholes in their offices during normal working hours. No, I know you guys are professional and will do the right job, but let me tell you, some of the jobs we subbed out—forgetaboutit! Complete nightmare jobs, and the district paid big money for a bunch of shitty work.

Look at my fucking colleagues. You see the fucking morons I work with; you've met some of them.

They are nice guys, but these guys can't paint, they can't fix an electrical outlet, they can't do simple plumbing—they can't even sweep and mop if you don't stay on top of them. I don't know what is happening in the world today. I don't think it's a question of pride and people not giving a shit, I think it's a question of most people just being fucking morons. The only people that still work are those that aren't too Americanized yet, or off the boat and they have nothing.

You like the art work in here? Yes, some of these kids are really talented. Every hallway showcases student art work—and for the most part the students amazingly respect the artwork. It is incredible what the teachers do here, and what they have to work with. Don't get me wrong most of the teachers are fucks. They think they're better than us, or they think they are above working here, and a lot of them don't do or give a shit. But the art, music, and English teachers here are amazing—probably some of the best in the country. This district wins all sorts of awards all the time, and a lot of famous people went here.

Like that painting over there—the one behind the glass. That guy was a Supreme Court Justice that went to school here, and he painted that picture of himself and sent it back here. He's long dead now, and when he painted it he was rather old, but what a nice memento right? It's something for children to aspire to I guess, or it's nice to know that a Supreme Court Judge studied in the same school you go to. It makes you feel good knowing a Supreme Court Judge walked the very halls you walk down. What is that school in Virginia— it's on the tip of my fucking tongue. I took my kids there, we went to Busch Gardens—it's William and Mary. Something like six Presidents of the United States went there. That was an amazing place to walk around.

This school, I went here, my brother and sisters went here. My father went here. When he went here it was a totally different school. He knew a few gangsters, a few economists—oh yea, a lot of famous people went here when he was here.

When I was going to school here, that guy— what the hell is his name? That guy with the big dick, doggy-style, you know who I'm talking about? Ron Jeremy—that's right, when I was going to school here he went to school here. His name wasn't Ron Jeremy yet. He went by something else—I think he was Ronnie Hyatt. I think his middle name is Jeremy and when he got into porn he just cut the Hyatt. I saw him around. I really didn't know him, but he seemed like a nice, funny, regular guy. I wish I was better friends with him back in the day. Maybe I could have gotten a lot of pussy with him or he could throw me a few fucking dollars. God only knows we could use a few more fucking dollars.

You've got to go? Where are you going, you just got here? No, I'm just kidding. We got everything squared away—you and I are on the same page. You know all the shit you and your guys need to do. You know the time frame. You got my number—we just need to communicate to get all this shit done right.

The school is closed this week for the winter recess. No, your guys are great. I've been watching them here and there. They work fast and good—but realize this week you can get here as early as six if you

81

like. You don't have to start working after five at night. Am I going to get to see what you and your father could do? I would like to see what you and your father could do. Are you guys going to be doing any of the work here, or just your guys? You've got that many jobs going on right now! Holy shit man, you must be all over the place. Well then I'll let you go.

Why didn't you tell me? Why don't you start your car, warm it up, and smoke a cigarette in here? Don't worry about it. As long as there are no children in here, I smoke cigarettes all the time. Here I'll walk outside with you for a minute, light one up, and then we'll come back inside.

I know smoking cigarettes is ridiculous. I was just thinking about it yesterday. I also can't believe how long I've been smoking for. I would never have believed I'd be smoking for as long as I have, but it's not like I put a time limit on it or anything. What the hell kind of cigarettes do you smoke? Those are real strong butts. I smoke lights mostly — and occasionally I'll treat myself to a pack of menthols.

Knock on wood I don't get cancer, but if I do I deserve it you know. I know I could quit; I just really enjoy it. I don't smoke cigarettes around my wife and kids, and when I'm here I really enjoy nine or ten. Just a half a pack and a few coffees gives me at least a little pleasure and enjoyment. If guys like you and me had to break our asses, and not smoke a few butts, and have a few coffees — we'd probably start running around cracking people in the head with a wrench. We'd lose our shit man — I'll tell you.

Look, smoking can be a solitary and peaceful activity, or it can be a social activity. I hate these

82

fucking computers. My kids are on the damn thing all of the time, and I don't even know what the hell they are doing. I'm sure they're not doing anything that any other kid isn't doing—I know they chat with their friends, and play games and shit, but it's not the same.

Don't get me wrong, I don't want them to start smoking because it's bad for you, but kids today really don't know how to socialize anymore. It's like they're getting colder you know. They either don't give a shit, are in their own worlds, or are just arrogant bastards that don't show anyone respect. And smoking cigarettes is the least of a parent's worries. You wouldn't believe what these kids are doing today. I know times are different, but we weren't like the kids today.

Well, I just about finished this butt, you're finished with yours, and I've got a lot of shit to do. I think your car is warm by now. What kind of car you got—was that an Infinity? Yea, it's definitely warm and toasty by now. Those Jap cars heat up quickly. I don't know how you keep that car so beautiful running around doing the type of work you do. I would have that car all shitted up by now.

Listen, when you get out of here, if you are hungry and you want to get some good Greek food— and I'm talking good Greek food—the real shit—it's very close. I know you're hungry and you aren't going to hit any traffic now, so you might as well. You remember the name right? "In Cahoots," that's right. The place is awesome—it's also a bar, but you won't be having any drinks if you got a long drive home. Anyone that lives around here knows that when you say, "I'm In Cahoots," you are either In Cahoots having something to eat, and a few drinks; or you are up to no good. Either way you're understood, know what I mean.

Yea, you take a left out of the parking lot over here—you go four lights, take another left—and then you'll see it. You can't miss this fucking place—it's on the left hand side of the street with a big bright blue fucking awning that doesn't say anything.

And the bitch that runs the joint—she's nothing to look at, but she's clean and the place is fucking immaculate. You could eat off the fucking floor, you can see right into the kitchen, and that's rare anywhere let alone around here. One night maybe we'll get a few drinks if everything goes good. The bar in nice, it's made of glass and copper. I probably go there just about every other day. Tell her you're one of my friends and I sent you over there. She'll take care of you.

Alright, I won't see you tomorrow because that's my one fucking day off this week, but I'll catch you on Sunday because I know your crew is scheduled to be here, and I'm definitely scheduled to be here. And another thing, if your guys don't want to bring their own lunches, or dinners, or whatever you want to call eating at this time—me and the guys usually order up food from the place you're going to.

They are more than welcome to sit and eat with us, and they don't have to go outside to smoke cigarettes as long as there are no children in here, which clearly isn't a problem this week.

I know this school is huge and there is a ton of shit in our contract, but you see no reason why it can't be completed right? That's great. Everything you have told me sounds wonderful. That's really great man. I think we are going to do business in the future.

If you're good, I'll spread the word. I'll tell everyone about you and your father. I know a lot of people around here. I can get you a lot of work just by word of mouth and recommendation. Believe you me; I know people and I have lots of friends. If your guys do right by me, meeting me might be the best thing that ever happened to you. The best thing, or as I said, your absolute worst fucking nightmare, because I don't play around.

Before I let you go, just out of curiosity, who are you voting for? Me too, the other guy is a real asshole. I really don't believe any of these mother-fuckers! All I know is day in, and day out, I have to go to work and bust my ass, live an average life, and exist in a world of garbage and paper. Fucking paper man! Money, and contracts, and checks—everything—all of life is paper. They're trying to make everything electronic, but thank God we still rely on paper.

I'm never going to have a lot of money, and I'm never going to be able to do all the things with my family that I want to do regardless of who the President is. Retirement—right? Where the fuck am I going to live? I won't be able to live in this part of the country not working with inflation and shit. And my kids are young. No I'm really fucked. But that's a story for another time. Have a nice night man. It was a real pleasure. I will talk to you soon! Bye now. Bye guys.

-Bring Your Own Lunch

I know what I have. Today it's two peanut butter and jelly sandwiches. I also have two pints of 2% milk, chicken soup in a thermos, a banana, an orange, and a snickers bar; but that stuff is irrelevant. You can't really mess those up. It is all about the sandwiches. That's the main staple in a homemade school lunch. What do you have and was it made properly?

I have a 'p' 'b' and 'j' because I asked for it. I asked for it because it's simple. I want to enjoy my lunch. Lunch is my favorite part of the day. Scratch that, I like eating in general, and regardless of what I'm eating in order to truly enjoy it—I expect it to have been made with respect. I expect a certain amount of care, consideration, thought, and a hint of preparation to be put into the food I eat.

In the end, I don't really care if you make something well or poorly; I just care about your conviction. If you want to bet on something, everywhere everyone is making mistakes consistently. Whether they are conscious of these mistakes, whether they care about them, or whether they are actually learning something is yet to be known.

I assure you given different circumstances there is a correct way to make a peanut butter and jelly. First of all, what kind of bread do you have, what kind of peanut butter do you have, and what type of jelly or jam are we talking about? If the jelly is mass-produced processed shit don't even talk to me. I rather not have it. If you want the sandwich to hold for half a day without the bread becoming disgusting and pink, and you don't want to toast the bread, there is only one way to do that.

A peanut butter and jelly sandwich is different than an egg salad sandwich, and that's different than a tuna or turkey sandwich, or a corned beef sandwich, and on, and on and on. No two sandwiches or situations are the same. And don't get me wrong, if I had the craving for a 'p' 'b' and 'j,' and I was in the comfort of my own home—I want it on hot toasted white bread. And I want to be able to eat it immediately. I want the peanut butter melting and dripping a bit because it's on such hot bread. I want the bread hot to the touch and hot to the mouth—but not burnt.

Burnt bread is never good on a peanut butter and jelly. I don't want to see any black whatsoever on the bread. If we were talking about a grilled cheese sandwich, a sandwich that must be made slowly, on the stove, with lots of butter, low heat, and any good bread and cheese—my favorite is rye bread and American cheese—but regardless, a grilled cheese sandwich needs to be burnt a little. Perhaps some other time I'll make a few grilled cheese sandwiches and you can watch me. But I need a craving for that, and I always make a fresh tomato and basil salad to go along with it. The salad is mandatory.

To get back to peanut butter and jelly sandwiches, regardless of when you are going to eat a "p" "b" and "j," and regardless of what type of bread you put it on, or if you toast the bread or not, or if you wrap the sandwich in foil, plastic, or paper—you always put the peanut butter on the inside face of both slices. Cover every square centimeter of the bread with peanut butter from crust to crust. The peanut butter seals the bread, so later when you spoon on the jelly or jam, it doesn't destroy the integrity of the bread. No one likes to have their fingers make the bread a purplish red everywhere they touch the sandwich — or worse yet, when you look at the sandwich before you even eat it, you see the your "p" "b" and "j" already started turning pinkish.

So you would think everyone on the face of the earth by now through trial and error knows how to make a peanut butter and jelly sandwich the correct way dependent upon the circumstances, but you would be surprised. People just don't care. People really don't give a shit, especially about the little things. And things they could have obviously prevented, or things that should be enjoyable, they rather neglect and later complain about.

I've had peanut butter and jelly sandwiches with a smidge of jelly in one corner, the peanut butter spread sporadically — let me put it to you this way. I've had food served to me, given to me by straight-faced good-intentioned individuals — and the food looks regurgitated. If it looks that bad, smells nasty, and you can tell it is comprised of store-bought long-lasting processed shit that comes in industrial sized containers — don't eat it.

Even something as simple as salsa — salsa is so easy to make. I only have a few dear and lifelong friends in San Clemente just outside Madrid — and they make salsa. They make everything! I wish everyone could experience eating in Spain. Or eating in Italy — forget about it! Food and eating in Spain and Italy is an entirely different story; it is unlike anything you have ever experienced. The food is superb and the company is equally as marvelous. You are not going to have a bad time with the regular people of Spain and Italy — it's just impossible — their love, compassion, passion, and generosity is by far unparalleled.

I've had an egg salad sandwich where instead of mixing the hard boiled egg with some mayonnaise, pepper, oregano, pinch of salt, maybe some bacon — it was just slices of hard boiled egg with mayonnaise soaked into one half of the sandwich. I mustn't forget; there was one thin slice of cucumber on that sandwich as well. A cucumber slice that had a plastic like translucent consistency, not to mention it was tasteless. Even better than that, I once had a tuna fish sandwich that was just dry tuna on toast. It didn't even have olive oil or anything. It was like trying to swallow sandpaper.

Speaking of trying to swallow sandpaper, listen to the shit that I put up with on a regular basis. My girlfriend wanted some fancy chrome license plate covers all chromed out for her car, with of course the BMW logo. They were beautiful, they cost eighty-one dollars a pop, she wanted and needed them, and so I bought them. She is my girl, what else was I to do?

I was ready to put them on, about to take off her old covers and screw these new ones on, when I noticed something. Upon opening up the package of the first one, I realized the BMW logo was a bit wobbly. It seemed like over time, or once a little water or ice got behind it, it would pop right out of the frame. So my girlfriend not being completely brain dead, but watching my every move said, "Is it supposed to do that?" She knew with my sighs of disgust it wasn't supposed to wiggle. My girlfriend told me to stop wiggling it, and we'll just have to bring it back.

We'll just have to bring it back means I'm going to have to go out of my way to bring it back. I decided to open up the other one; it couldn't be any worse? Low and behold wouldn't you know the same fucking thing. The BMW logo was loose. So, I said to her, "Give me a knife please; I'm going to need a knife to fix this."

Instead of giving me a knife, I had to listen to her interrogate me. What are you going to do? What do you need a knife for? You are going to ruin them? If you ruin them we won't be able to return them and we'll have to get new ones. She was driving me nuts all in a matter of ten seconds. After she said, "I agree with you. They shouldn't be like that, so that's why you should just go back to the store? You are going to waste your money, and they aren't going to let you return them. I'm telling you."

That's when I lost it. When the 'we' turned into 'you,' I couldn't remain idle. I just looked at her and said, "I'm doing this for you. I bought this for you. I want the damn things to be perfect. I won't settle for anything less than perfect regardless of how much money I spent. Get me a fucking knife. I assure you when I get done with these license plate covers the BMW logo won't come loose for 20 years." She tried to say something and I just took my key, pried the logo out, and told her to forget about getting me a knife.

Now these license plate covers obviously don't come with directions because a moron should be able to put them on. It turns out, there was some type of temporary glue, and the backside of the logo was

90

actually a shitty adhesive. It was meant to come out to begin with; and if you were only to use the adhesive on the logo, water and dirt would certainly slowly get behind it, and eventually a bump would knock it loose. So I drove three minutes away to a convenience store and picked up some epoxy glue. The chrome will come off these plate covers before the logo does.

I wonder how many people just put the plate covers on and three days later had the damn thing pop out pissing away eighty-one dollars. You'd think BMW would affix the logo in place to begin with? Well I'm going to eat these sandwiches my girlfriend made me in-between classes. From the looks of them, well, I'm not even going to comment because I'll get myself into trouble. What the hell, she clearly can't even make a peanut butter and jelly sandwich worth a shit. What is it with people today? Can anyone make a proper old school paper bag lunch?

-The Housekeeper

"Where do you come from in Africa?"

Well my baby, I come from a place called Ghana.

"Why do you come here to Italia, so far away from your homeland?"

Why do you think I come here?

"I think you come here to make money, well that's what my Daddy says. But you know I love you, my entire family loves you, and I hope you will be my housekeeper and nanny when I grow up."

That's so nice of you my baby; I love you and your family too. Don't you worry about not seeing me in the future; and when you grow up, if my body isn't too old feeling, I'd be happy to work for you."

"No, I don't want you to work for me, I just want you to live with me and my own family, and keep the house nice, and tell my children stories of your homeland, and I will give you all that I have."

You're so sweet my baby, how about you just come over here and give me a great big hug my little boobala.

It is true when I tell you I've been blessed. I've been coming over here to Italia now for 15 years. Yes, this will be my 15th year working for the Cavalli's. And little Guglielmo, isn't he a precious doll baby. You know I've taken care of him since the day he was born. He's almost six now.

I was even in the delivery room with Mrs. Cavalli; yes I most certainly was. I was in the delivery room for the births of all our babies except Gianna. She was born in July, and in July I am in Ghana with my family, my people. Gianna's actually the oldest of the bunch, she's fourteen now. Yes, there is Guglielmo who is five years old, Evelina who is eight, Riccardo who is twelve, and Gianna whose fourteen — Lord have mercy how quickly the years go. When I first started coming over here to Italia I was a young lady, yes I was.

I am truly blessed I tell you; I work for a wonderful family. I actually work for Mr. Cavalli five days a week, here at his home, and on Saturday he drops me off, or I drive first to his mother's house, then his sister's house — and I tidy up a bit at their places, do a little food shopping — whatever's required of me for that specific day. And Sunday, Sunday is my day of rest, but I usually spend it playing with my babies, or reading to them, or doing their hair, or telling them stories about my villages — really whatever my babies want.

    I am glad I only have to work for his mother a few hours, one day a week though; I'm not going to lie, she's really not a kind or tactful lady. I always feel her weight; feel her eyes burning into me, even if she isn't in the same room. But I don't hold it against her; she has a closed mind and it isn't her fault.

    Once, I overheard her talking to her son, telling

him how he shouldn't let a 'nigger' get so close to his children and corrupt their minds. Mr. Cavalli assured his mother he had the situation under control, and said that his family was just that, his family.

I remember him clearly saying, "Mama, I am free to hire and bring into my house whomever I want. If you have a problem with her, or a legitimate concern with the job she does at your house, I'll get someone else for you; but as far as I'm concerned that 'nigger' has been a wonderful asset and extension of my family, and hiring her was the best decision I ever made. She is free to stay in my house, and work for me as long as she desires, and there is nothing you can do about that."

Boy oh' boy, I wish I could have seen the expression on his Mama's face, because I didn't hear another peep out of her mouth. The next thing that happened was he came and found me, and told me we were leaving, and I was done for the day.

I don't blame his mother for not liking me, it's quite obvious that her own grandchildren prefer my company more than hers, but I don't like that. Your blood is your blood, and I drop them off at her house kicking and screaming sometimes because they should spend time with their grandmother, after all she does love them, and in entitled to some quality time. Who knows why she is the way she is?

"What's that coin you wear around your neck all of the time?"

—

Well Evelina, my baby, this coin is currency of my nation, my seven tribes.

"Can I touch it, and have a look at the back?"

Sure you can, but you are actually looking at the back. I wear the front of it against my chest.

"Wow, it sure is beautiful. There are lots of little pretty symbols. And who is this picture of, this lady who looks a little like you? She's so beautiful!"

Well, she is the Queen of my nation. She is actually the ruler of seven tribes in Ghana—a very revered, and highly respected lady because she brought peace and prosperity to the seven tribes.

"What do you mean by peace and prosperity?"

She stopped everyone from fighting and hurting each other, and she created a sense of order, and created jobs for everyone. She is the most famous and most loved person among all the tribes.

"How did she bring peace and prosperity?"

Well with money my baby. She brought money from Europe, and with that money, she created this currency, which is a source of national pride, and is accepted as payment for all debts. People are happy to have currency that is their very own, and shows pictures and symbols of their tribes and homeland. And with this currency, and with the money she

—

collected from Europe, she was able to create jobs, and get medicine, and get food, create a police station, and firehouse, and do many many other wonderful things for all her people. You see, my baby, my nation, it's a matriarchal society where the women have always ruled, and the women have the power of tradition, but no queen before her ever left the nation to try to make it better—most queens turned a blind eye to all of the horrible things going on, and believed there was nothing they could do to change things, and make things better.

"Wow, do you think Italia will ever be like that? Do you think we will have queens?"

I know in your homeland's past, you had a number of queens. And I think Italia is already like that. Just think, who is the boss of your house? Who is really in charge?

"My mama."

Exactly correct my baby; your mama is the boss—your mama is the queen of your house.

"So when I grow up, will I be the boss? Will I be the Queen?"

You most certainly will, you are a very strong young lady, and you mustn't ever let anyone make you do something you think is wrong or don't want to do. Never let a man boss you around. Will you promise me that?

"Yes, I promise. Do you know the Queen? Do you think I can meet her? Do you think I can be a real Queen in your country one day?"

My baby, you're asking me an awful lot of questions today, and I must clean all the bathrooms, scrub the floors, the showers, and toilets still. Later we can talk some more. Later I will tell you anything you want to know about the Queen of my nation.

"Can I help you clean so you can finish quickly? I'll start with the bathrooms on the third floor, and then you will be able to tell me another story."

Oh, aren't you a precious doll baby. You want to help me; you want to make me happy? Come over here and give me a hug, then go run along and have some fun. Enjoy this beautiful day, and tonight before you go to bed I promise to tell you a wonderful story.

Really, I don't mind cleaning the bathrooms. Do they need so many, I think not, but it gives me time to sing, and to think about whatever I want. Quiet time is important, and usually when I clean the bathrooms, I get a lot of it. I wonder how my daughters are doing back in Ghana. Perhaps tonight after I put my babies to sleep, I will write them each a letter. I'm so proud of them. I have three beautiful babies back home, and some day they are going to make some men very lucky—but not to soon I hope. My youngest is nine, and my oldest is seventeen. One day I'm going to bring them all over here to Italia, so they can have a look around at all the wonderful things there are to see in Roma.

"Hey what are you singing?"

Gianna, my baby, you scared me white. Please don't do that again, you know I'm starting to get old.

"You're not getting old. I saw you kicking around the soccer ball with Riccardo just the other day."

Well, I must do something other than cooking and cleaning to keep the blood flowing, and you know when I was a little girl, I was the very best soccer player in all my villages. I could beat all of the boys. Why do you think your brother is so good? Who do you think taught him how to control the ball so well? And how to kick it so it hooks into the goal?

"I want to go out tonight, and I was wondering if you could help me braid my hair. You know make some of those little tight braids you do so well."

Those are called corn-rows, and sure my baby, you just let me finish up a few more things, and when I come back from the grocery store, that's the first thing I'm going to do, so be ready.

"I will, O.K. see-you later."

Wait, wait, wait, where do you think you're going?

"I'm going shopping with my mother. Oh, I'm sorry, I

know, you need a big hug."

Of course I do, I always need a hug from all my babies. Thank you. I'll see you later sugar.

It's kind of strange, she's the only child I didn't see delivered, and yet we have an unbreakable bond. Perhaps it's because I've been a part of her life for so long and been brushing her hair ever since she was a little girl. Boy how she has grown up! She wants to come with me to Ghana, and I told her I would take her when she is woman and she is finished with her studies. She can hardly wait. What a precious one she is. She's actually counting down the days to her 18th birthday because Mr. Cavalli told her when she's 18 she can return to Ghana with me and spend the summer. She's going to love it, and she's so much like my thirteen year old.

You know they are pen pals and write back and forth to each other. My baby back home in Ghana is very close with Gianna, and they are looking forward to meeting each other. They send photographs back and forth, they make drawings for each other—my baby back home actually makes beautiful jewelry and sends Gianna her newest creations. It's really something beautiful; I'm truly blessed that all my babies get along and see no color.

Boy, I sure am going to miss my family here in Italia like I always do when I go to Ghana for four months. And, it's almost about that time, I will be returning home in May. For May, June, July, and August I go back to make sure everything is running smoothly and going as planned. It is also very important for me to spend time with my daughters; after all there is still so much they have to learn from their mother you know.

"Do you think I can talk to you for a few minutes?"

Of course you can Riccardo; what happened to your face my baby, and where have you been all day?! Tell me while I clean you up.

"Do you promise you won't get mad at me?"

Have I ever gotten mad at you my baby? Don't be silly. Just tell me what happened, and what's on your mind, and everything will be O.K. I promise.

"Well, I've been playing soccer with some of my friends, then something happened, then something else happened, and then I had to walk around for a while because I didn't know what to think."

What's wrong my baby? What's troubling you?

"Today when I was playing soccer, a black boy wanted to play with us. I could see that he was just hanging around, walking back and forth, so I invited him to play. And when he started to play with us, some of my friends left because they 'had to go home;' but we were only playing for 15 minutes. It bothered me a little that some of them left, but we still had enough people to have a game, so I just forgot about it.

Then, Lorenzo, you know that really big kid who looks like he's 18; well, Michael, the black boy, beat him fair and square, out maneuvered him, and scored a goal. It was an amazing move; I must admit he is much better than me, and all my friends. When Michael started to run towards me to celebrate, because we are on the same team, Lorenzo tackled him for no reason, flipped him over, and started punching him in the face.

Lorenzo is much bigger than me, much bigger than all of us, and even though I was telling him to stop, and even though I tried to push him off Michael, I was able to do nothing at all. I couldn't help this poor boy whose only problem was wanting to play with my stupid friends."

Baby, you did help him. The first thing you did was invited him to play with you, when no one else would ask, and you allowed him to play on your team. It's not your fault you couldn't stop Lorenzo from punching him in the face—the important thing is you tried. You tried didn't you? All you can do in life is try to do what's right my baby. So what happened to Michael?

"Well, I asked Michael where he lived, and I offered to walk home with him. Lorenzo told me if I didn't continue to play soccer, and if I walked the 'nigger' home, to never show my face again because I wouldn't be welcome."

And what did you do?

"I took off my shirt and gave it to Michael to wipe the blood off of his face, then I walked home with him of course. I did what I thought was right. And, I also told him the truth. The truth is, deep down inside I know I could have tried harder to stop the fight, but I was very afraid. I was so afraid of Lorenzo, I was so afraid he would hurt me next, hurt me even worse than he hurt Michael. I could hardly move.

Michael told me that if I am ever afraid like that again, I should put myself in a different place. I should imagine myself as someone in a movie, someone who is capable of doing anything, and think around my fear. He told me to go to a different place in my mind—that's what his grandma said to him once."

I would say that's very wise advice. But you still haven't explained to me what happened to your eye and your face?

"Well, when we arrived to Michael's house, and when his father had seen what happened to him, and saw Michael with me, before we could say anything his father pushed me away, jerked Michael into the house by his arm, and slammed the door. I could see his dad through the window beating on him, hitting him more and more, harder and harder—I saw and heard Michael crying out in pain. His father was hitting him much harder than Lorenzo, and I thought maybe he would even kill Michael."

My God, that's awful. So what did you do?

"I pretended to be Bud Spencer, and I picked up the biggest rock I could find. I ran inside, and hit his father in the face with all my might. Then his father punched me in the face, and I smacked into the wall face first. I guess that's how I hurt myself. When I fell to the ground, and saw that his father was going to come after me with a bottle in his hand, I made eye contact with Michael and pushed the rock over to him without even thinking. Michael hit him in the temple, and he fell to the ground and stopped moving."

Where is Michael now?

"Michael and I decided it would be best for him to go to his grandmother's because he did not want to be around when his father got up. So we walked and walked, and when we got to his grandma's house, she hugged him, hugged both of us, and she listened to our story. She promised Michael that he could live with her, and that his father could never hurt him again. She was very proud of both of us, and even invited me to have something to eat with them, but I explained to her it would be best for me to get on home because my family would worry."

Come here and give me a hug my baby. You had a very difficult day.

"Are you mad at me for hitting that man?"

Well, why did you hit him?

"I hit him with the rock to protect my friend; Michael didn't deserve to get beaten up more."

I'm not mad at you my precious; I am the exact opposite. I'm so proud of you for so many reasons. You are growing up so quickly, and one day you will be a great man. You hit Michael's father not because you wanted to hurt him, that would be very bad; you hit Michael's father because you saw he was beating your friend, he was hurting someone much much smaller than him for no reason — and that takes guts. You were willing to sacrifice your own safety and well being, for a boy you just met.

Sometimes my baby, the only way to fight evil, to fight violence, unfortunately is with more violence. In my county, within my seven tribes, before we could have peace and prosperity, although it is very sad, the Queen had to make the decision to declare war. She didn't want to, and she cried every night because she saw her fellow brothers and sisters die, regular people die, but it was necessary — there was no other way around it. She had to. If she didn't declare war, the bad people would continue to kill, to rape, to steal, and the nations could never be productive without any kind of justice, law, and order. Just remember my baby that violence should only be used as a last resort. If you can get out of a situation without lifting a finger, then do so.

Even if someone hurts you, and you are capable of running away, it doesn't mean you are a coward — it means you are wise enough to use your mind with the help of your legs. But, don't let someone hurt you repeatedly, and if you cannot resolve the situation on your own, then get help. Ask people you love and trust for help, ask the police. Never be too strong of a person to admit you need help. And that's exactly what you did today; you went to Michael's grandmother's house and got help.

"What do you think I should tell my parents?"

You know the answer to that my baby. Go run along, and talk to them, but I know they will be very proud of you, and say the same things. They are very wise. I'll see you after dinner, now give me a hug, and run along. I still have much to do before I start to prepare supper.

You know, I don't mind physical work. I don't mind cooking, cleaning, working outside with my hands in the earth—I think physical work has a certain value, and everyone should know what it's like to get their hands dirty, and get some sweat on their backs. Don't get me wrong, I don't love scrubbing toilets, or picking up outside after the dogs, but I know these things must get done, and I'm not above these kinds of tasks.

I just cannot believe people! Events that are so traumatic, they really make the young ones grow up a lot quicker than they should. They rob the children of their youth. I can't even count all of the horrid events that have happened in the past ten years globally.

"Can you please go into the kitchen right now, and

drop whatever you are doing?"

Sure thing Mr. Cavalli, is anything wrong?

"Just get into the kitchen please."

"SURPRISE!!!!"

Oh my God, what's all of this my babies?

"All this! All of this it is nothing compared to what you've done for us these past 15 years."

Oh my, I'm truly blessed, I am truly blessed.

"We've all decided that for your last few days here before you go back to Ghana, we are going to cook, and clean, and serve you. It is 15 years today that you have been a part of our family, and you will always be a part of our family. Besides, you already cleaned all the bathrooms."

What's all of that?

"All of that? Those are all gifts for you. Fifteen gifts for the fifteen beautiful years you've been with us. Gianna and my wife did the last of the shopping today."

Oh, my babies, how did you keep such a secret from me? Gianna, you sneaky devil you; you got all dressed up, and made me do your hair so you could look beautiful for me tonight. I can't believe it. Everything is so wonderful. Thank you so much. All my babies come over here and give me a great big hug.

That night was one of the best nights of my life. I had such a wonderful time with my Italian family, with all my sugar pies. And the next few days went quickly, probably because everyone waited on me hand and foot. It was quite nice, and very special. The entire family took me to the airport, and now I'm on a plane to Ghana. I'm so happy because shortly I'll see my family, my people, but I'll surely miss the Cavalli's.

When I arrived to my nation, I was greeted as always by thousands of people throwing flower pedals chanting:

"HIP HIP HORARY! HIP HIP HORARY! THE QUEEN IS HOME! THE QUEEN IS HOME! LONG LIVE THE QUEEN, THE QUEEN IS HOME!"

It's so nice to be back home and see all my babies, my nation in Ghana, and my seven tribes doing well. Perhaps one day I will tell both my families about my double life, because I'm certainly not ashamed to be both a Queen for a family in Italia, and a Queen of Seven Tribes in Ghana.

There is an underground movement of do-gooders fully camouflaged fighting a humane battle. They realize hunting laws exist, although they do not agree with the killing of innocent animals. They kill humans cloaked in orange or turkey camouflage shooting at God's beautiful creatures.

How many hunting accidents do you think really happen? The government has individuals in the woods picking off hunters that break the law, and cloaking it under the shield of an unfortunate hunting mishap. If they break hunting laws so easily, or hunt turkey without turkey tags, who is to say what they will do next?

No, that really doesn't sound that crazy. I'll believe anything. There are so many brain busters it isn't even funny. That's why you cannot concern yourself with the fate of the world, or you will just go mad. You will go completely mad.

So, you believe in God, and you believe 'thou shall not kill.' But you also believe in your country, and you rationalize killing. We have humane wars. We have social sciences. We have hypocrisies on all levels. How could a good person justify it is not right to hunt animals, yet at the same time they hunt and kill the hunters that shoot animals? Does that make any sense to you?

The sad thing is, it could get better, but it needs to get a whole lot worse before it gets any better. Just look at civilization! Look at what we have allowed ourselves to become, and look at how we have always allowed one percent to control. And that one percent controls with philosophies, structure, economics—you name it—if it is in our reality they have created it. Even the definitions and significance of words in our society have been created by this one percent.

I saw a mother cover her ears when her son told her his 'penis' hurt. This is a three or four year old, communicating to his mother a pain, and articulating precisely where the pain is, and she is reprimanding him. "We don't use that word. Say my privates hurt mommy." I never knew penis was a bad word, I just thought it was a part of a body, or a particular type of person. Does that mean vagina is a bad word?

We are all in prison. I will give you a number of examples. First, a literal example; you are behind bars, trapped in a five by five cell with a bed, and you get to eat, sleep, piss, shit, read, shower, watch television, talk, smoke cigarettes, exercise, wear clean clothing, break laws like do drugs, work, and talk to loved ones. You can never leave this jail because you are confined to the walls of the prison for a life sentence. It would be fair to say that you are locked up in prison.

Now let's say you have a nice house, a three car garage, five bedrooms, three bathrooms, tremendous kitchen, dining room, living room, den, recreation room, sun room—you have everything. And you eat, sleep, piss, shit, read, shower, watch television, talk, exercise, wear clean clothing, break laws like roll through a stop sign, work to pay all of your bills and expenses, and talk to loved ones. But you are afraid of flying, and boats, and you have no desire to leave your town. You spend all of your time either at work, or in your house. I'd say you were locked up.

The biggest forms of imprisonment aren't in a literal sense — they are in a philosophical sense. That's why the more I think about it; sure there were a lot of great people in history, and sure there are some great people today. I think DaVinci was great, I think Picasso was great, I think Einstein was great — I think all the great ones could be graphed on the same chart except for one man. The greatest man by far has to be Christopher Colombo, or Christopher Columbus — by far!

I said his name twice because he is that great. I know the arguments against him, and I know about all the immoral things he did — immoral by our standards today mind you. I know so much about him, trust me I can tarnish him more than anyone ever could, but I won't and don't because of one thing he did.

He went against everything and everyone for what he knew to be true. He had no proof, but he knew he was right and the world was round. The church believed the world to be flat, astrologists believed the world to be flat. Civilization has always used the most powerful form of imprisonment. The most powerful and deadliest form is what has crippled us for thousands and thousands of years. And it is an effective tool. It keeps control. FEAR. FUCKING FEAR! You want something to go away, or you want to suppress something, create hysteria.

Columbus would rather die, he would rather have sailed off the edge of the world and been proven wrong, than to not try at all. If the world was flat, when he got to the end he would have said, "Son of a bitch, those bastards were right," and he would have sailed right off into the abyss.

He wasn't afraid of anything. He wasn't afraid of being called crazy. If he couldn't explore, if he couldn't realize and support his philosophies and beliefs, he would have rather been ostracized or killed. He embraced the unknown, he believed and was comforted while in the unknown, and he never doubted what he knew to be true. There was no way in hell he was coming back to civilization empty handed or proved wrong.

Humans are very closed-minded. I'm sorry to say it, but for the most part people are ignorant, and their ignorance makes them stupid. People are selfish. If you had a room of money, let's say you had a room with hundreds of thousands, and you really didn't know how much you had. I guarantee you, the trusting soul that you are, you would believe your family and friends when they said, "I'm going to the bathroom," or "I was just in the kitchen," and they would slowly rob you blind.

The sad thing is, if you are a good person, and you had a ton of money, and someone asked you for a couple dollars — you would give them a few thousand. Why steal from those willing to give — it makes no sense. I'll tell you why? The only ones willing to give are those who ain't got nothing. The rich want to get richer, and the powerful want more power, and the happy want to be happier, and on and on and on. We have no ceiling when the sky is the limit. And we fail to realize all the stupid things we believe, all of our selfish behaviors — it just infuriates me.

Would you let a perfect stranger from another country stay in your home for a night or two? I don't think you would. And you wouldn't be wrong in not allowing a perfect stranger to stay with you. I'm not making a judgment. There are a lot of very dangerous, evil, and malicious individuals out there. And you never know. The most normal looking person can be a cold-blooded killer.

But what I am saying is that I don't believe most regular people are out to fuck others. When Pope Giovanni Paolo II died, Vatican City was a mad house. A mad house — there were millions of people crowding every possible cranny of the city. On the news, the Italian government asked the citizens of Rome to allow at least one visitor paying respects to John Paul to stay in their home. The government asked — and when I say the government asked in was in the news papers, on the television, on the radio — the media asked the citizens of Rome to provide tourists with a toilet, or a meal — because the restaurants were overcrowded, there hotels were booked, and the government tents/beds were full, there was no place to go to the bathroom — it would be like trying to create order with three hundred adults packed into a school bus. Even though they are all God loving, when you are standing on line for a few days, and you see some mother fuckers cut you on line — it is going to piss you off. When you are cold, hungry, and sleep deprived, you become easily irritable.

That funeral is another topic of discussion all together. I will conclude with saying I think John Paul was a good man who really tried to do some good and believed himself to be doing good. I think the way he went about doing good is horrible, and I think it is sad that such a nice man lived his entire life in a complete lie, and in a hypnotic state. As far as a competent thinker, or an intelligent man — I can't say he was because he was naïve enough to believe in a heaven and hell, in a God in the sky, a God in the sky punishing us for things that are our own fault. He was a nice man who was fucking crazy — like a crazy uncle. And the people that waited for hours and hours just to see a dead body for less than a second are even more pathetic and sad. They are imprisoned. Can't anyone see this? Holy shit! You're working me up!

If you think we are better off now than we were fifty years ago, or better off now than we were one hundred years ago, or five hundred years ago — I'm going to tell you I think you are wrong. The same problems and travesties have been going on for thousands of years. Do we have more comforts? Sure. Are we less savage? We don't club our wives over the head and drag them to our caves.

But we have legal drug dealers. We call them doctors. We have doctors getting people doped up, keeping them stupid. Take antidepressants, take some pain-killers, take this for your heart, and this for your cholesterol, and don't forget to take this for your weight.

We impair peoples' judgment and vision all of the time, and it is legal. What's the difference if you hit a bitch with a club and drag her back to your cave, or you give her a few smiles, tell her a line or two of bullshit, and pour her three glasses of wine. You still hit her with a club. Two thousand years ago did people kill people for beliefs, territories, governments, or for no reason at all? I think they did. Do we still do that today? I think we do.

And Huckleberry Finn is just as real to me as George Washington, or Alexander the Great. Our reality is so fucked up, are you going to tell me Jesus is more real than Holden Caulfield? I don't think so. It just all should be classified under the category of human experience and art during the "former eras." Something needs to happen, there needs to be an evolution of the mind, or who knows what's next? I'll tell you this; someone asked me if I've ever read the bible, and I just said I prefer to read non-fiction. Their mouth dropped, and they instantly left me alone.

And no one is talking about the changes in the weather patterns, or the dying of many species because of climate changes. No one is talking about the melting and moving of Greenland's glaciers, increased wild fires, and catastrophic weather calamities.

When there are 60-degree days in the heart of winter doesn't that seem strange to anyone? We are contributing to every known problem on this earth because we are allowing ourselves to be controlled, and we are allowing the fat cats to get fatter. It has already been happening, and it is coming. Does it really seem that ludicrous? You don't think we could be lead to believe that the controlling of our weather systems is for the greater good of civilization? I already happen to know for a fact that the government has been experimenting with and shooting electromagnetic waves and lasers into various levels of the earth's atmosphere in Alaska. There is so much they don't tell us, and so much we don't care to find out.

If you want to purchase a computer, a computer that will be competent for a few years, get ready to spend a few thousand dollars. Don't take a chance with the cheaper models, or the special deals because those computers are nothing but a headache and five years obsolete the second you buy them. I heard Bill Gates speaking, and he was talking about the technology he has, and the technologies that will be coming out within the next 15-20 years. Technologies he already utilizes, but they are too expensive at this point in time for the average, every day consumer.

He was talking about cars with navigating software that could drive themselves, three dimensional holographic computers; he was describing some of the features he has in his house, and much more. Everything he discussed sounded like it was out of a sci-fi novel, or worse yet Orwellian. I was actually driven to throw up after hearing him speak because what he had to say so nonchalantly was sickening.

We have technologies today, nanotechnology — we have cures today, cures to "incurable" diseases, and we are being jerked around for the sake of a profit. There are no profits in cures, only treatments. There are no profits in selling the best technologies, only in the upgrades. Do you mean to tell me that computers should be expected to get progressively slower and worse with time? Does that make sense to you? Shouldn't the longer a computer is connected to the web having the latest software and upgrades continually downloaded make your computer better?

Look at the printer industry; you know printers for computers. No company is in the business of selling printers; they are all in the business of selling ink. That's where the real money is made, and it is sickening. You know rape is illegal, but in the business world you are allowed to rape consumers all of the time.

How many people remember records? They became obsolete when 8-tracks took them out. Then 8-tracks were short lived because tapes wiped them out. Then we had laser disks that were obsolete before they ever really sold because CD's came out, then DVD's. Now we have MP3 players and satellite radios. Probably as soon as you read this there will be another must have for consumers to run out and purchase like the *iPad*.

And we are pissing away thousands and thousands of dollars, only having to purchase more and more to stay current, and trendy. Satellite radio is the one that pisses me off the most. Now, we are starting to pay for something that since its conception has always been free — the radio. On top of that, it is just a matter of time before the government starts controlling satellite radio.

And look at Howard Stern. He has become everything he has despised, everything he hates. I've always liked him, and I still do. He amuses me, and that's all he has ever been to me is a source of amusement. And I could appreciate the things he tried to do with freedom of speech, our first amendment. He went about things in what he'll have you believe to be his own unique way — but all he did was wear a cloak of controversy. Controversy and unorthodox mannerisms really work. But he has never been a leader, or a role model, or a God — I've never wanted to be like Howard Stern, I've always wanted to be me.

With satellite radio, he had the opportunity to give it to the people. The mass media is obsolete. Television, newspapers, and radio — it is all obsolete. Computers and Social Networks are the new future. And our society is slowly preparing us for that. Our cable is becoming more and more digital, more controllable, but they are still fucking us with advertisements, and jerking us around.

Why should we pay Howard Stern, or Larry King, or Oprah when we could be supporting and paying each other? I'm sure there are a lot of funny bastards I'd enjoy listening to for twenty minutes or an hour a day. Satellite radio could be free for everyone to have a little piece of the airways and project portions of themselves.

I'd have a show; I'd call it the "News in News." I'd talk about the mass media, and all the crazy shit they are talking about. Then I'd talk about the real news, and things that are directly going on in my environment, and the environments of other regular people. Anyone could have a radio show in today's day and age. And I'd throw them a few dollars. Just in Howard Stern's defense, on September 11th, and for some months after that he was brilliant.

Think of telephones and long distance. Long distance doesn't exist. If my telephone has a nine one seven area code, and you are a friend of mine visiting from Boston, so I call you to see where the hell you are on your cell phone, a six one seven—just to hear you say, I'm five minutes away—I had to pay long distance. What long distance; we are dealing with satellites that can send, transmit, and bounce signals around the world with ease. There are no more operators manually changing wires in switchboards.

Think of movies and the talent-less or complacent actors that we are led to believe are superstars. Fuck Spielberg and Lucas. I know there are directors in your town that could make better, more inspiring movies. Their early stuff was great, just as everyone's early stuff is great. Now what separates them is the technologies at their disposal, their wealth, and their ability to publicize their movies. If you want to go out to see a movie, it's difficult to find good independent films in local theaters. It's much easier to see a bastardization of an H.G. Well's book or *Episode I* with so many special effects that there is nothing special about them whatsoever. Lucas's last few movies are a disgrace to the film industry and purely made for kudos and monetary rewards.

What I'm trying to say is that we don't need to support these conglomerates that dictate the trends. Sony and MCA records should tell us what good music is? You see the Internet; it has been groomed towards consumerism since its conception, and will soon be regulated and controlled for "our benefit." It is already controlled today, just look at all the filters and blocks imposed on us. I think it isn't too late for us to take control because anybody can be somebody on the Internet. But I hate the entire thing, and I hate the thought that my every move is monitored and traced. Not that I'm doing anything wrong, it just feels as though I'm being violated.

I'm going to go buy Kraft cheese when I could get homemade cheese? I'm going to buy juice from concentrate when I could make my own? I'm going to see a band that sucks when I could support good local singers? The Internet could be a collective, a network — of knowledge, human experiences, ideas — and we could all pool together.

If you like to make blankets, we all need blankets. I'm sure there is one person in every town that likes to make blankets. Over the Internet we could support and find our local blanket makers. Let's say you like to set off fire works, and you are proficient at it. I've had a few parties where I would have liked to have had fireworks. I would support someone who did that. I support my local pizza parlors everyday — I'm going to eat pizza from a chain restaurant?

What I'm saying is that if we all supported each other, we could all do the things we want. There will always be a person that likes to clean, and sees cleaning as fun. There will always be people that like farming and gardening. Not everyone wants to be an artist or a rock star, and if they do that is sad because all people are valuable and should be driven to find what makes them unique. All people want is respect, to provide for their families, to not be harmed, and to work. Humans don't like to be idle. Idle hands are the Devil's play things. But finding work, finding a way to contribute to society and do something that doesn't feel like torture is important. Or doing something where money isn't the only motivating factor.

You will never hear about the truly revolutionary breakthroughs and discoveries the way the world is now. Those ideas are suppressed, or those individuals are killed. The person with the cure to AIDS in the eyes of those in power is a very dangerous individual. The individual that condemns and tries to bring down establishments and philosophies is a very dangerous person.

In the eyes of many, Martin Luther King Jr. was a very dangerous madman with crazy dreams. What they didn't realize is that through assassination they made him more powerful than he could have every hoped to be, but they still did kill him. I bet his family would rather have had him enriching their lives and be alive another forty years than have him be remembered. What is being remembered? What is dying with fame, or wealth? What is having your own national holiday? Who really cares?

Actors, musicians, and athletes — they give people enjoyment. And this is important, and enjoyment, like love, like friendship — there are many things that a price cannot be put on. Well, we put a price on our environment. We put a price on our medical treatments. We even put a price on death. Everything in the world revolves around money, beliefs, philosophies, or religion. We need an evolution of the mind. There is no reason for us to be miserable.

Look at all the people with diseases. There are more people today sick with something than ever before in history. There are more people depressed today than every before in history. There are more people today who want to die and just don't give a shit than ever before in history. There are more people today who believe that's the way the world is, or I have to do what I have to do to survive. There are more lazy people today. And we will blame the individuals. We will say that the person who killed him or herself is weak and crazy. We will tell the person who doesn't give a shit anymore that they didn't try hard enough. We will put the blame on others, but never blame ourselves.

I'm not going to blame the conglomerates. I'm not going to blame religion or government. I'm going to blame myself. The sad state of the world is my failure as a human. I'll give you the perfect kick in the ass. Look at something like the automobile. I don't drive anywhere anymore. In actuality I'm only hurting and crippling myself because me not driving in the realm of things isn't going to make any difference whatsoever. But doesn't it infuriate you? We are using gasoline. We are using gasoline. We are still fucking using gasoline. The automobiles engine really hasn't changed all that much since Henry Ford's version.

That doesn't make you sick? Technology is available today, and I'm not talking about hybrid technology because that is just another upgrade, another money-making-get-rich-quick scheme—hydrogen technology exists where the waste the engines produce is water; good ole' fashioned H_2O. In the 1950's at the New York World's Fair they had a car that ran off of corn oil, and people are talking about bio-fuels now like they are something new. Now if I don't use my car, and you don't use your car, and everyone stops using his or her car—now we have something.

Sure, a tremendous luxury we would be depriving ourselves of, but eventually we will have a form of transportation that is in harmony with our surroundings and environment. I'm not saying we should all start riding horses again, or live like they lived in the

Middle Ages. All I'm saying is that now, more than ever, we are capable of making this world a utopia. And the only way this can happen is through unity, and embracing the unknown.

Fuck Bill Gates! Fuck the automobile industry! Fuck the pharmaceutical companies! Fuck the lawyers and the doctors! Fuck the politicians! Fuck the banks! Fuck Home Depot, and Best Buy, and Target, and all fucking conglomerates! Do you want to be a slave for the rest of your life? Do you want to have your place in society and know that you will die mediocre? Do you want to continue to live on a chain?

And no one takes pride in anything anymore. Instead of making a sandwich, we'll get one made for us, or get some processed shit that we've convinced ourselves tastes good. Keep going to McDonalds. Keep going to Burger King. This is why there are no more good restaurants. How can a restaurant compete with places that sell enough food to feed an army for fewer than ten bucks? And people today don't even know good food when they taste it.

Yet with all these advances in technology, advances in medicine — we have more sick people, more people in need than ever before. How the fuck can homeless people be starving when after food is ten minutes old McDonalds throws it away? I once went to a McDonalds and asked for the old food so that I could give it to some homeless people. They said absolutely not, it is against our policy. So I had to wait in the back for these bastards to throw the food out into the dumpster, and when they went back inside I fished it out. There were over thirty miscellaneous burgers and half a garbage bag of French fries.

What the hell is wrong with the world and wrong with people? My favorite is the computer virus or worm. Computer viruses don't just create themselves and spring up out of nowhere. Some sick bastards dream up ways to wreak havoc in computer systems. The Internet, the Internet is like a pool of piss, shit, puss, and blood. It is a festering disease and unless you want to do something mindless, or unless you want to buy something — it's fucking chaotic and really dangerous. The information highway — what a scam that is!

Just as individuals have created computer viruses that destroy, why can't they create computer viruses that assist? I know I mentioned this before, but I just don't understand why they can't go throw your computer and make things better. A computer getting progressively worse with age makes no sense to me! But then we'd only have to buy one, or maybe two computers and all these fucking computer chop shops like Dell, and Gateway, Toshiba, Panasonic, and Sony would be losing a lot of revenue.

I urge people not to purchase anything new. What I mean by that is, if you were to buy a new car, a car made after today's date — then you are an asshole. We can beat them if we ban together. We can make the world a better place in spite of them trying to control us. Now a car from 1995, or from 2010 already exists so there is no harm in buying those — but if we stop buying these hybrids, and these new regular cars with combustion engines, the car dealerships will start reducing the prices dramatically. Then you will see that a Mercedes could still be sold at a profit for three thousand dollars. Mercedes, BMW, Cadillac—they all skull fuck us. They pull our eyes out of our heads, and then fuck our sockets and our wallets. I'm sick of it.

I know what will happen though. People won't be able to resist buying a bran new Mercedes for three thousand bucks. Oh, I'll just buy one—just to have it. Then the prices will go back up, and the conglomerates will have waited out the storm. But if we cause these car companies to go bankrupt and shut down, if we don't succumb to our temptations, or at the very least force them to release and produce technologies that are far superior and environmentally friendly we will once again be in control.

Don't let corporations fool you. There is no such thing as opening up new markets. All a company can do is provide to an open market what it is willing to accept. If I am selling the greatest pink shirts in the world, the greatest pink shirts in the world mind you, and you do not want a pink shirt, what would I have to do to sell you one? If I said to you, fine, the pink shirts are free— you still have no use for, nor do you want a pink shirt. Now unfortunately when we see free, most people will take what is free regardless of what it is. People see free, and even if it's shit in a bag they want two.

I see it all the time; people putting packets of sugar in their pockets, or saving those little creamers in the plastic containers. How fucking pathetic? The best part is, they never even use them. They went through all this trouble to take them, and then they just throw them away. It's the same thing with leftovers. Ninety nine percent of the time, I wind up throwing out what I got put in a doggy bag.

I do have the answers, but I have little or no faith in people anymore. They are selfish, self-serving, and really only care about themselves. We wait around for help that never comes and grow more and more calloused. We don't look at the big picture, and that is because most people are stupid and could receive immense pleasure sitting around with a finger or two in their ass. And we expect things, we believe ourselves to be entitled to things, and we bottle inside of us a lot of anger and disgust.

Let's say you are a good person. And let's say you are the only person in the world that witnessed a large corporation burying toxic waste in containers that were leaking shit. And the corporation saw you. First thing they'd do is probably kill you. That's what I'd do, I'd save myself the headache and bury you right along with the toxic waste. But let's say for some reason they didn't kill you. Let's say even though they had no respect for life and our planet, they had a conscience and just couldn't kill you. You would have a price, and you'd probably settle for something too low.

Think about it. They say, "Listen, you didn't see any-thing, you don't say anything, we don't say anything, and ten million dollars will fall into your lap." Are you going to turn down ten million for your principles and beliefs? I would, but that is me and you aren't me. Here, the ten million is now in front of you, you can see it, you can smell it, and you aren't going to take it? Let's say it's one hundred million? Are you going to turn that down? Think of what you could do with one-hundred million? I hope you would turn it down, but I don't think you would. And that is why there are so many rich executives getting rich off of people that have nothing, or don't know any better. Money shuts people the fuck up — money stops people from being human.

Get out of debt. You heard that one before. Just take out a second mortgage. Sure, suck all the equity out of your house, have all of your credit cards paid off, charge your credit cards back up to their limits because you cannot live within your means, and find yourself in the same situation you were prior to pulling all the equity out of your home. The only difference now is you have no more equity to pull out of your home. This is provided you even own a house.

I'm sorry. I see a very grim future, I really do. And sadly, I know what's next. People will still be making pledges to the CBN Network; people will still be casting votes for uncaring candidates, and buying machine processed cakes. People will still be putting on uniforms, fighting wars, and listening to the latest boy band. And people will have smaller and smaller vocabularies. The Internet in a sense is destroying language — all language. In the process of destroying language, we are simplifying and destroying thought.

I see a world where there is no such thing as privacy or free thought. GPS devices, cars that drive themselves, anything that is deemed destructive or unhealthy to be illegal. I see a world where people still believe in right and wrong. Where people still fear differences and rather fight each other, or profit off the weak than just get along unselfishly.

I just want to say, yes, I had records. I was lucky enough to have a record player, but I don't really remember it. I only remember images and snapshots. CD's I lived. I thought CD's would be the next records. Records were around for a good long while. We studied records in school—learning about album cover art was one of my favorite scholastic experiences. Then when they shrunk the album covers down to fit onto a CD jacket, just about all the minute details were destroyed and invisible.

Gregory Hines wherever he is now is either tap dancing or taping that ass. I wish I was a fearless dancer. I'm already at a point in my life where I am overcome with fear. And it is because I am a perfectionist. To my demise, I am a perfectionist, and perfection doesn't exist anywhere other than nature and human experiences. I have aches and pains that exist everywhere in my physical body. The minutest things I fixate on when all I am really trying to do is transcend, forget, and live more simply—live each moment.

Why do my joints hurt? Why do I have pain, physical

pain? Why is my mind never at ease? Why do I think about so many things out of the realm of my control? Why haven't I met someone who feels the same way about the world as I do?

I mean, they've got to be out there right? There has to be some people who feel the same way I do, that I just haven't bumped into yet.

-The Scarlet Freckle

I never really thought much about it. Lots of people have freckles. I personally happen to think freckles are very sexy. I've known women whose skin was a soft sea of freckles. Some were very subtle and barely noticeable; others strong, memorable, and pronounced.

Could a tiny cut develop a scab, and later turn into a freckle or a slight skin discoloration? I once developed a tiny pimple, a piece of extra skin. One day, I woke up and just had it. It never got any bigger, or smaller, but it used to irritate me because I would pull at it. I actually cut it off a few times. My hope was that the skin would just grow back naturally, but this tiny pimple of skin came back.

After some time, I went to a dermatologist because this extra pimple of skin was on my eyelid. It wasn't noticeable when my eye was open, but I felt it. The doctor said, "Oh, that's nothing. People get those all the time, and all over their body. That's a skin tag." In a matter of one second it was gone, and it hasn't come back since.

So, a tiny cut developing a scab, and later turning into a freckle sounds logical to me. And could that freckle after two years or so turn into a tiny raised mole? That makes sense to me as well. My grandmother had many moles; Cindy Crawford's mole put her on the map and made her famous.

I developed a mole smaller than the size of the space within an "o" one might find on the page of any soft covered novel. It didn't bother me, and I actually kind of liked it. Little did I know that what I had was no ordinary freckle? What I had wasn't a freckle, a birthmark, or a mole at all?

I remember it like one second ago. I was making love with someone that had been in my life for many years. We were always the best of friends, always very close, always very attracted to each other—but before that moment we were never intimate. Somehow, somewhere, on something, I got the tiniest little cut on the shaft of my dick.

It didn't hurt at all, and it was barely noticeable, so I paid no attention to it. I thought possibly the friction from her closely shaven pubic hairs did the damage. Three days passed, and it was all gone. I had forgot all about my tiny cut; it never crossed my mind again.

Some months passed, and I had a freckle on my dick where I once had that tiny cut. I thought what a coincidence. My lady friend brought it to my attention. She said, "Look, I never noticed, you have a cute little freckle over here." I thought perhaps I've even had it my entire life. When I say a little freckle, this thing was barely noticeable to the naked eye.

Years had passed; two to be exact, and one day my freckle turned into a slightly raised mole. And this mole had another little freckle friend. This is no longer cute, and a mystery to me. Very, very strange because I know for certain I did not get another cut. And even if I did, what are the odds of developing another tiny freckle on the shaft of my dick where I once had a tiny cut?

I started thinking about nicking my face when shaving, and no freckles or discolorations there? My face, my hands, and my dick are the cleanest parts of my body. I am certain of that. And I take phenomenal care of my body and skin; my hygiene is impeccable. I am a perfectionist, I am meticulous, and now this mole and freckle were driving me crazy even though they were barely noticeable. When I am erect, they are virtually invisible.

Ever since I was a young child I have been plagued by some type of rash—skin cirrhosis. First it manifests under my armpits. If I am sleep deprived, or getting run down, or stressed to the max, you can see it appear and spread right before your very eyes. My stress rash recently has become out of control—now it is even starting to occasionally appear on my stomach right where the elastic from my underpants rests, and on my inner thighs.

For years and years I had been prescribed topical solutions. All they have ever done for me is provide me with temporary relief. And if they are used on a consistent basis, or used as a preventative measure—they are no longer effective. So, I only use them when absolutely necessary.

But I'm getting tired of having this stress rash. And now I've got two freckle things on my dick. On top of that I have a series of other physical ailments that are taking a toll on my physical well being. I don't know why, I've never had them before.

It was never difficult for me to keep my mind and body healthy. I just eat well, sleep well, and exercise naturally. I never force myself to do these things. I've always done them because they feel right, and just are a part of who I am.

I would think nothing of playing basketball for an hour, or reaching to pick up a tray of lasagna to put it in the oven. I don't care how many bags of groceries I've ever purchased — I pack efficiently in paper and plastic, and make one trip. As long as I can hold the bags, I can pick them up. Twenty bags with gallons of water, two-liter bottles of soda, and lots of other heavy stuff has always been no problem.

I know my ailments have nothing to do with growing older because I'm not that old, and even older people don't have all these pains. My upper back, lower back, and neck is killing me. My shoulders, my wrists, my joints feel horrible. I have no strength, no strength whatsoever. I have a permanent low grading migraine all of the time. And occasionally it becomes so severe that I cannot see.

I have tremors — situations where my hands shake uncontrollably. The base of my skull hurts all of the time. I feel compelled to click and crack neck and shoulders all of the time. This constant cracking and twisting provides less than a second of comfort and is highly annoying. I feel like I have Tourette's syndrome. The worst thing is that I no longer can sleep. Even when I am exhausted, I can sleep for an hour or two.

So these two freckles on my dick put me over the edge. They were the straw that broke the camel's back. I decided what the hell. Let me at least go to the dermatologist and inquire about all of my skin ailments. Perhaps he can help me. I'm even at the point where I would consider oral medications to suppress or prevent outbreaks of this rash. I cannot function when my armpits, stomach, and now crotch are raw meat.

My main priority was what I've come to call a stress rash. All the doctors in the past have told me different things all amounting to they really don't know, or there isn't much they could do. This dermatologist I've went to on one prior occasion is a young Harvard Medical School graduate and he seems to know his shit. He could see that my rash was in full swing, and said, "I understand the pain and discomfort you undergo on a continual basis. Unfortunately, there is nothing more that I can do for you than give you the topicals you've already been using. We just don't know enough about your skin condition."

Then I figured, while I was there, I might as well show him the two freckles on my dick. It was a difficult thing for me to do, but I said, "And Doc, if you don't mind I would like to show you a mole, or a freckle I noticed on my privates. It looks like nothing to me. I once got a cut, and the next thing you know I got a freckle."

This dermatologist happens to be a cool guy. He has all sorts of modern art scattered around his office, and any room you are in, you are certain to hear some form of classic rock. He's a big dead-head. So, he said to me, "Alright, you've got one, I've got one — just show me your dick." He took one look and said, "My friend that ain't no freckle — that's HPV."

I said, "What the fuck is HPV Doc?" "Don't worry about it. Many different types exist, and you happen to have a mild case. You will continue to have a normal and healthy sex life. Are you currently involved? Don't even answer, just if you are engaging in sexual activities, you must wear a condom because what you have is a contagious STD which there is no known cure for, and even if no visible symptoms are present, it is still contagious to others. Has it been itchy or painful?"

I couldn't believe my ears—what he was saying to me is that I had a scarlet freckle, a fucking stigma—a genital wart. I have a genital wart. It doesn't sound right? How could that be? On top of everything, now I have fucking genital warts! And that one bitch, the one who promised me I had nothing to worry about. The one who assured me she was clean. That's always the way it is—the one you least expect.

The doctor asked me if I know how I contracted HPV, and I had a pretty good idea. He said, "You know, perhaps she doesn't even know. Some people are only carriers of HPV, and show no symptoms whatsoever. In some people, genital warts don't start to develop for many years or never at all; and with women sometimes it is solely internal. If you are still in contact with her, you should inform her to see a physician. But once again don't worry; there is nothing you can do, and HPV is very very common among young people like yourself. I think a cure is forth-coming in the near future."

I felt like I was in a silent move, and what was happening to me, wasn't really happening to me. I felt like I was in seventh grade health class and Mr. McCourt was discussing how the safest sex is no sex at all, abstinence—but if you are ever going to engage in sexual activities it is important to always use pro-tection. And the most effective contraceptive for both pregnancy and disease is a condom.

I don't remember learning about HPV. HIV, AIDS, hepatitis, pregnancy, the dangerous of drugs and alcohol—yes we learned about those—but what the hell is Human Pamplona Virus? Why the hell is there no cure? In fact the medicine he gave me for my dick you can only use every other day, and keep it on for six hours. Right in the directions it states, "We don't know why this drug works. We don't know how it works. All we know is in 6-12 weeks your warts should fall off. That doesn't however mean that you aren't contagious. The virus eventually retreats into the nervous system and lies dormant."

So now I had a special dick cream, a questions and answers booklet about herpes, a lot of anger, a lot of sadness — but fortunately no regrets, and no remorse. I love that I received this booklet after the fact. What is herpes simplex? How do you get genital herpes? I got it. What happens when you first get genital herpes? When can genital herpes reoccur, and what are the symptoms of a typical recurrence? What triggers a recurrence? And the best question — what about treatment? There are no effective cures or treatments known for their effectiveness. It did go on to say that with liquid nitrogen the warts could be burnt-off.

I just find this so disturbing. A virus, the herpes virus that can easily be killed with soap and water, can just as easily be spread to other places on the body by touching the sores. How great is that. Could you imagine touching an outbreak, rubbing your eyes, and now infecting your eyes? Infecting your eyes with a sexually transmitted disease? Is that even possible?

But now all of the pieces of the puzzle were starting to make sense. Of course she knew. Of course that bitch knew. She just didn't want to tell me for one fear or another. But how could she allow me to have sex with her unprotected? How could she put me at such risk? How do I know she knew?

The pieces came together while reading the informative information package. She once told me an interesting statistic I paid no attention to because I could give a shit less, it didn't sound true, but now I see all too clearly where she got the statistic? "In the U.S. an estimated four out of five adults have one form of herpes. And did you know one in six adults has genital herpes?" I responded with a, "That's interesting and horrible. I'm glad I don't have it."

Then another time she told me that she is at a high risk of contracting cervical cancer and she regularly goes for pap smears. I still didn't put two and two together. Usually when women talk about womanly things I listen selectively because they'll just talk the ears right off your head. I don't feel I need to know all the details and stages of a period.

She's old news, and what's done is done. I can't really blame her can I? Would I have had sex with her if I knew — of course not, but it was me that stuck my dick inside of her. I would be just as sick and just as evil if I was ever to infect someone unknowingly. Just because a woman in the future might willingly want to have sexual relations with me, that doesn't mean that she should unknowingly be put at risk, or worse yet add to a statistic. I also really have nothing to be ashamed about because my scarlet freckle is not how I define myself and already disappearing. Soon these warts will be gone completely and there will be no physical evidence whatsoever.

If those statistics are even remotely accurate, I've must have had extraordinary luck in my lifetime. The next person I'm with will probably already have some form of herpes. At least there is one less thing I have to worry about because there is nothing more I can do. Now I guess I'll move on to my other ailments. Number one on my priority list is figuring our why I can't sleep anymore. If I could just fucking sleep I'd be fine. Perhaps it's because I might have just a few things on my mind?

-Tap Dancing Out of a Burning Ring of Fire

All situations are always more than only words; and this situation was no exception. I felt my spirit break. Something essential died. I was no longer "me." My eyes welled up with sadness, with anger, with hurt, with a feeling of lifelessness. And everything hit me the instant I opened the door. I didn't know whether I was going to move forward, or fall to the ground. Perhaps my friend was dead.

Judging from the butt filled ashtrays; the smell of sweaty clothing; the empty bottles of Jim; packed out bowls; and a bent soot covered spoon, blacked by days and days of continual cooking—the signs weren't looking good. And all of that I noticed within a half of a second. It really took the wind out of me.

Then, as I worked my way towards the bedroom, I saw lengthy apologetic letters to all his loved ones; dried blood all over his clothes scattered throughout the hallway. And then I saw him, lying on the floor face down; a Spyderco serrated knife on his belt. I knew he was a millionth of a millimeter away from the edge if not over. Not only had he been getting fucked up for days cracked out of his mind trying to touch God's feet, but in doing so, he was inching closer and closer to his ultimate demise. Perhaps it has always been his destiny.

Lately he seemed increasingly more logical, happy, and optimistic. He looked healthy and sounded good. I always knew he believed that an individual has the right to kill themselves as long as they don't hurt another living soul—as long as they don't infringe on another's well being. But this has been going on for one week, and every time I'd spoken to him on the phone he sounded fine. I never thought he'd turn to this! I never thought he was hiding out in his apartment torturing himself.

Can I help my best friend? Can anyone help him? Why did this happen to one of the finest human beings I've ever known? I am enraged, I am saddened, I am going to geeeeeeeeeeerrrrrrrrrrrrrrrraaaaaaaaaaa—I am empowered—I am charged up! No one likes to walk on broken glass; no one likes to file their genitals down to bleeding pulps.

While I looked at him, an intense indescribable pain filled me—I realized one of my reasons for living, my best friend, my confidant, was slowly leaving me. I'm not ready for this, I'm not ready for this, I'm not ready to see another lifeless body in a fucking box. Especially because of his own doing. He isn't only hurting himself. He's hurting me now.

I never understood how people who hurt themselves cannot see that they are also hurting their loved ones. He is not only destroying himself, he is destroying me—he is taking me down; he is giving my demons power. But I can't get mad at him. It isn't his fault. It isn't his fault. It is no one's fucking fault in particular. The weights and the burdens of the world, the fallen heroes, the voice in his head saying "you must strive to be the best—if you aren't the best your life is a failure—if you aren't the best you will never be able to make the people you love happy"-- along with many many many other factors drove him to this.

I must try better than my best; I must do

everything in my power, even if it means killing myself, to save him. If I couldn't save someone I love, someone I hate—what purpose do I have for living? Perhaps this is another test. Perhaps this is my final examination. I am choosing to do this because I have to, because no one else can, and because no one else will.

Really, I don't blame him. Western thought has destroyed the right hemisphere of the brain completely. Drugs will never be laid aside until individuals have inner balance and peace. And the drugs are not bad, the criminal is not the drug user—the politicians, the doctors, and the educators are to blame. The politicians, the doctors, and the educators are the real fucking criminals. The people with money, power, and influence are the individuals with sick minds—they have allowed their right hemisphere to control all.

I have experienced many demons. I used to fight to suppress them daily. I know what it is like! I know how it feels to be crawling around on the carpet with your fingers raw and bleeding because, you are picking up every crumb, every piece of lint off the carpet smoking it--thinking, hoping, wishing, praying it is that fucking piece of crack you dropped two, or was it three days ago when you had a rock the size of a baseball?

But the difference between us is that I liked the high. I enjoyed getting zooted and booted. I was trying to fill myself, to feel something I felt I was entitled to feeling every second of every day. I was happy high. I wanted to always be high. And I functioned perfectly in society high. I never ever lied about taking any drugs. I never stole anything to get drugs. And when I say drugs, I don't mean marijuana or alcohol. Those aren't real drugs. I mean drugs that grab you. Drugs you dream about. I never wanted to die. Never in my mind did I want to die. I just wanted to feel like a rock star.

My friend isn't a drug addict. He wants to die. He sees no reason left to live in this world, and I don't understand why exactly. He doesn't want to be a father, he doesn't want to be a grandfather, and he doesn't want to see tomorrow because it doesn't matter to him. It doesn't make a difference. He doesn't believe he can achieve his goals, so he just wants to die. He sees no reason to live in what he believes to be an awful world; a world of evil and greed. A world that people cannot, or don't care to change.

He wants to feel again, or he wants to die. I wanted to feel a particular way and live. He just wants to feel again. He feels nothing when he interacts with people—he doesn't see himself as progressing forward. In fact, he feels he is already too far behind and will never be able to catch up.

I will never know what it is like to want to die, to want to embrace death. When I turned him over, I had noticed deep gashes on his chest, his stomach, his sides, his upper arms—and either these gashes weren't completely scabbed over yet, or when I turned him over, I ripped them open because they stuck to the carpet.

Now I don't know anything about cutting and stabbing myself. I can understand it, but I don't have any first hand experience. I knew he was still alive. I also knew I could help him. It crossed my mind to call an ambulance but with these kinds of wounds, and with illegal drugs in his system—that would involve the police, and my friend isn't dangerous to anyone, or any living thing other than himself. Yes he is capable of hurting himself, and he has—but he would never physically hurt another individual—he would never lie, cheat, or steal. He would give up his life in one second to help anyone. And I don't want to see him locked up, or worse, in a mental hospital.

The police ruin peoples' lives. They don't help anyone; don't let those bastards fool you. They do nothing that ordinary good people—regular citizens—not only could do, but would do better. Putting someone in jail, putting someone in a rehab isn't helping anyone. They have to help themselves, see light again, see the error of their ways. And that isn't achieved by punishing someone or proselytizing them. So I said fuck the police. Fuck talking to those assholes.

And with bogus blemishes on one's record, opportunities and avenues are closed. People are closed-minded. They think once you use a drug or any drugs you are a drug addict; and once a drug addict always a drug addict. They think everyone that takes drugs are the same. They also make distinctions as to what is or is not a drug; and I would argue pharmaceuticals are just as, if not more, dangerous than illegal drugs.

My friend is a lot of things, but he isn't dangerous. And I knew if he was in a rehab, or a mental hospital, or a prison—he would do whatever he needed to do to get out. He is brilliant, more brilliant than anyone I have ever met. As soon as he got out, he would be so angry that his autonomy was taken away from him; that he was forced to do something he didn't want to do or believe in—he would kill himself with immediacy.

He has very few beliefs. The older he has gotten, the less he believes in; the less he views as legitimate. But his strongest belief is that people have the right to hurt themselves—but only themselves. He also believes if a person does not want help, or wants to die—you don't help them, or let them die. You do not force someone to live. You do not force anything. He told me if someone was drowning, and he jumped in to save them, and they said, "Don't save me! I want to die! I want to drown!" He would "have to" swim away.

I will have to help him learn how to live with, instead of fighting his demons. Too often we try to fight disease, or fight mental ailments, and fighting has nothing to do with it. I will have to become the pain in his ass he never wanted until he is strong enough. He knows I don't judge him, he knows I could never think differently about him, he knows that I love him, and my life is richer—is fuller because he is a part of it.

He knows everyone whose life he is a part of thinks the world of him. He also knows his secret is safe with me. No one will ever know of, or see his scars unless he lets them. He has to view himself as something other than a failure and has to start believing in and loving himself. I hope I can get through to my good buddy and he listens to me. Let's just leave it at that for now.

-A Part You Cannot Touch

There is a part of every person that one can never touch; that one can never share; that one can never access. Sometimes that part is better left untouched. Sometimes that part isn't necessary to be known because it is ever-present or unimportant.

When we find a soul mate, the part we cannot touch is virtually nonexistent, but more often than not we are not with a soul mate. More often than not we rationalize, or we tolerate, or we go against what we feel and know to be true.

Usually we are attracted to individuals where the part you cannot touch is tremendous, is hidden, is secretive, is unconsciously manipulative, and virtually undetectable. This is a deceptively alluring attraction.

I've had relationships where I've heard and felt a mumbled boiling of perversions in my partner's mind. Thoughts, feelings, and energies contrary to every action, gesture, and uttered word, existed in my so-called love's being. I knew this. I knew something was not right, yet I convinced myself otherwise. I convinced myself I was off, or incorrect and persisted forward reluctantly because of what I believed to be an illogical caution. In many senses questioning or doubting what you somehow know is bad.

When the very essence of the person you are with is the part of that individual that makes them unique; that would allow you to become close to them, and them to become close to you; that would enable them to truly love and be intimate; that would enable you both to "know" each other. When that part is the catalyst and it cannot be accessed, you are in serious trouble. It is hard enough to be intimate because one must drop all of their defenses, and without defense mechanisms there is no cushioning whatsoever.

There is no one alive that really knows anyone. You don't know your mother, your father, your best friend, your partner, or anyone else for that matter. How could you when most individuals don't even know who they are, and we don't know ourselves? We might think we do, but we don't share with each other, we are not honest with ourselves, and our hidden thoughts and feelings become cancerous, destructive, and denied.

I think one of the problems is that no one remembers we are fragile animals. Our entire lifespan is approximately twelve degrees. That makes me laugh. Our body temperature must remain within a twelve-degree-range or we are dead. Although truly morbid it is a simple truth that we are only on this earth for a brief moment in time. We are only on this earth the way we understand and know ourselves to be for a flash in the pan.

We are unique, we are human, we are fragile, and something within each of us just is not right. Because of something not being right within each of us on an individual level, even if that something is miniscule—all of us collectively have contributed to the gruesome reality we call life. All of this miniscule negative and destructive energy shifts everything off-kilter for all of existence; and the horrid states of the world and individual's personal lives are directly affected.

I don't even know where to start, and to be completely candid with you I'm a bit emotional to be speaking so coldly and philosophical, but right now it seems to feel right. When I feel, I remember I'm an animal. The very word animal is actually derived from the Latin word "anima." It just so happens that "anima" means "alive." It isn't a bad thing to be alive, to be an animal. I'm not going to say if we thought like an animal, but if we felt like an animal, if we lived more simple and natural lives, perhaps we'd feel a little more alive. This is part of the reason why we all unconsciously have a fear of intimacy. This is part of the paradox. This is part of the high.

I like to think that at least in the company, at least in one person's presence; the two of us could and should be totally nude, totally exposed to each other. This must not have to be contrived, this should not feel dangerous, and this must not be bargained with—used as a bartering chip. I want to live rather than living to be remembered. I want to be free of fear, so I expect trust to be an unspoken given. I am tired of hearing sweet nothings, having my ears massaged, and watching life slip through my hands because I'm too busy existing. I'm tired of having to play games and read in-between lines.

Massaging my ears with meaningless words really upsets me. It isn't because I think the words are meaningless, it's the exact opposite. I don't want to get into that. I can't get into that now, but I will say I'm really starting to appreciate the silence more than ever before. I think in silence, just as in darkness our senses are amplified, and everything becomes increasingly sharper.

Could it be true that only in darkness one's true self is revealed? When making love, we prefer to occasionally make eye contact, but I'd say for the most part we keep our eyes closed. We try to feel ourselves with our bodies; we try to feel and see another person, using a different mechanism.

And I don't know if you've fucked before, but when we fuck, we are looking with our eyes wide open. The eyes are the windows to the soul, and when fucking you can see just how tainted and sick some souls are. Visual stimuli are received in a desensitized, yet domineering manner on an individual and societal basis. From my perspective, and I think you will agree, that which is not visible to the human eye is what's meaningful, coveted, desired, and considered by many: priceless.

Getting back to being remembered; remember Alexander the Great? From what I've read and seen in history books, movies, and documentaries I always found him very sexy, strong, intelligent, and sad. He conquered the known universe—the known world. He was a spectacular, strong, and fearless warrior. He had a vision of unity and equality that was far before his time, and even before ours. It is yet to be realized.

The precise moment in Alexander's mind when he realized, when he believed he conquered the known world—what did he do? "The Great" wept like a little princess that skinned her knee. He completely exposed himself and broke down. It has never been suggested that this was a sign of weakness, and that is because it clearly isn't. That proves to me that he was a normal individual with aspirations, goals, and feelings. He believed to have accomplished his unachievable dream, and now had nowhere left to go. He had nothing left to do.

Alexander lost so much to gain everything, and now his heart was empty, he was empty, and ultimately unfulfilled. He did conquer the known world and bring about an awareness and hope. He did lead an adventurous and fearless life. He didn't use knowledge because knowledge is the enemy of faith, the enemy of one's belief in themselves. He understood best the win/win/lose/lose scenario. It really doesn't matter if you are searching and the object/state/destination does exist, doesn't exist, may or may not exist—during the search you are incomplete, unsatisfied, and have a feeling of emptiness; yet you are motivated, driven and crazed. Upon completing your quest, you are still empty. The intrigue is the unknown, the raw experiences and feelings, the chase.

Generally speaking men approach everything in a methodical manner, and women are extremely emotional. And I'm speaking about real men, not Neanderthal men using their dick's brain—remember this is generally speaking. Life is not an equation to be solved, nor is it something to always be wonderful and well received. Life is a beautiful mystery to be lived and enjoyed. We as humans have become conditioned to not trust the unknown, unless of course it is an approved truth making some sense of the unknown.

There is nothing more beautiful than simplicity. Simplicity can often be coupled with the ordinary, with the natural, with the intimate, with comfort. Simplicity is often absolutely exquisite harmony. And dreams; dreams are beautiful, but must ultimately be viewed as nothing more than unlived thoughts, unlived desired, and unlived longings. The unconscious mind must be realized and shrunk. That will bring "dreams" to the consciousness and they will evaporate, be forgotten, be dropped, or accomplished and realized.

I am tired of deluding myself with fantasies and dreams. I am tired of reality falling short of expectation. My thoughts, my dreams, my logic, and emotions are perpetuating my state of disconnection. I know I am still not capable of being alone and in a joyous relationship with myself. If I am not capable of being fulfilled, if I don't feel in harmony with myself, I can never be in an intimate and fulfilling relationship with another.

How many people are truly at peace and in love with themselves? I know I have more to go on my individual journey, and I know everyone has mountains and plains to cross; but in the mean time I don't necessarily feel like being alone. At the same time I don't feel like engaging in something fake, or feeling as though I'm wasting my time, or a part of something that doesn't feel right.

Perhaps the only thing that matters in life is that one must develop an intimate and viable relationship within themselves. Maybe not the only relationship, but at the very least the most important relationship one should nurture. Maybe, just maybe, we were all meant to be solitary creatures, never becoming so attached to anything we couldn't leave in under thirty seconds. Or perhaps we were meant to be so open and loving that we are so attached and a part of anything, we never feel detached. Usually when you take the left to the extreme, you become so far left you are right. I don't know. The only thing I can say with certainty, the only thing I truly know is that everything is grey, and I know damn near nothing.

———

Is the essence and appeal of life the romantic and poetic aspects? The essence and appeal of romance is the irrational, undying hope that for a moment you can stop the process towards death; and for a moment you can escape the confines of the primal loneliness that each person lives. Romance is a mystique and concept that on a rational, realistic level humans reject.

The paradox of romance is that the moment you transfigure the real by combining it with the ethereal, this ultimate high and beauty transfers into pain, suffering and loss. Romance is a double-edged sword; one isn't sure if they should go out with, or marry "Madam" or "Monsieur Right" because the apocalyptic high only lasts for a brief moment and is rarely ever achieved again. However, one must live life and create experiences that are revered as incredible and keep them the locket of their hearts and minds.

Romance is another dimension added to love because there is only one type of love. A heightened emotional state is what romance is about, not just the physical aspect of sex. Making love is the consummation of this temporary emotional state. Sex isn't a consummation of anything, and an individual can fuck inanimate objects if he or she desires.

Romance is in the eyes and mind. When romance hits, it is a high; a high that is maintained as long as possible. Romance is a surreal fantasy brought to life. It is when two people are hopelessly in love with each other's mind, body, and soul.

Romance is about ice cream, candle light dinners, red wine, Swiss chocolate, picnics, carriage rides, poetry, holding hands, dancing, dining, taking long talks and walks on the beach, and wanting to be close to the one that you love. When any couple is involved in a romantic episode time is irrelevant and the night is always young.

Romance has no boundaries and knows no color, race, sex or creed. It can be achieved between any two people. When romance is achieved however, it takes the human brain one nanosecond to recognize, but a lifetime to comprehend. I know I am a hopeless romantic. I know I'm searching for that special some one, and I don't know if this is a good thing. I don't think it is healthy, but yet I desire it.

I'm just tired of all the ups and downs, ups and downs, ups and downs. Will we ever stop being afraid? Will we ever stop comparing our realities, our perceived realties, to the fantasies and preconceived notions in our minds? Will we ever stop thinking we did something wrong? As a good person, what have I done to deserve to be alone, deserve to be lied to, deserve to be manipulated?

Will someone please tell me! I just don't know. I just don't know, and that doesn't even bother me. It is the fact I feel powerless and helpless to change anything. I feel powerless and helpless. I fear I will never find someone on the same page as me reading the same words. I fear I will always have a part of me not only that no one can ever touch, but that I will never know.

There is nothing like the sheer madness of a coffee station in 7-Eleven around six, seven in the morning; or half past six, seven at night. Every one scrambling to make the perfect cup of coffee; some rude bastards paying no attention to common courtesies and just satisfying their needs as quickly as possible.

But at the same time, there is a real art to it. Everyone likes their coffee a particular way. No one is going to convince me differently; I do like coffee many ways, and many different types of coffee, but I'm not going to say that black is the only way to drink it. Once in a blue moon, yes, I want a strong double shot of espresso strait up, but a regular coffee black, no way. A tall American coffee can be made so much better by adding to it.

And the folks at Sev's are always trying to get the freshest pot and never sacrificing the proper levels of sugar, sweeteners, cream, milk, and so on and so forth. People using half a packet of sweetener, one and a half packets of sugar, and a dash of half and half, followed up by a dash of two percent. And if there is only a dash of half and half left, they'll ask an employee to please get another few half and half's over to the coffee station.

Only those who don't know much about American coffee, or pure masochists drink it black. Why would you drink a 7-Eleven, or more specifically a tall coffee black? The only coffee you would drink black would be an espresso, and Sev's doesn't have an espresso yet. They should, I heard a rumor that some are starting to now. Black coffee isn't even black; it is light brown, the same color of shit water. You need to cream it up, give it some love.

You know there are a few 7-Elevens, and I don't know why they all don't do it, but some have the plastic bears of 100% natural honey. When I'm in the mood for a tea, I love putting honey in it. Just thinking about it makes me want to get a tea right now. But, I hate those little packets of honey — I hate them and I'm not going to waste my time telling you so because you've experienced them or could imagine what it is like to try to get a small amount of honey out of a small plastic and foil package that you must rip and squeeze.

So, back to the sheer madness — at this point in my life, I'm not going to drink a coffee at Sev's if I cannot have cinnamon hazelnut flavored creamer, and when it is low and warm, or when there is none left, and I kindly ask a gentleman who works there to go in the back and get me another, if they don't have any — they don't have any.

When I want a coffee, and I'm going out to get a coffee, I'm going to Sev's and that is what I want. I expect them to have cinnamon hazelnut creamer at all times. It's not the same as cinnamon hazelnut coffee with cream. I know the difference, and I don't consider it to be an adequate substitute. I like regular caffeinated coffee. I use the 20 ounce ups, and I know by eye how much sugar to pour in, creamer, and half and half.

Then I add the hottest and freshest batch of coffee I can find, or if I'm not in a rush I wait the entire two minutes it takes to brew up a piping hot fresh before your very eyes batch.

If they don't have cinnamon hazelnut creamer,

"I'm sorry sir, we are all out." I try to contain myself, I often think of driving to another Sev's and try my luck once again – but I often switch to Lipton's tea, but for God's sake they better have honey.

When it comes to tea and me, there is nothing better than having tea with a little honey. You always have to have honey if you operate a 7-Eleven. Some things you just can't run out of as a franchise. If they don't have honey, well, I settle for nothing. I'm not going to drink something just to drink something.

Part of my daily ritual is going to Sev's. I go in the moning, I go in the mid afternoon, and I go late evening. I'm usually always going for a coffee, and it's just because I like some of the folks who work there, and I like to get out, sometimes bump into folks and catch up, or coordinate schedules. It's just nice being kind of social, and Sev's seems to be the only type of social environment I like or have time for.

Everyone usually grabs a drink, or some kind of candy, and hangs out in front of Sev's for ten minutes or so, socializing, looking around, and taking a little down time. My buddy every time I see him it is 12:55 p.m. and he needs to be back at work for 1:00 p.m. He always says to me, "I need to get back to work; oh well, I guess I'm going to be 5 minutes or so tardy."

I've never understood those people who drink those healthy shakes that taste like chalk just because they are healthy. Those people who actually convince themselves that they like drinking these shakes. Listen, anything you put in a dog's bowl, and the dog won't touch it, you know there is something wrong. A dog enjoys the taste of antifreeze, something that will kill the dog, and yet a dog rather die of starvation than drink a health food shake.

And why don't we have coffee houses? I'm talking high quality coffee bars that are sociable places with reasonable prices. Italy, Spain, England—just about all of Europe has wonderful cafés and bars. Why don't we have that here?

And I'm not talking about a Starbucks where you feel as though you were actually violated. Teenagers can't even go there because you have to spend twenty fucking dollars for pretty much nothing.

I love the people who work at Starbucks though, they are some of the nicest people. They do a great job, and they make the drinks just how you ask for them. I have three drinks that I really enjoy at Starbucks, but I never fucking go there unless a girl I'm with goes, "Oooo, can we get some Starbucks?" And then I say sure because I never mind dropping unnecessary money on women.

But if I'm by myself, no fucking way; going to Starbucks is never by my choosing. Starbucks is completely ridiculous, and a complete failure. There espresso is some of the worst tasting espresso on earth, but unfortunately most people don't know what espressos exist out there in this beautiful world, and Starbucks has a lot of people in America convinced that their coffees are the best of the best and worth every penny. Starbucks is laughing all the way to the bank.

The worst coffee I ever had in Italy is infinitely better than the best coffee I ever had at Starbucks. Their coffee sucks. No, no, I never said that. I told you I have three favorite drinks there; I never mentioned any of them being coffee.

I would never drink a Starbucks coffee, I rather

buy and drink an overpriced bottle of natural spring water. But I will say again, some of the loveliest people work in Starbucks—and I'm talking both men and women. All the employees seem to have their own personality, and they let it shine through, while at the same time never being angry at the world or sharing negative downer shit with you. "Yes, I guess today is a nice day, but for me it sucks because I don't feel well and I still have to work here for another three hours, then go home and make diner, do some school work…"

I hate when people air their personal woes, and I have to hear their fucking sob story when I'm trying to get a coffee. It's not that I don't care, but I don't. If they are my friend, that's another story, but some person I just met, I don't want to hear your problems.

Well, the employees at Starbucks, they don't have problems, and they always seem jovial. I've gone out with many a beautiful Starbucks' female employees, and they were pleasant and wonderful girls. Enough about that. I can't believe that I talked about the employees and had to make it clear that I felt this way. It should be clear that just because I hate the monster doesn't mean that I hate his children.

It was no ordinary day. It was the day of what I guess you would call a "Beer Marathon." You see in my small village, in the Czech Republic, we have this thing. It happens once a year, and what you do is you make a team, and drink all day. Your team consists of three people in total and you literally run from pub to pub. Each person on your team must drink two pints of ale, and then off to the next pub you go. The team of three that gets to the last pub and finishes their beers together wins the marathon. Oh, and the prize is wonderful. You each get a keg of the very best Czech beer.

Me and my two girlfriends were really looking forward to it. We had participated in this event every year since we were twelve, and every year we half seriously, but jokingly would say this is our year to win. It started off wonderfully as it always does, and in case you didn't know, the people in the Czech know how to have fun, and also know how to drink more than your average person. I mean look at me. I'm as thin as could be, and I could drink way more than any person I have ever met, man or woman, from any other country. That saying the Irish can drink a lot in my opinion is a complete myth because they drink nothing compared to the Czech, Polish, or Russian people.

As I said before it was no ordinary day, and I had no idea it would be the worst and final day of my life. It was the day my life was stripped away from me, as well as my two girlfriends. Although I don't know what happened to them, or where they went, I think of them often. I think of what would have happened if we didn't participate in this beer marathon? I still believe the end result would have been the same. These men would have abducted us anyway because I now know they were studying our every move for some time.

They knew about me, about my family, about my friends, about my friends' families — things like where we lived, how old we were, where our brothers and sisters went to school, where our parents worked. If we didn't cooperate with them, or if we tried to escape, they promised we would go home only to find a dead family. They would kill our entire family — everyone.

It was horribly awful, we were jogging to the final pub, laughing having a great time, and the next thing I knew, something crashed into side of my head, and I was unconscious. When I woke up I was completely naked, and so cramped I couldn't move at all. My legs and my arms were bound together in the same fashion you might tie a pig before roasting it, and fabric was stuffed in my mouth making it impossible for me to say anything, and difficult to breath. I was in complete blackness, and I knew there was someone next to me, because I could feel the warmth of another body. I also knew I was in a car that was moving because I could feel the vibrations from the street.

After what seemed like an eternity, the trunk of the car opened, and I couldn't see very well because I had been in such darkness with my eyes open for a very long time. I realized that myself, and my two friends had made this horrific voyage together, but where we were I had absolutely no idea. This tremendous man put his arm in-between our legs and arms picking each one of us out of the trunk and dropping us on our backs on the floor. I noticed there were many women in the same position as me when I regained my vision as I looked around with my cheek on cold wet cement. All I could hear was women moaning and I saw many tears rolling down many eyes.

I will never forget the eyes of my dearest friend Susan, she looked like the woman in Hitchcock's *Psycho* after she had been slain in the shower; Susan was catatonic. After some time, once again I don't know how long, we were picked up, and slid across this rusty iron bar, now suspended and hanging next to each other in the air like meat. I could feel warm blood start to trickle down my arms and legs, and all the circulation to my feet and hands was cut off. I felt as though my back and neck were breaking, and I couldn't imagine what was to happen to us next.

I wished to God they just killed me already, and in fact that is what I thought they were going to do, but I suffered a much worse fate. I was starting to get dizzy, because I had a day of drinking, and now I was suspended with all of my blood rushing to my head. I was tired, and it was impossible for me to hold my head up anymore so I just had to let it hang, and I could see a whole bunch of men in suits joking around approaching us.

One man in particular, although I couldn't see him was inviting all these men in suits to have a look at us. They were walking back and forth, and I don't know how many of us there were, but I could hear the moans were growing more intense. By this time the pain I felt was so intense and all encompassing, I felt nothing. The girl next to me was crying because one man was punching her in her legs, arms, and ass, and pulling on her nipples as though he was going to rip them off. He remarked, "This one is firm and strong, she looks like she will be a good earner; so far she is my first choice."

All of these men in suits were speaking different languages, and although I didn't understand everyone, I understood most of them. I can speak proficiently German, Italian, Russian, Czech, Polish, French, Spanish, Portuguese, and English. In school I studied languages because it has always been my dream to travel the world and learn about, and communicate with people of different cultures in their native languages. The Arabs I had no idea what they were saying because their culture and their language never interested me; and prayed none of them came near me. Fortunately they didn't because they obviously have a thing for only the blond haired, blue-eyed girls.

Next, this pole we had been suspended from violently and suddenly went crashing to the ground. I remember hearing many shrieks of pain, and a lot of laughing from the men. Fortunately for me, I unconsciously lifted my head and landed on my shoulders and not my head like most of the women.

Our feet were cut away from our hands, but our arms and legs were still bound together. We were now each allowed to stand, although it was very difficult because we were bound in balls for God knows how long. The girls who refused to stand, or two weak to stand, quickly stood when an example was made out of one of them. One of the girls refusing to stand had her throat slit, and her tongue pulled through the opening so it looked like she was wearing a man's tie. After viewing that, all the women stood on their own accord.

While standing, I caught a glimpse of the man who had invited the men in suits to have a look at us; I knew it was him because I recognized his voice. I'll never forget his voice. He only spoke in English, and I'm guessing all the gentlemen in suits had a basic working knowledge of English, the universal language. He said, "Why don't you test out the women you fancy free of charge. Feel free to do whatever you want to them, just don't abuse their faces."

These men in suits proceeded to drop their pants to their ankles, and if anyone tried to resist, they would slap us repeatedly being sure not to damage our faces, or punch us in our ribs and stomachs making it impossible for us to breathe because we were all still bound and gagged. Occasionally, they would cut us with razors under our armpits or on the souls of our feet, or stab us with keys in our ribs and lower backs.

Then we were violently fucked over and over, so many times that I just blacked out. When I blacked out or when any of the girls lost consciousness, the tremendous man who picked me out of the trunk would shoot ice cold water on us from a hose, just laughing sadistically. I suppose that was his job for the moment, to revive any women who passed out from the trauma and torture.

After being fucked, and fucked everywhere, with not only dicks, but with broomsticks, or hands, I could see blood coming from my vagina, and knew blood was coming out of my rectum because it was very warm. Now, I guess I'll call him the host of this sadistic escapade for lack of a better term, he said, "Give me twenty minutes or so to clean these bitches up, and during that time you think over your decisions, and then we will let the bidding begin."

We were all pushed and shoved into this tiny room, and the only way we could move was by hoping because our feet were still bound together. With every hop we left a trail of blood because most of us had gaping slits in the souls of our feet. At this point in time, beyond feeling pain, I wasn't even in a hellish nightmare. What was happening to me was impossible, and I convinced myself that I was sleeping in my parent's home. I would have to wake up shortly.

Now with a fire hose that had so much pressure we were pushed into the concrete walls, and later to the ground, we were hosed off with ice-cold water all together. Everyone was standing in puddles of pink water.

An old gentleman, with sad and compassionate eyes, toweled each one of us off, rather delicately, and I remember the tremendous gentleman holding the fire hose telling him to hurry the fuck up because he didn't have all night, he only had now less than twenty minutes. I could see that this man was just as scared as we were, and how he got caught up in all of this, God only knows. He feared for his life as well, but he made sure never to hurt or scare any of the women, and I remember with me, he dried my intimate parts in the same fashion you'd dry a baby, and he made sure to occasionally make eye contact with me to make sure he didn't do anything to hurt me because after all I was profusely bleeding. I felt so sorry for him.

After toweling us off, a bathrobe was draped over our shoulders, and we were instructed to move back into the other room of this warehouse. Some of the girls, exhausted, and in tremendous physical pain just fell to the ground, and instead of being picked up were just kicked and rolled into the other room by that tremendous gentleman who was really enjoying himself. He reminded each of us of the woman who had her throat slit and assured us that there was an endless supply of young tight bitches. The master of ceremonies told him to have fun, but try not to break anything on the girls because that would bring down their value. "Nobody wants to buy a bitch with a broken arm or leg, then they won't be able to work." That guy was all about business.

When in the room for the second time now, the master of ceremonies said, "Let the bidding begin," and that is exactly what happened: This master of ceremonies would hit us behind our knees and push us one by one to the cold concrete ground and start the bidding.

For each of us, the bidding began at 5000 euro; that is 5000 euro to purchase a person. And it was a bidding war, men were going back and forth fighting with each other, or negotiating with each other—if you let me buy her, I won't bid against you on the third bitch from the end. Alliances were formed, and much money was changing hands. More money than I had ever seen before.

The master of ceremonies would give a little biography on each girl telling her age, where she was born, assured her teeth were hygienic, and would provide the highest bidder with all of her background information so that if she tried to escape her family could easily be found and murdered. The information was insurance because these men wanted to be sure to protect their investments.

As each woman was bought, she was thrown into the back of a truck. I'm guessing each one of these men came with their own box truck as to transport the women to their new destinations. My beautiful friend Susana was bought for 11,000 euro by this disgustingly grotesque and fat Arab mother-fucker, and it came as no surprise to me because she is a blonde haired, blue eyed angel. My other friend was bought by a Frenchman; I could tell he was a Frenchman by his accent when he tried to speak English.

My father always told me it is easy to spot a Frenchman when they speak because when the French were born, they were born without mouths. Their mother would take a pin, and poke a tiny hole where their mouth should be, and that is why all French people when they speak sound like they are talking out of an asshole. I think French is a beautiful language, but it is true, you must keep your mouth somewhat more closed and they are a very arrogant, snobbish, cowardly people. The French don't even really like the French.

I was bought by a little-fat-balding Russian; and he was little in just about every way from what I remember. Except of course his rage and temper. That day was the last time I saw any of my friends. I don't know what tragic fates they suffered, or are suffering. I don't know where they went, or what has become of them, all I can do is pray and hope that the bastards who bought them are murdered or tortured, or I pray that they are dead because I wish this life of being forced to fuck on no one other than the bastards who use us like pawns in a devilish game of chess.

While in the truck with these eleven other girls from all over the world, the Russian came in the back and gave us a little speech in his very best English. He told us, "You all belong to me. I kill you if you make noise. I kill you and your family if you try escape. You belong to me, you work for me, I your new father." Then he closed the doors to the back of the truck, I heard them lock, and off we went.

It was a long voyage; I think it was many days, many days of once again being in complete darkness. I was beyond weak for I had not eaten anything in some time now. My head was spinning, and I could hardly move. Some of the girls had to go to the bathroom, and even though we all tried to relieve ourselves in the corners of this truck, the stench of for lack of a better terms, shit and piss was nauseating; and in fact many of the women started vomiting up what little they had in their stomachs, or just dry heaving. The souls of my feet were burning because I was stepping in all this bile.

When we arrived at this new destination it was night, and we were instructed to one by one climb out of the truck, and once our feet were unbound, we were told to walk through a door. There were two men with machine guns, there was no where to run, so all twelve of us walked into this building, and up many fights of stairs, all being directed to a little room with a toilet and a shower. The Russian who bought us, and the two men with machine guns proceeded to take off all of their clothes, and freed our hands now. They told us if we tried to take off our gages, they would torture us, so no one dared move their hands near their face.

They each fucked us once again, or tried to stick

as much of there hands and fists as they could into our vaginas, and rectums, or would laugh and take turns seeing how far they could stick a broomstick into our vagina or anus, and they were taking crude measurements as to who had the deepest anus, or the most flexible pussy. This went on for many hours, and occasionally more gentlemen would join in, some would leave, some would come back. I was one of the lucky ones, what was happening to my body was not happening to me.

At this point in time, I felt nothing, I was dead, I had lost my will to survive. Although my eyes were open, I didn't see anything at all. Everything was a blur.

Although I'm not deaf, somehow my brain shut off my ability to hear. I was conscious, but unconscious. I suppose that was their goal, to completely break us, and break us they did.

I was dead inside I tell you, I was bleeding from everything except my eyes and ears, and there was nothing more they could do to hurt me. I remember thinking about when he said he would torture us; if this wasn't torture then I don't know what was. What more could they possibly do to us!

When they were finished abusing us, our new daddy told us to get into the shower and clean ourselves up. Just as he was saying that, another gentleman entered the room with a box of clothes, and our new daddy told us to put on some clothes, and he would be back in one hour and expected all of us to look presentable. He said if we were able to stay quite, we could remove our gages, but he was leaving one of the gentlemen in the room with us, and instructed the man to beat us and break our ribs if he saw or heard any talking of any kind.

The box of clothes that was presented to us really wasn't clothing at all. It was all this lingerie, and we were expected look very sexy. After dressing and cleaning ourselves, we went into a kitchen and there was food everywhere with our daddy and other gentleman eating.

He said to us, "You girls must be very hungry. You can eat, but you can only eat just as soon as you start making money. Nothing is free!"

We were given a long trench coat with not much lining in it, a cheap digital watch, and were on our way out of this building to have a tour of our surroundings. I knew we were in Russia, but exactly where we were I had no idea; all I knew is it was beyond cold outside; so cold that I saw birds frozen on the street dead, so cold that a tear would instantly freeze on your face and split your skin.

While on the tour, he explained to us the rules. He said, "I trust you ladies. I trust you never disobey me. I trust you be good earners. The more money you make, the more food you eat, the more freedom you have. These streets you work. These streets you find many customer. I know all police. The police never bother you, I give money to police and they watch you for me. If you ask Police for help, or if you ask another person and he go to police, they will say to me this, and I will hurt you more than you've ever been hurt in all the life. If I no trust you, you have nothing."

Then he introduced us to a beautiful girl wearing sunglasses and a glove on her right hand that was being escorted by another Russian gentleman. He said, "Have a good look at her. Isn't she beautiful? She still work for me. She still a good earner. She ask a man for help one time. This man try to help. This man dead now. She write a letter to family. Family never get letter. Have good look at her. She look no more."

He proceeded to take off her sunglasses, and remove her glove. Her eyes had been scooped out of her skull. She had no eyes, no eyelids just two holes. All of the fingers on her right hand except her thumb were cut off at the knuckles. He told us this isn't even the worst fate we could suffer, and if that wasn't the worst fate, I don't know what in God's name could be.

So we learned about the streets, where we were, and he told us that we all must go back to his building at six in the night, then six in the morning. He told us as well that there were lots of wealthy Russian and Chinese international businessmen in this town, so we always better come back with money, or we would be very sorry. He said, "Each one you bitches I pay good money for. Until I get back money I spend on you, right now I have negative money and I very mad. Never take less than 20 euro each man, and when you have 200 or more, come back fast."

I was thinking 200 or more euro is a tremendous amount of money for me; me being Czech. In my village a beer cost 10 cents you know. I remember thinking if I was to earn money like that, I could certainly find a good spot on the streets to hide some money here and there; I could certainly outsmart this Russian bastard, and save my family. Although I was dead inside, I was still physically alive, my brain still worked—I just needed to become a machine for a few years, or until I figured something out. I needed my father and mother, my sister, and brothers to know just how much I love them, and that my disappearing was in no way their faults.

The days were cold and long and all seemed to blur together. I was ageing tremendously before my very eyes because being fucked by ten to twenty men a day takes a lot of life out of a person. But I was a master of my craft and knew just what to say, and how to get much more than 20 euro from each gentleman. All the men desired me, and none of them could last very long sexually.

I found a loose brick on a building in a rather dark alley, and I started to save money. Twenty euro here, fifty euro there, and the money was adding up. I never gave that son of a bitch more than 200 euro for a ten-hour shift—never ever! And why should I? He had no idea how many men I was fucking, or what I was earning for him.

Yes the police were everywhere, and yes I could always feel their eyes watching me, and I was fearful that I would be seen hiding money behind that brick. I never thought of the ramifications of my actions if I was to be caught. I never told anyone, and never initiated a conversation with any of the women who worked as prostitutes. I figured they all must be for lack of a better term completely fucked up, and I don't want to know anything about them, or what they are thinking, or doing, or trying to do—I only want to be concerned with myself. I never spoke with anyone, until of course Justin.

I remember seeing this gentleman once in a while. I suspected he was just a regular guy because he drove a beat-up car, and was always dressed with very thin clothing. His boots had holes in them, and he lived in a building that to the eye would appear to be abandoned. He would always look at me with an intrigued look on his face, and I got the impression he really thought I was beautiful. He really thought to himself, why is this woman doing what she is doing?

After many months of making eye contact with me, one day he approached me, and asked me what my name was. I told him my name, and I could see he just thought I was playing with him because he didn't believe me. He found it strange that I had the same name as a famous American icon.

I told him I didn't care if he believed me or not, my name is Madonna and I have no reason to lie to you, or anyone else about my name for that matter. I also told him he should feel privileged because he was the only person who I ever told my name to. I didn't have to tell my name to that Russian bastard who bought me because he had a full biography of who I was, and where I was from; I never told my name to any of the bastards I fucked, I always just asked them, "What do you want to call me big boy," or "who do you want me to be?"

He said to me, "You are a very beautiful woman, and I don't know why you are doing what you are doing? I see you almost every day and always wanted to ask you this: would you like to come to my home because it is very cold outside and drink some hot tea?"

I was a bit suspicious; in fact I was always suspicious of everything because how could I be sure he was a genuine individual after all. Perhaps he worked for my new daddy, perhaps this was his ploy, and when my daddy found out that I went to a kind man's apartment for a cup of tea, and didn't receive any money, just chatted with some gentleman, I would be tortured.

So I needed to find out more information about him in a manner that didn't seem to invasive. I asked him if he wanted to know why I was doing what I was doing, and he replied, "One day, if you would like to confide in me, that's fine, but I just want to get us out of the cold for a little while. I just want to have a cup of tea with a beautiful woman."

Something in my gut told me to trust him. Something told me that this man, this man of twenty something new nothing about the injustices and sadistic practices in my world. I looked around for police, and saw none, so I decided to trust this man. I had already made more than enough money for one day of work, so I certainly had some time to spare, and when I returned back to my daddy's building I would have nothing to fear.

In his apartment he did just what he said. A fire was roaring so it was warm, and he started to boil water and brew some tea. The tea was so delicious, and I was very grateful. It was the first cup of tea I had in Russia. He apologized for the condition of his apartment, and he wished he had more to offer me than just tea. He also apologized for not formally introducing himself.

His name was Justin Cavior. I asked him what nationality or ethnicity he was because I never heard a last name like that, and he told me he had no idea. He was an orphan, and had no known family. When he was 17, he was given the opportunity to change his name before being sent out into the real world, and something in his soul told him that Cavior was his last name. But, he had no idea why. He laughed at me when I told him it sounded a bit French, he told me of all the ethnicities he possibly could be he knew he wasn't Chinese or French. He said he always felt as though he was an American, and one day dreamed of living somewhere in California or Hawaii where the weather is always warm and beautiful.

After chatting with him for some time, and really just learning about him, and what he did for work, or how long he had been in Russia for, or what was his favorite artist or classical composer—just as I started to feel like a normal human being again, having normal conversation, I realized it was getting late. I started to get my things together. He begged me not to leave, to just stay a bit longer, but I assured him it was the best time I had in a long time and we would do this again soon enough.

For the next few days, I didn't see Justin, and I was worried. Yes, perhaps I was wrong; perhaps he did work for my daddy. Perhaps my daddy was just waiting, waiting to torture me; perhaps my daddy was just waiting long enough until he could kill my family and show me evidence of there deaths. But then I started to recall the short story by Edgar Allen Poe I once read about the tell tale heart or something, and I knew it was just my imagination getting the best of me. No heart was beating under my floor. That Russian son of a bitch knows nothing, and that is what I should be telling myself rather than hearing a beating heart in a dead person, and trying to act nicer than usual, or looking deeper into the meanings of words that were uttered and subtle gestures.

Finally, I saw Justin again, around eight o'clock at night, and he asked me how I was. I told him I was as good as I could be given the circumstances, and asked him where he had been in these days, and what happened to him because he looked extremely sick.

He told me he was in the hospital because he had a terrible accident. He appeared to be fine other than his pale complexion and his hands bandaged up in gauze, but when he lifted up his shirt for me, I could see that his stomach and chest had been completely burned. "The burnt skin you see on me isn't from a fire, it is a chemical burn. You remember I work unloading trucks? I never know what I'm unloading, but I unload whatever is on the truck. One of these containers had in it some kind of acid, and while carrying it, it ruptured all over my hands, arms, chest, and stomach."

I felt so sorry for him. He is such a beautiful young gentleman, and I assured him he was still handsome with the face and body of an ancient Greek God. He laughed, and said to me, "Please don't make me laugh again because my skin and body hurts too much. Sheets of my skin have been coming off." He then asked me if I wanted to accompany him for some potatoes, cabbage, bread and tea, and I explained to him that it was still early in the night, and I needed to work, but if it is possible, I would meet him at his apartment for midnight.

That night at midnight, I knocked on his door, but he wasn't answering. Just as I was about to walk away, he came to the door sweating, and I could see he was sick and in much pain. I brought him to his room, and laid him on the bed, and placed cool rags on his head to try to bring down his fever. He just kept saying to me, "I don't know what I am going to do? If I cannot work, I cannot eat, and if I cannot eat, I cannot live, and I am not ready to die just yet. I'm not ready. I'm scared. I have no one." While he was lying in his bed, I noticed a bit more of his body was burnt by these chemicals than just his hands, chest, arms, and stomach—in fact the entire front portion of his body was horribly mutilated, all except for where his belt was fastened upon his waste, where he wore his wrist watch, his ankles, and his feet.

"You know I'm only 24 Madonna. I'm 24 years old, and look at me; I have nothing. I have nothing and who will ever want me now? You are the first real woman I ever spoke to. I don't know why I spoke to you, I guess it is because you are the first woman that I ever found attractive, and something about you just felt familiar and comfortable.

I never approached you because I know what you do for a living, and I don't associate with prostitutes. Something in my heart told me you were different, so one day I said what the hell, let me just talk to you. Now, you would be disgusted to be with a man like me. Look at me Madonna! My entire body is destroyed. Even if I were a rich man, you wouldn't be with me. You couldn't be with me! I haven't even had enough courage to look at my dick yet; I don't even know if it will still work, all I know is it feels like it is on fire along with the rest of my body. I appreciate all that you have done, but please just leave me now. Let me die. I don't want you to remember me like this! Please just get the fuck out of here and never come back!"

I didn't leave him. How could I leave him, he

was my only friend. I just leaned over him, looked into his eyes, and gave him a kiss on the forehead. I didn't want to stop there, for some reason, for the first time since I was in the Czech Republic I felt love, and I gave him a kiss on the nose, on his eyelids, and on the lips, and assured him that everything would be O.K. He fell asleep, and I left him a note telling him I took the keys to his apartment, I want him to stay in bed, and when I had time, I would check on him during the afternoon.

The next day, I decided to take all the money I had been saving over the past few months, and without telling Justin, I hid it in his house. I figured it was better to hide it in his house, than to just leave it behind some loose brick in a building. I went into Justin's room, and he told me he had been feeling a lot better, but I knew that was a lie and he was saying it just to be polite. He thanked me for everything, but I explained to him that what I did for him was nothing; it is what any normal person or friend would do. He said to me, "If there is anything I can ever do for you, now or in the future, just say the word, and consider it done."

During the course of the next few months I continued to work, and twice a day I would visit Justin. He preserved my sanity and gave me hope. He was getting better slowly but surely, and he had enough energy to take himself to the market to buy some food occasionally, but his skin couldn't bear being out in the cold for prolonged periods of time.

At first he had a problem taking money from me, and he remarked, "You work so hard for this money. You do so many things you don't want to do." And I told him that is all the more reason why he should take it—it was blood money. He promised to pay me back little by little just as soon as he could work again, and I told him just his company and his friendship was enough, but I'm sure I would be able to think of something.

One day, and I knew it was going to happen, he said to me, "Do you remember when I told you I don't know why you do what you do? Well now I'm asking you, why does such an intelligent person like you, such a compassionate person as yourself do what you do? Why are you so far away from your home and your family?"

I explained to him my current situation. I explained to him how I was abducted the day of the beer marathon. How I had to check in twice a day with my fucking daddy. How I had to bring him money. How we were abused and tortured. How I couldn't run away because these were dangerous men, and if they couldn't find me, they knew the whereabouts of my family and would kill all of them. He was filled with rage, and told me that he wanted to kill the Russian son's of a bitches for me, but I told him that would be impossible because there are many of them, they know and pay off all of the police and government officials, and they have machine guns and sophisticated surveillance systems.

He asked me what I was going to do, and I explained to him that I didn't know just yet. He asked me why I just didn't write my family a letter, and believe me I already thought of that, but I do know besides the girl whose fingers they cut off, one of the girls told me she had written her family a letter back in England, and was going to get out of this mess within a few days, and don't ask me how, but the very next day, she was murdered by our daddy. I am only lead to believe that our daddy knows some men in the Post Offices in this zone, or knows some government officials who monitor all mail traveling to other countries; perhaps somewhere there is a record of our last names and our family's addresses.

Our daddy makes a lot of money. And at this time his has sixty something women working exclusively for him earning on average at the very least 120 euro each ten hour shift, which means he makes approximately at the very least 7200 euro every ten hours, but probably more like 15,000 euro—plus God knows what else he does. There always seems to be an ample supply of cocaine around for him and his cronies, also for daddy's "privileged daughters."

Justin had a wonderful idea, something I never thought of. "When I can, when I have enough money, I am going to go to the Czech Republic. I am going to find your family. I am going to help them to move far away from your village, and I am going to come back here and take you away from all this madness. In these months, I have grown to love you Madonna, and just as you gave me my life back, I want to do the same for you."

At that moment I knew for certain he was the only person on earth I could trust, and I showed him all the money I had been saving and hiding in his apartment. I had thousands of dollars, and told him to use the money, to use the money to help me. I passionately kissed him, and for the first time I had feeling again; for the first time in over a year I felt alive. We kissed and kissed, and finally we were about to make love when I stopped him.

179

"Oh, I'm so sorry Madonna. I know, I know, my body disgusts you. I am so sorry to think you could be intimate with me." I explained to him that I loved him so much; I explained to him that he was the most beautiful man I had ever known. I explained to him that the reason I didn't want to make love with him was that God forbid I was sick with some awful disease from being repeatedly raped, or for having to fuck so many men, so many times, I would have to kill myself if anything ever happened to him.

After saying that he said, "So that means you could make love to me? That means you would want to make love to me?" I told him, "Of course so Justin. You are the only man I could make love to. You are the only man I would want to hold tightly inside me." At that moment, he gently slid himself inside me and said, "Madonna, I love you. I don't want to be alive without you. If something has happened to you, it has happened to me — until death do us part my love."

We passionately made love, and I was amazed that I was able to feel pleasure. I thought my intimate parts were destroyed and capable of feeling nothing, but I loved this man so much, that I truly felt safe. I felt warm. I didn't feel alone. I felt strong. I felt complete. I remember thinking I never want this to end. I wish I could just stay here with him forever, and soon enough I would be able to. We made love with our bodies; we made love with our minds, souls, and hearts.

The time was getting late once again, and I needed to check in with my daddy. Tomorrow I would see Justin, give him all the necessary information he needed to find my family, and off he would go. When checking in with my daddy, he said to me, "You have a man you see two time a day do you?" I knew he must know something, someone must have seen something. Why did this happen now? Why when I was so close? I said, "Why yes daddy, I do. He is one of my very best customers. I make a lot of money for you off of that poor son of a bitch." I was so scared; I didn't know what would happen to me. I didn't know what else he knew. I didn't know what he would tell me to do, but then he started to laugh. "Come here. Sit here, on me." I proceeded to sit on his lap, and he proceeded to squeeze the back of my neck, squeeze the front of my throat, and my chin, while gazing into my eyes, trying to get a better look into my mind.

For the first time ever he offered me a little cocaine; he offered me to sniff it out of his disgustingly long pinky nail. I had to. I wanted to seem as though it was my honor to do that, it was my absolute pleasure— I needed to seem grateful. "You love your daddy, don't you? You no lie to daddy right? You know if you lie to daddy, daddy torture you, or daddy kill you family?" I said, "Of course I know. I love my daddy. I never ever lie to you. Aren't you happy with me? Can I do something more for my daddy? Have I not been one of your very best earners?"

I proceeded to massage his little genitals, telling him how big and strong he was. I proceeded to suck on his tiny dick and balls, making him feel all warm and fuzzy inside. I proceeded to fuck him in his desk chair, saying to him, "I love my daddy. My daddy is good to me. I love my daddy. I trust my daddy. My daddy love me. My daddy trust me."

After an hour or so with this disgusting greasy son of a bitch, I laid all his concerns to rest, and he told me that if I ever feel myself becoming close with anyone that I must tell him immediately and stop seeing that person, or allow him to kill that person because a prostitute can love no one except their daddy. I assured him with a girlish gaze that I hated seeing and fucking any man other than him, and everyone else just looked like money to me – money that belonged to my daddy.

The next day I went to see Justin, and it was a brief visit. I just needed him to go on his way because I knew perhaps they were on to us. He told me he thought it would be suspicious if he just left, or if I stopped coming by his apartment, and I agreed with him. He would leave in the night undetected, and I would continue to, once a day, go to his empty apartment.

For the next few weeks, I was a machine once again, and continued to go to his apartment to rest for an hour or two. I continued to save more money for myself. I continued to appease my daddy, and started to make him believe I was his very best girl. I started to gain more privileges. I could eat whenever I wanted, and my daddy told me I didn't need to wear a watch anymore, I didn't need to check in twice a day. He trusted me. He started to have me take some of the newer recruits out on the street; he started to have me tell the girls what to do, and how to earn. I had a sense of confidence that everything was going to be just fine.

Finally after a little more than two months, Justin came back. He told me everyone in my family was alive and well except for my father. My real father, my real daddy was dead; I learned he died shortly after I was abducted. When I asked how he died, Justin just said, "Is that really important, I'm sorry Madonna he is gone; he is dead." Justin had moved my entire family to Poland; he had given them the majority of the money, and just kept what would be necessary for him to reach me, and for us to reach them together. He told me the apartment they have in Poland is beautiful, and it will be a wonderful place to make a life just until we all had enough money to move to Hawaii or California. The only thing he didn't know yet was how to get me out of Russia undetected.

That was something I never thought about. After all I was illegally smuggled into this country. I had no identification whatsoever. The police were definitely corrupt, perhaps some government officials, how was I going to get out of Russia? He had an idea. Remember in the past his job was to unload trucks, but in the facility he worked in, on the other side of the compound the folks loaded trucks with various exports. He still knew some people there, and he said one gentleman in particular is a guy he grew up with in the orphanage for a few years. A guy he could trust. What if we were loaded into one of the trucks whose destination was Poland? We would be part of the cargo.

It sounded like a good idea to me. Now that I knew my family was safe, what did it matter? I could reach them in one day, two days, two-weeks — just as long as I got there. Justin assured me he would make all the arrangements, he assured me everything would be perfect — he assured me that this was the best way to get us out of the country. Over the next three days, Justin implemented this plan. We were going to travel to Poland in a truck delivering what other than Russian

Vodka. We would be packed in a box. The voyage would be three days. It sounded great to me, but just incase, God forbid something were to happen, I wanted to know where my family was in Poland, and Justin apologized for not telling me, and gave me a piece of paper with the address.

On a Sunday night, we were packed in separate boxes, and I fell asleep only to be woken up because I knew I as being picked up, and slid way into the back of a truck. I have no concept of how long it took to pack up that truck with all of the vodka, but once we had been on the road for some time, and I heard the truck moving along not stopping at a rather fast speed, I started to cut a little flap out of the side of the box with my nails, and started to say in a soft voice, "Justin? Justin? Can you hear me?" I wanted to be certain he was on the truck with me. I didn't hear him, and was starting to cry.

How could he not be on this truck with me? Where was I going? Where the hell was he? Just as my heart sank into my stomach, just as I was filled with all the fear in the world, just as I felt my life being sucked right out of me once again, I felt his hand touch mine. His hand came through the flap I had cut into the box, and I saw some light, for he had a cigarette lighter in his pocket. "Shhhhhhhh. I told you sweetheart, everything would be perfect. Enough of these fucking boxes — let me get you out my love."

I was afraid, what if were to be spotted when they started to unload the truck, it would be obvious that we were packed onto this truck and trying to cross the boarder. He assured me everything would be all right, and I could do nothing but believe him. We were in the extreme back of the truck, and Justin told me it was hell getting out of his box because the boxes had been packed so tightly together, and each of us had boxes on top of us and all around us, but even if the truck stops, or even if someone is to gaze in, there was at least 25 feet of Russian Vodka in front of us.

He told me the plan was to get us out of this truck before it would ever be unpacked, and when I asked him exactly how he planned on doing that, with a smile on his face he said, "Guess who's driving this fucking truck?" His friend, his friend was driving the truck. His friend had been promoted, and in these months was obtaining the necessary certifications in order operate such a large vehicle, in order to drive over country borders.

Justin's friend was going to pull over to the side of the road and open the back up for us and let us out when we were safely in Poland, but that we weren't to move or make a sound, even if we heard the doors open. We were to start moving only when his friend said, "Free yourselves!"

Justin also explained to me however that there was another gentleman in the truck with his friend, an individual he did not know. That concerned me a bit, but Justin assured me once again not to worry because if anyone jeopardized our freedom, he would kill them or die trying. I asked him how he planned on doing that, or what if they had a gun, and he said, "Well, what if I have a gun? What if I have a gun that only you know about?"

He really had thought everything through. I wasn't worried in the slightest bit. He passionately embraced me, and we made love in the back of that truck, in extreme blackness, but I knew he could see me, and I surely could see him.

The next day, someone opened up the doors to the back of the truck. We were sure to make no noise, and it was a wise decision because we were still in Russia. It was the police, and they were just checking out the cargo, opening a few boxes here and there, and letting drug sniffing dogs have a few sniffs just to make sure that what was supposed to be in this truck was in this truck. Justin's friend was just laughing and trying to joke around with them. He asked them if they knew his uncle who was a Police officer in this zone, and both officers in fact new him, so they immediately closed the doors, and I don't know what was said after that because I couldn't hear anything other than a bunch of faint laughs.

Once the truck started moving again, I was able to breath more easily, and my muscles became relaxed. It was really happening, I was really escaping and soon after such a long time I would see my family again. I would be able to live with the love of my life, the man who saved me and got me out of my horrible nightmare. I dreamed of us one day getting married on a white sand beach under palm trees in Hawaii.

Everything was happing. Everything was perfect just as he said it would be. Then all hell broke loose once again. But I was too close, we were too close, and Justin wasn't going to let us get caught. We were most certainly getting to Poland and there was nothing anyone could do about it.

The truck stopped again, the doors opened, and boxes were being slid away at a feverishly fast pace. I could hear my daddy's voice, "I know you in there!

Bitch when I see you I kill you! Bitch I kill you!" How did he find us? How did he know? Justin under his breath uttered, "That son of a bitch." He was speaking about his friend driving the truck. His friend had some reservations about the whole "plan," and Justin said that his friend probably asked his relative, his uncle who was a fucking cop about the whole plan, and that cop in turn relayed the information to my daddy." I heard a gunshot, and my daddy screamed in Russian at the top of his lungs, "Kill everyone but the driver! Don't kill the driver!" That very phrase confirmed our suspicions.

Perhaps there was only five or six feet of vodka in front of us now, and Justin started to open up some of the bottles of vodka, and rip off portions of his shirt and stuffing them into the tops the bottles. He looked at me and winked, and said, "Don't worry Madonna — it works in the movies." As soon as he could see a man's head, he lit one of the bottles up, and threw it in that direction setting the man on fire. The man was screaming, and ran off the truck. Daddy said to another gentleman, "Get into the truck. Pull them out alive. I want them alive! I want them to pay for this!" Just as Justin saw the other man approaching, he lit and threw another bottle of vodka, and once again another man was on fire.

Justin and I both heard a little click, and when I made eye contact with him, he quickly grabbed me, and pulled me to the ground. A barrage of bullets from a machine gun was being fired through everything. The fire was growing more intense. I heard my daddy say, "Just pull out the bodies. Come on! Just pull out the bodies. No one survive that." But we did survive it because I think the expression you would say is, "we hit the deck."

When the third man approached Justin lit up another bottle of vodka, threw it at the man's head, and in the same fluid motion started running outside the truck firing his gun away. I heard many shots, I heard the machine gun start to go off again, and then all I could do was hear the fire growing more intense, the smoke building up inside the truck. I needed to get off, so I just closed my eyes, and ran as fast as I could off the truck jumping into the street.

When I landed and opened up my eyes, I saw my daddy crawling rather slowly to a black limousine, and Justin was barely moving. Justin had been shot in the legs, and in the stomach. He couldn't walk, he couldn't talk, and all I could do is tell him to hang on. I picked up his gun, and I ran over to my daddy holding the gun against his temple demanding the keys to the limo. He said, "You stupid bitch. You stupid bitch! The limo is on. Can you not hear you stupid bitch?" Once I realized the limo was on, I said, "I can hear, and I no longer need to fear you." That was the last words my daddy heard before he got his brain shot out the side of his head.

I drove the limo over to Justin, and Justin said to me, "I love you. I love you. Are you O.K.?" When I told him I was just fine, and when I told him to hold on, he said, "I will always be with you, now go find your family" and then he closed his eyes and died. Just as he died, and I was screaming and crying, and kissing him passionately hoping that my kisses would somehow bring him back to life, I could hear Justin's friend saying, "This wasn't supposed to happen. None of this was supposed to happen."

His friend was crying a little bit, and with open arms I invited him over to me, I motioned that I would embrace him, and embrace and hold him I did. Then I shot his brain out the side of his head as well because if he would have kept his fucking mouth shut and just trusted his friend, my love, my savior, the man who gave me back my life and helped reunite me with my family, he would still be alive and right now.

Justin I will never forget you. I will never love another man. I have no words to describe what you did for me and just how much I love you. To the fucking bastards who buy and sell women, who psychologically and physically torture them, who make escaping that sadistic world virtually impossible — your day is coming!

-Monumental Crap

Never will I understand it—shelves and shelves of shitty books. Whether it is in a library, or bookstore, or an acquaintance's home—always do I see books that would better serve as kindling wood in the peak of summer on the hottest of days, or as doorstoppers in a hallway, than as books to borrow, books to buy, or prized possessions.

The monumental crap people read, or tell each other to read is beyond me; and the funny thing is most of the time they defend these bastardizations of literature instead of admitting they read half-assed abortions. Perhaps they are embarrassed? Perhaps they are simpletons? Perhaps they enjoy cuddling up with a heifer or two?

How on God's green earth can people say, "I don't like Shakespeare;" "Yeats is alright;" "Virginia Woolf is nothing special;" or "I don't like Faulkner;" "Mark Twain isn't that good;" "T.S. Eliot, I've heard of him;" "Who's Edith Wharton;" "Steinbeck, didn't he write a book about a retard or is he the misogynistic bastard?;" "Dickens, I never read an entire book of his because he got paid by the word, and they're very lengthy;" "Arthur Miller, he wrote plays, and I never really cared much for plays;"—I won't dare go on anymore because I'm sure you get the point. The truth just drives me mad. People today just don't want to, or are incapable of taking the time to digest and understand an *Unbearable Lightness of Being*, or *The Plague*—so they rather just say, "That book sucks;" or "It could never happen in today's society so it really doesn't interest me."

Just look at that book *Bridges of Madison County*. A man wrote that book on the toilet as a joke just to prove that he could write a best seller, and he did. He sold infinite copies, made loads and loads of money, and even inspired two of the most revered actors to produce a movie. I hope to God good old Clint jumped on that carriage and did it for the money. Certainly not because he thought it was a beautiful story or brilliant work.

I'm not criticizing Clint because he's a great actor and director; in fact he is one the absolute best, and my favorite. Just look at five minutes of the masterpieces *Mystic River*, or *Unforgiven,* or *Gran Torino* if you already haven't and you'll understand.

And I'm not criticizing the author who wrote that trashy love story; he played the game. If authors want to sell out and create crap that the masses will buy, then that is his or her right. Have a few million in the bank, play the game—or—stay true to your passion, your vision, and eat tuna out of a can on Sundays.

Until people stop reading crap, we will have authors and publishing companies with no integrity making tidy little profits, and everyone involved will be driving speedy little imported sports cars, and drinking *Cristal*, buying the finest of caviar just to say they have it. They perpetuate all of this nonsense. They are the one's telling us what to read, & who the next hottest author is.

Recently, I met a beautiful woman. You can tell a lot about a person from the books they've read, the books they love. She was working on an atrocity; I don't want to tell you the title of this book because if it sticks in your mind for even one tenth of a second, that would be too much. The cover of this lucky find was visually appealing, and had a quote stating that this book was written by the critically acclaimed author of *The Lovely Bones*. Critically acclaimed by what, a rock? Did a conscious person read this? Was it one of Oprah's "books of the month;" after all she knows everything including great literature right?

I forced myself to read the first 30 pages, 15 pages in the middle, and the last 20; and let me tell you—reading a piece of dog shit bubbling on hot asphalt would have be more stimulating, and creates more visual imagery.

When I told the girl this was one of the worst books I ever read, ever seen, ever looked at—she said, "How could you say that? She is one of my favorite authors. She's writing about her past. About being raped." She wrote about a rape with the same fervor as a person writing about an 18th century tea party.

When I read the very first sentence of the book aloud, and when I read a few sentences of 'crucial importance,' and explained to her that my eyes had been raped by this visual assault of elementary and chaotically scattered words, she said, "That's because you are a man, and you can never understand what it's like to be a woman or feel like a woman, now can I have that back?!"

I'm a man. I hope so, because last time I checked I still had two testicles and a dick. Isn't that the only real difference between men and women, the repro-ductive organs? Women fought so hard for equality, and rightfully so, and now this bitch is going to have the audacity to say to me that I can't understand because I am a man! Perhaps I can't experience exactly what that author, or that character experienced — no, I've never had a dick forcefully pushed in my pussy; that much is true, but I most certainly can envision, comprehend, and sympathize. I've unfortunately known too many wonderful girls that have been brutally raped physically and mentally — and they have shared and communicated their horrific experiences with me, and although enraged for them, at the same time I've been honored they shared something so deep with me.

When I asked her if she ever read any of D.H. Lawrence's novels or short stories, she told me he wasn't that good. When I asked her what she read of his, she replied, "I don't remember. Only part of one of his books; and besides that, two of my friends who are English majors took a course of his work and told me to 'stay away.'"

D.H. Lawrence wrote more like a woman, and understood women, better than most women. If someone was to rip off the cover of the book, and never told you the sex of the author, you'd never know, you'd never guess, it was written by a man. If you tell me so, I'll call you a liar!

The problem of today is we have no more people like Joseph Conrad or Fitzgerald — contemporary writers are developing an increasingly shrinking vocabulary, and really don't know how to organize and use words.

Publishing companies understand that the average person doesn't know what 'apathetic' means, or what 'pragmatic' means, or what a "dolt" is. Perhaps there are a few hundred copies of books by contemporary authors that would blow my mind away like a *Cat's Cradle*, but I will never read them because I don't know they exist.

It's sad but absolutely true that you can find more people who have read every *Better Homes and Garden* and *Vogue* for the past 15 years, but never read or know of *Valpone*.

Magazines filled mostly with advertisements and scattered articles explaining important information like this fall's fashion, or how to get the body you've always wanted, or what placemats would be just perfect in your kitchen are collected like Superman Action Comics from the early 1940's, saved and stored in secure locations. Reading an old Superman comic would prove more useful in life than peeling back a little tab in a magazine and smelling the latest fragrance.

Don't you dare misinterpret me, I'm not saying that *Time Magazine*, and *National Geographic* are a waste of time, because they clearly aren't; I'm just saying people don't choose wisely what jargon to clutter their minds with. You can go to the newsstand and pick up a *USA Today*, or you can go to the newsstand and pick up a *New York Times*.

What do you want to spend your time reading? Maybe you should just read the contents of your favorite cereal on the side of the box to learn about what is happening in the world, what is happening in your country?

The other side of the coin might just be that society has imposed so many burdens upon us that most people just want to have a mind fart when they read, hence we have grown adults reading *The Hunger*

193

Games, or the *Twilight Saga*. What a load of crap.

Why do people want to read *Sophie's Choice*, when they are having trouble making ends meet, and trying to figure out how to provide for themselves, or their daughters? Why do people want to tackle a *Metaphysics of Morals* after they just worked a ten hour day and are completely exhausted, and on top of that still have to cook diner, do some laundry, and make their lunch for tomorrow — oh yes, and they still must sleep a bit? I mean people in general are exhausted just because we're all chained to that big wheel — we are part of a grotesque economic machine.

I don't understand because I'm a man! Yes, and you don't understand great literature, and wonderful writing because you are a moron — that's what I should have said.

I had an English teacher in eleventh grade who, and this is no joke, she never read *The Adventures of Huckleberry Finn*. How the hell can you be an English teach, or a teacher of literature, and never have read about good old Huck Finn?

Did you ever eat a piece of apple pie? She said, she never got around to it in college, but she is going to take a look at it one of these days. In eleventh grade, I was explaining Holden Claufield to the class, and she was regurgitating what some asshole wrote about the book in *Cliff Notes*.

Perhaps paradise is lost, perhaps people have just become so desensitized and calloused that all they can do is watch some soap opera's, or infomercials about a product that can cook meat perfectly because that's all their brains can bear to handle.

Perhaps these novels as inspiring as flea farts are

the precursor to the annihilation of books all together, and one day we will go to the museum and look at books behind glass, the same way we look at fossilized bones—with utter amazement. "Wow mommy, look at that beautiful book by the critically acclaimed author of the *Lovely Bones*, and look at that old ugly book next to it called *Fahrenheit 451*. Books surely were very different weren't they mommy? Did people really pick up those things and look at them?"

-The Woman Who Involuntarily Killed Me

You won't think that it's unusual if I tell you we met in Italy on *Via Veritas*, directly across from my cousin's home. Apparently, she is a neighborhood girl. A neighborhood girl I've never met before because I don't live in this town. I just moved to the center of Rome; and I'm trying to meet people outside the circle of my family. And there she was.

My night wasn't exactly going well. I had been at a bar, an Irish Pub that I frequented, and I wasn't even inebriated when I spilt my third perfectly poured Guinness. It was just a clumsy accident where I knew I was about to knock it over, even before I knocked it over.

I could have asked for another one, but with three bartenders looking and seeing all the action, why should I? I figured one of the bunch would be a logical enough individual to do the right thing, but I figured wrong.

A normal bartender would have said in addition to 'don't worry about it,' 'here's another Guinness.' How could they not? Especially when a Guinness is 7.50 euros a pop? I mean, what does it cost the bar, nothing—less than one euro?

And I had not even had a single sip. Not one sip! That's the biggest bitch of it all. It's not like any of the bartenders own the place; and even if they did, it would have been a wise business decision, considering I've been going there all of the time since moving to Rome. I was disgusted to be honest with you; and since I really didn't have anything to drink, with a little coaxing, I convinced my cousin, who had decided to visit me, to leave the bar, and head on back to his house just outside of Rome.

"What luck! You've been talking about wanting to meet people right? We just got here man, and here she is. This is the girl I told you about. This is the girl you are going to love when you have a good look. I'm telling you this girl is fucking beautiful. Wait until she comes into the light. She is your type. She's fucking intelligent to and I know she speaks a little English. Come on! There, you see her...amazing right! Didn't I tell you? You have to play your hand smart; don't show too much too soon. Intrigue her a little. You know what I mean. I can tell by your face, my English amazes you right! Who do you think I am? Am I good, or am I good. It has been a long time my cousin."

He most certainly was right; upon first glance when I could see her, under the streetlight, I noticed her straight blonde golden hair and the bluest of blue aqua colored soft amicable eyes, with a smile that felt familiar and sexy. From the beginning I knew it not only could be, but it must be. I had to get to know this girl. Sometimes all the stars just seem to align correctly, and this was nothing short of one of those occasions.

The only problem I would come to learn was; we were in different places. Although I was only one year her senior, she was happy "enjoying the life," going out with different kinds of people, having fun, being "single but active." I was a little stunned because I knew this from the beginning, and she knew it as well. Perhaps that was her game with me, playing hard to get; I don't know.

For the first three days after our initial contact, she and I most definitely communicated very closely — and enjoyed each other's company for the majority of every day. She cooked me Calabrese pasta, and it was wonderful — actually the best dish of pasta I ever had. When she asked me how I liked it, I joked and told her she made the most amazing glass of cold ice water I'd ever had. We shared endless cocktails and dozens of joints and explored too many tiny clubs and bars to remember. She and I went for walks around Rome, and she accompanied and helped me with various errands necessary for me to accomplish in order to live, work, and be comfortable, in this ancient city.

We never became physically very close. She gave me two kisses hello, and two kisses goodbye, that most definitely landed on the center of each cheek. Would she laugh and touch my hand, or my arm, or my leg...sure...but she never initiated anything other than that.

Even on the couch, she kept her distance, and didn't give me even the slightest opening to get close to her, and possibly get a little kiss. I always thought Italy was full of very touchy feely people — I mean I am, and I'm not even a real Italian. I guess you could say I'm American, but that wouldn't even be very accurate.

Well, on the third night, I initiated first contact. We went to a typical Roman *lago* on an extremely *caldo* Roman summer day. She brought along with her, one girl friend, two guy friends, and me. I was thinking: why this ratio, but it's fine; whatever. Friends are just that, friends; and regardless of their sex, they pose no threat to me.

Upon arriving, the other people we came with

went off doing their own things; and she and I went back and forth at the food concession stand treating each other to things like: *Acqua Claudia, Yoga Aldicocca, Arancia Rossa, pannini con mozzeralla i pomodoro, procesitto, birra, gelato, caffé* — at one point, I don't think either one of us could move.

The day was jam-packed with laughing, eating a ton of food — we kayaked, walked are holding hands which was a new change of pace, spent time alone sitting together on a blanket, and occasionally jumped in the lake for a swim to cool off. I didn't enjoy going into the lake all that much, because upon exiting, you were walking in and through mud. Who the hell wants to walk around with mud caked all over their feet the entire day? Anyway…

At some point, we once again found ourselves in the vicinity of the folks we initially arrived with. She went to talk to one of the dudes that came along with us; a person she told me during the course of the day was a nice guy she had met only one time before this.

When I first saw him, I would have bet one million dollars he was a faggot. Anyway, after literally five minutes of them talking and laughing, she was making out with him. On a blanket, virtually feet away from me, after having spent the entire day and days before together; and this is where I found myself.

I don't even know how they were breathing; she was wrapping one leg around him, pushing herself against his cock back and forth, while he was grabbing her ass. Then the two of them go right to the hammock I pointed out earlier as a beautiful place to read a book, or do something. She certainly did do something, and escaped the eyes of others, for what seemed to be a very long time. I was beyond words and felt an assortment of emotions to say the least.

I even wrote her a little something the night before, which I gave to her just before she went over to the douche-bag. And she took that note, and put it in her bag, without ever reading it.

At the lake with her all day, I was surrounded by lots of foreign voices, but the only two I seemed to hear were — the sound of hers, and of course the sound of my own. I did also hear *The Eagles* "Hotel California" in the background and I thought that was a little strange.

Anyway, at some point, I said to myself, this is just one girl and here I am in Italy, at a lake, on a beautiful day. Fuck her, and fuck trying not to watch this. Why does she and most Italian women like these effeminate flaming homosexual looking guys; I don't get it. All these dudes in Italy; with their tight pants and chick haircuts; they even wear girlish t-shirts. It's the strangest thing.

So I said to myself; I've never been here and I should socialize with other people. I came here with this neighborhood girl I guess I don't really know and a bunch of tools I don't care to know; I don't even have to go back into the center of Rome with them. I can find another way.

And I had to get off that fucking blanket I was on because the ants were invading me. There were ants all over the goddamn place! There is nothing I hate more than having ants crawling all over your body — especially your face and the parts of your back you can barely reach. Ants; obnoxious people dry humping in bathing suits a few meters away; a man throwing a ball practically next to me, and having his dripping wet, smells like ass, "black - mutt - sheep - slash - wolf - dog" retrieving it. It was starting to get like a bad horror movie.

I was at the point where everything annoyed me. What I really wanted to do was break a few jaws, but I know that's never the answer. And I know it would make no difference. You can never change the way one thinks, even if you knock out all their teeth.

Eventually, while I was sitting with a book of paper and writing with a pen in my hand; she was still sitting with her legs wrapped around this guy who understood no English, she looked at me, and asked what I was doing? I quickly replied with a, "What are you doing?" Then, I motioned my index finger 360 degrees and said, "Writing a little something about all of this and my day." She said, "*o capito*," and went right back to speaking Italian with this fucking jerk-off for thirty seconds or so, and the show started again.

For the next few days I didn't see her. I didn't contact her. And I was starting to feel good again; in the sense I wasn't thinking about her and it really didn't bother me.

For my first ten days in Rome, I accomplished a lot, and if anything, during my time with her, I did eat the most amazing dish of pasta I ever had in my life. I learned where a lot of places to eat, to shop, to socialize were—everything wasn't a complete loss I suppose.

Then my phone rang. When I did not pick it up, I heard a voice outside my apartment saying, "I know you are home! I can hear your cell phone ringing while I call you! I'm standing outside your balcony in the street. Come down here or let me inside."

I proceeded to let her in and she said, "I think it's over." I said, "Think what is over?" I didn't really know what she was taking about. She explained to me, "that boy was just a 'beautiful fuck,'" and she was tired and over it already.

For the past few years she has only been interested in "beautiful fucks," her phrase, not mine; and this is because she once had a boyfriend she loved very much, he was her life, but he was a tortured soul and died of a heroin overdose. She never forgave herself for that, because that night, the one night she didn't spend with him, he said, "I want you to know that I love you, and I will always love you," and she didn't pick up on the fact he was in essence saying, "Goodbye. This is the last time you are going to see me."

She blames herself for his death in many ways; she blames herself for not being there; and she's never at ease thinking about the point right before he was about to die. Did he still feel like he wanted to die? Or did he want to live, but it was already too late?

So, we talked and talked like usual. And I made some caffé for us, and we smoked, laughed, and we shared real thoughts, and real emotions, learned much more about each other's past, present, and future plans; and things felt like they did before the lake incident.

She looked at me and said, "I feel at ease with you. I feel more at ease with my past now as well after talking to you. Thank you for helping me put things in perspective. I am ready to have a big kiss and make a nice story with you." Then she leaned in to kiss me, and every thought in my mind vanished. All I could do was feel her wet beautiful lips and tongue, her warm body and sticky sweet skin close to mine; her hands running up and down my spine, occasionally resting around my neck.

We kissed and kissed and kissed, for hours and hours touching each other everywhere; never saying another word. Then she just stopped. Just stopped and looked at me saying: "Why haven't you tried to take off my clothes and make love with me? Don't you desire me?" I told her, of course I desire you; there is nothing more in this entire world that I'd like to do than to physically be with you, but I don't want to be a "beautiful fuck." I want to be with you when I know you have feelings for me and want to be with me.

I told her I had too much respect for her, and for her body, and I was willing to wait until we became a little closer, and had a stronger bond emotionally and spiritually. She was in awe. She was so impressed that she said, "No one has ever spoken to me like that and now that I know how you feel about me, it's the best reason I need to make love to you right now."

She started taking off her clothes, and now I could really see, she had the most fantastic physique I will ever see in my life. She had very pronounced features — tone shoulders and arms, perky breasts, a six pack that was really an eight pack, an ass like a gymnast, a perfectly shaved pussy, long long legs, strong calves, boney ankles, perfectly manicured feet and toes, and a nice high arch. I was incapable of moving because I couldn't believe what was under her clothing. Seeing her in a bathing suit was nothing.

I knew she had a smoking hot body; I had some idea, but this was incredible. Not a single hair on her entire body other than her eyebrows, eyelashes, and head. She was, and I use this term as a complement, not as a knock, but she was a real life Barbie doll. That's the best way to describe her. That's the sort of body she had with nipples and without those hard plastic nude colored underpants the real Barbie is always wearing.

Even though I knew she fucked this guy I met and saw her with at the lake; and even after all she told me about being promiscuous and enjoying "beautiful fucks;" I couldn't help myself. I had too. I absolutely had to. She was a temptress and could turn even a gay man straight.

Only later did I find out, her previous boyfriend had AIDS and she was a cankerous sore in the making. The direct quote from my cousin was, "No way man! I can't believe you fucked her. I would have never fucked her. She sleeps with everyone man. There is no way that girl doesn't have AIDS or something worse if something worse exists."

I should have known better. And someone should have offered up this information a hell of a lot sooner. My cousin is a fucking dope. He really is. Why did he say to me, "You are going to love how this girl looks and she's really cool, but never fuck her." Why not offer up that little piece of information as well? What the hell is wrong with people?

Should have, could have, but didn't, right? She's that sort of person who doesn't even know she is sick, and thinks it's OK to just let a few guys here and there every week bust loads inside and all over her. It's fun!

What are the odds of me escaping this un-scathed? Assuming she does have an STD of sorts, I don't think you will always catch a disease, even if you have sex with a diseased individual once. Otherwise everyone in the world would have an STD by now.

It doesn't matter how many minutes you wait for the results of an STD test, each second feels like an eternity. But I'm glad I'm here. We slept together such a long time ago, and I haven't been with anyone since, and it has certainly been weighing on my mind. "Am I OK?"

This is the only time I want to get negative results on a test. What the fuck was I thinking? Condoms are so cheap these days. Well, it's too late for that. It's not like she forced me to fuck her, she just exhibited a very persuasive argument. Regardless of what happens, and especially if something horrible is to happen; it's all my own damn fault. I played with fire; and now I'm praying I didn't get burnt too badly.

-Lonely

As much as I'd like to say it and believe it; and I don't know if it's to inform the populous, or if it's to try to convince myself, or a bit of both, but I am not a loner. I have never been a loner. And I don't like being one now.

In recent years, yes, I have assumed the role. Who hasn't spent time being a loner? But I am tired of this and it's very uncharacteristic of me. It feels unnatural. I'm tired of being alone by myself; I'm also tired of being alone with people. And to tell you the truth, the computer isn't helping at all.

I find that I should be sleeping, but instead I'm online, doing something of no particular importance. The thing I rationalize most is catching up with "my friends" on Social Networks. But who are these people I call my friends? Who are they? And what is it that we have really? The truth is it all detracts from the life I should be living. It's a crutch. It's a safe place to stay.

And what happens when I go out? I either see people I've spoken to one hundred times before; people I already know everything about in a glance; people who have everything to say, and say nothing at all... you know just as well as I do, it's all the same old, same old. Same day. Different shit.

I'm in a beautiful major city; I am surrounded by people all of the time, most of whom I do not care to know, or care to see. And I don't think that is being cold hearted, that is just being truthful. But it has to be in my power to change this.

The genuine people here didn't venture out on their own to try to find something unattainable like I have. The genuine people here; they have their plates full, and are living their lives. For the most part they talk to me just because I'm a foreigner from a place that is strange and mysterious to them. They want to pick my brain and see if all people from my country really are the same and think alike. They have a model in their mind of what "all Americans are;" and we are amusing companions. "'Ha-ha' funny...funny like a clown? ...Do I amuse you?"

Last night, this couple will probably never know because I was somewhat rushed, and even though I promised I'd be back to speak with them more in a little while, unfortunately I couldn't. But last night, I met a genuine, loving, friendly couple; who I really got along with. Not only were they happy to interact with me, they were happy to speak my native tongue.

They weren't upset about me not speaking their language; they were exited to meet me as I was them, and for about seven minutes we shared experiences with each other, got to know each other, laughed and smiled, and we never said goodbye. We left off with a "see you a little later."

Who wouldn't want to know how to speak every language? Especially the language of the country you are spending time in! Sometimes, it isn't necessarily the ignorant American, trying to say, "Fuck you speak English;" it's the respectful American, saying: "I really wish I knew how to say something other than the words, "Yes," "No," "What," "Good," "Hello," and "Goodbye"...in your language. To have a command of many languages, that would be a wonderful gift.

Anyway, they don't know what an amazing experience it was for me to meet them. In short, I spoke about how much I loved their city, what I was doing here; and they spoke about how much they loved my city when they went to visit, and what they do in their city — but we said so much more with our eyes, and conveyed love and warm energy in-between words. Even though they had the largest English vocabulary of any person I had met up until that point, I could also tell they were really good people; and in many ways we were the same.

In the night, perhaps they mentioned me once again saying a few words to each other, or perhaps they filled in all the gaps and vocalized everything that wasn't verbally communicated during our time together. It always amazes me, how different people observing and or experiencing the same moment, can have such different perceptions. What is meaningful for one isn't necessarily profound or meaningful for another.

Roberto, Francesca, and I never shared an awkward moment. They gave me one of the most memorable conversations and experiences I have had since arriving here. It was smooth, seamless, and will last as one of those moments that is just as vivid in your mind, as it was when it happened.

You know that's the funny thing about major cities, once in a while you can meet very warm, friendly folks who are going out to enjoy themselves, and not necessarily looking for anything, other than just being who they are.

Sometimes you'll find people able to read your eyes; those who can see we are from the same stock; the same kind of people. With Roberta and Francesca we were old friends just catching up and reminiscing in

Saint Andrew's Pub—yet we never met before.

I believe as human beings, we think too far into the future. We think about so many things that are hypothetical and irrelevant. We have trouble just enjoying the moment and each other's company. And I'd like to think one day my family will be my wife and children. I'd like to think my home is wherever they are because people are people and the only people who will really matter are my family—but that's just not true.

I miss the guy who I used to see every Friday night cutting the pizza in the pizza joint I've been going to for fifteen years. I miss being able to see my mother and father whenever I want. No man can live on an island all alone without human interaction. That is impossible. You would inevitability go crazy and give up the will to live.

I don't even know what I'm talking about, other than to say; I suppose I'm lonely here. And I don't really have anyone to talk to in any kind of genuine or deep manner because I cannot bridge this language barrier most of the time. Hell, I can't even make a joke.

That's when you know you have some sort of command for a language; when you can make a joke in it. When you can make a joke in another language, or when you have a dream in another language...when a language becomes easy and fluid in an unconscious manner; perhaps that is when you don't feel so alone in another country with a foreign tongue? I don't know. I'm just spit-ballin'. I wonder how you would translate that?

Thank goodness for this bottle of wine, and those things...those simple pleasures, which don't need any translation. Thank goodness for the delicious aromas and food I've been pouring into my system. Food has been my only source of real enjoyment. When I feel connected during the day or at peace at night, I'm usually eating something. And I'm certainly starting to show it which is not good, because the warm weather is just around the corner.

-Could Have

I become so irritated when I hear someone say how much they could have done something, or could have been something. 99.9% of the time you know they are full of it.

If they could have, and they wanted to, then they would have. Of course it's a different story if you legitimately could have done something, and you just didn't want to. My father for example made the Olympic team for skeet shooting, and also made the New York Yankees, but he unfortunately was drafted and had to go to Vietnam. So there is a man who could have done something, but couldn't due to forces beyond the realm of his control.

I have a friend that could have become a professional basketball player, and that's a fact. The L.A. Lakers invited him to try-out right out of high school. They had been scouting him. He made the team, they offered him a contract, but in the end he chose a different path. For a number of reasons, he chose to attend N.Y.U., and later went to Stonybrook Medical School. Now he is a successful doctor. He decided to nurture his brain, because he realized that his body at some point in time might let him down. He chose to help people.

And everyone told him he was nuts. Everyone said, you can always finish college, or you can always become a doctor; but what window do you have to play professional basketball? His friends, his family members; I think they all just saw dollar signs, and wanted to be able to say when they saw him on

211

television, "Hey, that's my boy!"

And you will probably never know my friend's name because he never became a Michael Jordan; but I assure you the families and people he assists free of charge, the people whose lives he made and continues to make a direct impact on; those people know his name, and will never forget him. Those people are happy he didn't decide to dribble a basketball.

At first I thought I was a contradiction of sorts, for I know I could have been the greatest author the world has ever seen. I know I could have been the greatest novelist, the greatest screenwriter, and the greatest poet. This is a fact, and just about every teacher I ever had would tell you that, but I never had the time. I never had the time to concentrate all my abilities into my passion, and I've always believed that if you cannot do something to the best of your abilities, then it is better to do nothing at all.

I would never want to be remembered as a great author; I'm sorry, that just isn't enough. If people weren't comparing me to Shakespeare, if people weren't articulating strong arguments discussing how my genius far exceeds that of the greatest authors and philosophers the world has ever known; then I say fuck it! Being great, or one of the best, would never be enough for me personally.

And why, why have I never been able to create? Why have I never been able to translate the stories in my mind, the philosophies, the poems, and put them onto paper? I'll tell you why!

I have to eat. I have to pay bills, bills, and more bills. I have to work and accumulate and amass money. I have to plan for the future. I am already too old. I always said if I lived to be 150 years old and wrote for 18 hours a day, I wouldn't have enough time to even break off the tip of the iceberg.

And now, well, I'm about to retire, and I'm extremely tired. I'm not going to create a legacy, or body of work that is just a millionth of what I know I should have created, so I'm going to die a disappointed and frustrated man.

The world will go on without me, and will go on never knowing the greatest author to ever live, but never write. They will continue to adhere and cling to the past greats; they will continue to read the crap the mainstream media and press and social networking currents say is "cool" or "good."

They will worship false idols, listen to popular culture, and go through life as little engines that could, never straying from the tacks. I feel sorry for people; and this sorry-ness I've felt for people, I'm beginning to now see, I used as a crutch and excuse for myself.

It is different for painters and artists. I could have painted pictures of famous architectural structures around the world, or painted portraits, or made sculptures. I could have made a living painting, playing the game, creating things people would want to buy, while at the same time creating things I was passionate about. If my passions were to catch on, fine, if not, at least I still would have had the time to create them along with making a few dollars.

It is different for musicians. Musicians can play bars and clubs, and play cover songs of the Beatles, and Stones, occasionally throw in an original song or two. People will pay to see live music. And if they become lucky and catch the ear of some bigwig who thinks he can sell or structure their sound, then they will be known for a short period of time, and make a few dollars.

But for a writer, who is really reading anything other than newspapers, websites, and the occasional magazine? Most of the time, you don't even have to pay for these things because you can ask someone when they finish up with the paper to give it to you. Or you can hop on your smartphone and search any site instantaneously. I bet most people probably only read a few times a year when they are in a doctor or dentist's office waiting for an appointment.

I could sell one of my stories, and before you know it, it will be photocopied over and over, and in the end I wouldn't have made a dollar. Or I can write an e-book and self publish, and if it was something of value that people enjoyed, they would figure out how to copy it and share it, and I'd never see a dime.

Don't get me wrong, making the dollar was never the reason I wanted to write. If I knew I could live, I could eat, and I could satisfy all of my needs and the needs of my family writing; maybe I would have created some stuff for no recognition. I never wanted recognition either. I could have been like the Pearl Poet; no one knows who he is, but yet, he left a little legacy.

Instead, now I am a broken down man at the end of his life, full of regret, talking to you. Wishing I had the courage to say so many years ago, "You know what; this is something I must try for myself." At the very least, I could have found the time, to write ONE novel that I was proud of and happy with.

Why did I spend my life clinging to this stupid

"all or nothing" mentality? Because I couldn't "do it all" I had such a defeatist mentality. Because I got caught up in all the bullshit that every other regular person get's caught up in; I didn't even try to do something that really wouldn't have been all that difficult for me.

What I used as excuses, really are valid excuses, but so what? There are those people who "could have" been something; and there are those people who "were" and "are" something. I'm going to have to go to my grave knowing, I could have been more than what I was: because all I was, was a good man who worked every day until he retired and now I'm probably going to die soon.

You don't have to be a genius to figure out, I don't have too many healthy and good years of life left. And when I'm gone, the only people who are going to miss me, or remember me, are those who loved me. I guess that will have to be good enough. I have less life in front of me, than I do behind me, that's for sure; and there is no way I'll ever be able to write anything now at this point in my life. I missed all my windows of opportunity.

-My Hour With Sandra

I remember my only hour with Sandra. I still have vivid mental images of her. My mind sees her small slightly sagging ass; tiny breasts with dark pancake nipples; wrinkled and aged smile; stretchmarks adorning her hips, thighs, and upper arms; and a barbaric c-section scar... ...that is pretty much what comes to my mind when I think of her.

She was physically distressed, and worn out; but at one time, I could clearly see that she was more than beautiful. She was definitely magnificent! As a young lady, she had to be the object of many men's desires. Her profession just sucked the fire and life right out of her. The whites of her eyes were more cream colored and antique looking than white.

Such an intelligent, sensitive, caring woman—I know, because I spoke with her and we connected. She was only 26 years old, but you never would have guessed it. She lived a lifetime at such a young age. Twenty-something and she looked like she was in her late thirties.

She showed me pictures of the two beautiful boys she had, three years apart, with the same deadbeat Latino. She was a Latino. Don't make that face. That's how she referred to herself. I'm not trying to cast a shadow of discrimination; I'm just trying to tell you a story using the appropriate words.

Sandra was a beautiful Latino, a good person, but she was scared, she was aged, and she was unhappy. She felt like she never had a shot in life. She couldn't make ends meet any other way; she couldn't live and provide her boys with the life and education they deserve if she wasn't a prostitute. She explained to me that although she works all night and is always tired, she is with her kids from the moment they wake up, to the moment they go to school. Then she gets a break when they go to school, and during this time she finally gets to sleep a little; then they get home from school, she cooks for them, helps them with homework, and spends time with them, until they both go to sleep. One of the many benefits her night job gives her is the ability to spend time with her boys, which is of the utmost importance. And she also has enough cash to higher excellent and responsible baby sitters.

But honestly, the memories I have, how horrible! Why did she have to take her clothes off? She looked so much more beautiful with them on. Men pay to fuck her, and they pay her well, and I don't see how or why. I guess there are just a lot of men who prefer rather than wining and dining some bitch, spending hundreds of dollars and hours of time, they rather just spend a few hundred and know what they are going to get. I bet you a lot of guys in real life would never be able to fuck a woman who is this attractive, unless they paid for it. There really are a lot of slobs in this world.

When she first walked through the door, I was tempted to stiff her and send her on her way, but then I realized that wouldn't be right. She is just trying to make a living selling what she has left of a once godly face and body. I now know getting fucked all night every night by many men takes a lot out of a person. I never paid for pussy before, and I never will. If all you want is pussy, all you have to do is go out to a dance club, or a bar, and just be a little blunt with a few women. Wave around a big knot of cash, buy a few people drinks, look sharp, smile, and that's it. Most of the time you don't even have to buy them or anyone a drink; all you have to do is just wave around your knot inconspicuously. Women who like to fuck and have men take care of them have radar for that. There are women who are going out for the very same reason you are, to have a good time, and to go home with someone.

New York City, forget about it! Do you have any idea how many 'escorts' are available of every and any age and race capable of accommodating any fetish you fancy — you name it and it will be delivered to your door in under an hour. You just have to pay for it.

But Sandra, she has had sex with thousands of guys. Thousands! Sometimes, eight, nine, ten, or even eleven in one night! And she's a reasonably priced girl. But even with the money she is charging, do you know what kind of money that is? She makes more than most lawyers; and that's all cash money off the books mind you! I hope she's saving some of that for the future, because God only knows how many more years she'll be able to do this.

But I don't understand who in God's name is giving her all this business. Are there that many pathetically rich individuals able to shell out $500-$1500 dollars just for one measly little hour? On a slow night she said she'll make about $4,000, and on a good night she'll clear about $8,000; and on really great days a few times a year, she has made as much as $20,000. She said, sometimes you get dream customers who really take a liking to you, and just want to keep giving you stupid money.

I called her on a whim, as a fucking joke. I was

drinking Patron, thinking about the non-existent relationship I have with my son, and I saw a little picture on my coffee table of this exotic bitch, with a caption that read, 'Hot Latino dream girl available for you." It was one of those flyers you get on your car, or someone hands you while you are walking. And even though everyone always says, "I never did anything like this before;" I have no reason to lie to you. I never did anything like that before, but I figured I might as well try something like this once in my lifetime before I die; and who's going to know?

When she came to my door, and I saw her, I thought she was very true to her ad, but upon closer inspection, when I saw her naked, when I saw the make-up she had plastered on her face; I didn't fuck her only because of the nightmares I would have. She just didn't meet my standards cosmetically speaking. I'm always a skeptic of women who wear make-up — on their cheeks and their entire face — what are they making-up? She even had make-up covering up skin blemishes on her upper chest; that was very disturbing as well.

If you ever see a woman who puts make-up on other parts of her body, or on her breasts for example — be aware. Unless she's trying to cover up a tattoo for a formal occasion, what the hell is she covering up on her body under her clothing? And why even cover-up a tattoo or some pimples on your chest? Scratch what I said — you see a girl with makeup on her body, you fly like the wind.

As I lay with her naked body draped next to mine, for an hour we talked. I only tried to focus on her eyes, and we talked. I made her feel as though it was my fault, and she was everything a guy could dream for. And for the first ten minutes or so I was consciously aware of every part of my body she touched with her gestures while conversing. Then I thought to myself, this is silly because "a" I cannot get a disease from just being touched, and "b" as soon as she leaves I'll just take a scalding hot shower, and throw all of these sheets into the washing machine or garbage. So, there was no sense being too paranoid.

And I'll tell you what, she was an amazingly sexy woman the more I started really talking to her. She still can be for someone "the right person," and find someone good for her in a new phase of life. She doesn't have to settle for this profession and this life. And what will she do in a few more years? How many years does she think she can continue to do this? Does she have money saved up, or is she beginning to save — I really wanted to ask her those questions.

Why not do what every ivy-league schoolgirl does — shop for, then get a 'M''R' 'S' from a motivated 'destined to be successful,' or 'comes from money' soulless prick. I'm sure she can work her pussy and hypnotize a man.

It doesn't really matter what most women study in school because they have no intention of working very long. Once they get married, and want to start a family, they are done. Think about it? How many women do you know who are the sole breadwinners? I'm not saying women shouldn't have the option of working, but you either become career orientated or you become family orientated; you can't do both effectively. Don't let your family suffer because you want a career. That's the problem, once women started joining the workforce during WWII, family values in this country started to plummet and now are complete shit.

I'm not suggesting women should stay home. I'm only suggesting that one parent should be home to parent the children. If my wife could have run my company, and I could have stayed home with my fucking son for 18 years—I would have done it. Staying at home and being a parent is the most important job, but it's overlooked—and in most cases it has to be overlooked for economic necessity.

Anyway, I suggested to Sandra she try to get one of these rich bastards she could tolerate head over heals for her, and make that "Pretty Woman" story a reality. If she's going to work that pussy, why not work her pussy for some real security. Women do it all the time, they get the men head over heals for them, and make the men think that they're the only ones with the magic slit between their legs.

I gave her a business card. I mean if I'm able to drop $1,500 dollars for an hour of drunkard bullshit and not even get my dick wet, I might as well help her anyway she'd let me. But I could never love her, I could never desire her physically; put it this way: I wouldn't even fuck her if I could use Magic Johnson's dick and I was blind, so we are impossible—even as friends. The age difference and our backgrounds are too great to bridge. I'm not looking to try to mentor a reforming hooker.

But, even though I'm willing to help her, I never care to see her, or even speak with her again. Strictly casual, quick, and in an abrupt business fashion, speaking for New York minutes on the telephone. We could conduct business until she was where she should be; maybe send a few e-mails back and forth. I won't give her, but I will get her a job in a place where our paths and circles would never have to cross; where I wouldn't have to respect her as a business professional or even see her—only thing is, she makes a lot more money being a prostitute than she would with a respectable job. And that's a huge sacrifice.

No way no how she would give that up? She's really going to take a job for a few more bucks than minimum wage? Or even if she could get $17 or $25 dollars an hour; I don't think that would be enough. She wouldn't even make in one week what I gave her tonight.

If I had to shovel shit and make one million a year, and someone said why don't you work for me and cut roses for thirty-thousand, I'd say you know what, I'm going to continue to shovel shit thank you very much. On top of that some people believe prostitution is the oldest profession and should be legalized. It probably should be legalized, but if it were, I'll tell you this, a lot of these women wouldn't be able to make the kind of money they're making now. Who are we to pass a moral judgment on these individuals who make money using their bodies? And let me tell you, these are no stupid bitches—they know a lot about disease—mainly they don't want to get any.

Yea, what the hell was I thinking? No one in their right mind is going to pay some Latino girl with no education other than that of the street, and no business experience top dollar to do something as simple as answer a phone and direct calls. And I don't even think she could get a sales opportunity, or be part of a technical support team. Really, what can she do?

Not everyone is Jennifer Lopez you know; not every Latino woman without a pot to piss in can make it to superstardom. And if J-Lo didn't have that ass, and that body; with all this technology augmenting her voice; who the fuck would she be? She certainly can't sing or act; she was a good dancer when she was very young and skinny; I'll give her that. But she would probably be struggling, and doing desperate things just like a lot of people out there if she didn't have a lot of luck.

And now, because of mostly shit luck, she's so far removed from reality, she doesn't have a clue where she came from, or who she is. At least Sandra knows who she is, where she came from, and how she never wants her children to have to live in the world that most underprivileged minorities are unconsciously steered into.

Hell, most of the divisions of my company have automated systems to direct and traffic incoming calls—it's more cost efficient. I don't have to give a computer program benefits, medical insurance, a company car, cell phone, days off, listen to its bullshit—the list goes on and on. And the few secretaries I have, at least they are proficient with computers, typing articulate letters, and doing all sorts of clerical work. The more I think about it, the more I think you can't just transplant someone that comes from one world to live in another.

We all live in different worlds. It's nice having cash money in your pocket, everyone loves cash money baby. Money is power. Money commands respect. J-Lo, yes I said some things about her, but she could give a shit less. She has more money than God! She has legions of fans that love her. She wouldn't think for one second about anything I said because my comments would never enter into her psyche. And when her looks fade, no one will remember...or care for that matter. What she will have left behind certainly isn't timeless. Her music will be forgotten. But everyone will know who Madonna is.

If all you have to do is open your legs, let some pathetic bastard shake around for a few minutes — then that's all you have to do. I couldn't believe in this day and age that she felt safe from disease. I was just sitting next to her, and I didn't feel safe. She told me that she always used protection, she doesn't kiss, and she doesn't do anal. She has complete confidence in modern day contraceptives and uses them for both oral and vaginal sex. That's nice. I don't have complete confidence in anything or anyone — not even cold hard cash.

I'll tell you what I told my son, if you don't trust a woman, don't fuck a woman — and most women you cannot trust. If you think she might have a disease, or if you think she might want to get pregnant, or you want to play it safe — walk away from the pussy, it isn't worth it. You want to get a blow job, now that's another story.

But let's face it; contraceptives suck. Condoms suck. And if you can't ride bare back — there is no sense riding at all. I mean if you like fucking latex, then why not get a few of those medical gloves, fill it with Vaseline, throw it in-between your mattress and box-spring, give it a name, and fuck away. Thinking about it, I must have drunk a lot of Patron this evening.

Why did I even call Sandra?

I really can't believe it, I'm thinking about my son again and some of the girls he has introduced to me. There really are women with the brains of a chicken — no, that's too kind — peanuts for brains; and they think if they take some method of birth control, they can fuck everyone. It's amazing. These girls today are so dumb, and they are all in college, and they are all going to get jobs, and they're really no better than this Sandra girl.

I remember seeing all of the prostitutes on *Christopho Columbo* street in Roma, just walking back and forth looking amazing, and having no concept of how susceptible they were to disease. Especially eastern European women, or Spanish, or the Italian women who enjoy sex — they have no idea. And these people come from civilized countries. I can only imagine what it is like in Africa. How many people have diseases down there?

Hell, most American girls, and I'm not talking about slutty ones, sluts exist in every region, I'm saying regular good ole fashioned American girls — they don't have any problem with sucking dicks, and some don't even have a problem with anal — but sex, sex in the vagina — now that's a problem? How does that make sense? It's OK, just tank me in my ass, or cum inside my mouth...but no, you cannot fuck my pussy? That's absurd?

I'm afraid for my son's generation because it is really full of stupid pathetic little impish bastards who don't know shit about shit. I mean there were always

225

stupid gullible bastards since the beginning of time, but this generation more than mine has an invincibility heir about them, and they think nothing can happen to them, just because they are who they are, or who their father is. If you remind them of all the famous people who are now dying from some horrific sexually transmitted disease, they'll just say you always take such extreme examples.

And these little invincible bastards, they only feel like that because they are all to pussy to fight. No one fights physically anymore; they just throw words and expletives at each other, and have a sense of achievement at the end of a viscously long tirade, like they won something. Or worse yet they will grab a gun and squeeze off a few rounds. Back in my day, I'd let someone say about five words to me, and then the situation was going to end with either me unconscious, but more times with the other bloke seriously abused and deformed wishing he never opened up his fucking mouth. He would remember me for at least one week, especially if I got a hold of his throat and his eyes.

Kids today wouldn't last five minutes in my fucking world; not five. And the guys today, they wouldn't have been able to score with the women of my generation. Today you don't have to say much and a woman will allow you to toss yourself into her. Women today, women of my son's generation, they don't even look at the dicks they let into them. I don't know if the women today are more naïve or stupid, or if the advent of the pill gives women a false heir of confidence, but they trust everything the men tell them — and the men trust the women!

I'm not only saying the women now a days are

stupid, the men are as well because they don't even think a second time—a woman opens her legs for them, and whether they have protection or not—they are plowing away as long as she doesn't seem to mind. And of course she doesn't seem to mind because if her legs are open for you, and you just met her—well she's had many a men drinking at her bar during happy hour.

How do you think the straight men get these horrible diseases? The women fucking give them gifts that last a lifetime—and a lot of women know they have a disease and are infecting you. They feel like you deserve it in some sick way. If they don't reflect a second and consider what they do to themselves, they certainly won't consider how they can ruin the life of another.

Men will walk around and neglect their bodies, or fail to go to the doctor, or fail to get blood tests, but women are much more in touch with their body. If something doesn't look right or smell right they are in the doctor's office. And they want to know how to remedy the situation, hide the smell, and make sure no one can ever possibly know. My son, the first girl he was with he was with when he was 14, and I was proud of him. But I wasn't proud of him for being stupid. He told me his piss was burning. It turns out he got chlamydia, which clears up with antibiotics in seven days or so, but that's not the point. He confronted this bitch, told her he had chlamydia, and she tried to tell him he must have given it to her and it's impossible for her to have given it to him. How could his virgin penis give her anything other than pleasure or pregnancy? My boy knew to crank one out before he was with a woman for the first time so he wouldn't accidentally prematurely ejaculate.

I don't think the youth today really know about all of the horrible diseases there are out there. If you get an STD caused by bacteria, you are fine. They have cures for chlamydia, gonorrhea, syphilis, trichomoniasis, and vaginal infections, all caused by bacteria. But if you get an STD caused by a virus, it will plague your life and never leave you. Genital herpes, genital warts, hepatitis, HIV, or AIDS—good luck!

But I really don't know? I really don't know how the future generations are going to amount to anything, other than a bunch of assholes working for a bunch of assholes, and everybody knows everything, but the reason they are where they are is because they have no luck, or plenty of it.

I had no luck. I made my luck for me. I got married at a young age. I went to the University of Pennsylvania while working, while being married, and while having a young son. No one made me a millionaire; I did that on my own. No one bought my company for me—I did that. And although I did everything, my ex—wife still gets half of everything.

Now given for many years I was just scratching by, and I didn't always have a company. I mean I always worked in the field thinking I'd be president of a company, but never believing I would venture out on my own and destroy all the competition—some being companies that formerly employed me.

And I really wish sometimes that my wife didn't ask for a divorce. But she was right—she was totally right and deserved to be able to move on. When my boy got to college, she was tired of putting on the social face and keeping blind eye to my affairs, so she left. She served her purpose – she was a great mother and I have a wonderful son.

In addition to that, someone who never worked a day in her life, she has half of my fucking money. But I don't care, she's entitled to that for being supportive of me. I definitely wouldn't have been as successful as I am if I didn't have her in the past pushing me – nagging the shit out of me. Maybe I'll get remarried one day, but I see no reason to do so. I had a beautiful wife, and that lifestyle didn't seem normal to me. I tell my son all of the time, 'never get married – just live with someone.' You can have a successful relationship with a person for many years and not have to be married – look at Goldie and Kurt. They seem to be happy.

And that's why I don't understand the gay folks. I mean I understand they want to enjoy some of the benefits of being legally married, but the benefits aren't all that good actually. They are trying to do something that straight couples have been forced to do in the past. It's now acceptable to live with a partner, and that makes a hell of a lot of sense to me – it's also a hell of a lot cheaper.

If you want to be married, do it symbolically with your own ceremony, wear a ring, and screw the whole legality of the matter. You have to legitimize yourself in the eyes of others? What does that do for you? That's why this big thing with the fags and wanting to have marriage rights makes me laugh. What rights? They're better off not getting married. But they'll see. Once they get what they're fighting for, they'll see that they could have done so much more for themselves and others if they focused their energies on another crusade.

Well, it's time for me to go now—I have something else to do. But if you wanted to know more about Sandra, I don't know what happened to her after that hour we spent together. Even though we connected, she never called me thank God. She probably knew I was just trying to be nice. I'm sure she's probably doing what she does best—making money with her body and devoting her life to her children trying to give them all of the opportunities she never had, or at least felt she never had.

I've been around a long time now, and I've never judged anyone, and I don't think you should either. I am glad however that I will soon be retiring, soon be passing the torch to my son if he wants it, and I won't have to live very long in a world that future generations are continuing to screw up for the worst. How can there still be people who rightfully know that the only way they can provide is by performing or engaging in unscrupulous activities? *Ultima hora!*

-The Dream of a Warm Ice Cream

I spent time in a psychiatric hospital. Do you think differently of me? If you do, you obviously are a close-minded potato head. Don't you understand the real crazy people are the psychiatrists?

The real crazy people are the ones who assume they know more about you than you. The people who think they have an understanding of the human mind and how it works.

The people who can perform a psychological profile of you because you don't like to sweat, and you enjoy prime rib rare. Those who think they can prescribe something, or say something, or help you to achieve some heightened awareness, or give you a treatment to feel better; because the way you feel obviously isn't "normal."

So you read some books, so you go to church — and you think you know something? You invented something, you wrote something, you digested something — do you think you know anything?

What do I know? I don't really know anything. But one thing I do know is: these fucking bastards; these people who think they know exist. What do they know? Do you know how to regurgitate? Do you know how to make a few dollars? Do you know the names of your friends and family? Or the user names and passwords to all of your social networking accounts?

What do you know? You don't know a damn thing either. I'm not trying to be impolite; but if I don't know a damn thing, you certainly don't know jack shit.

I went to the Ivy League colleges for my undergraduate and graduate degrees. I graduated Magna Cum Laude and got to wear the gold tassels and stand behind a podium and say a little something. I have a doctorate.

You know nothing, and that's the most you'll ever know — nothing. The sooner you realize that, the better off you are. The sooner you realize that happiness is a warm ice cream — the sooner you realize that most things in this world are warm ice creams, the better off you will be.

I cannot give you a warm ice cream. I cannot give you something that doesn't exist. But that doesn't mean you will stop dreaming of your warm ice cream; that doesn't mean you won't desire it.

Until we find a more direct way of communication, until we can do away with language, this barbaric form of communication, we will never know. We will always have yearnings and dreams, desires for philosophies, feelings, and emotions that just don't exist because they cannot be defined in a cut and dry manner. How can we universally define energies?

I will tell you this. I can feel. I can feel energies. I can anticipate thoughts. I can smell emotions. For lack of a more exacting phrase, "I love." I've always been in love...In love with my family, in love with my friends, in love with the sand beneath my feet, but that has never been enough, nor do I know what love is.

It is something I feel, or think I feel, because I've been conditioned to think that this experience, this energy, this moment and experience, is love. Why has it never been enough? Who cares, it just has never been enough. Something has always been missing. And that something that is missing; is the very same thing that is ever present. The things we long for are the things we have. Those things we cannot see, are the things we see perfectly, but don't know.

A warm ice cream, how wonderful that would be! What flavor would you want? I've always been partial to strawberry. Why? I don't know once again, I just know strawberry is my preference. Actually I do know why; because to me, it tastes yummy!

So why did I spend time in a psychiatric hospital? I checked myself in. It was during the part of my life where I knew too much; when I knew it all and saw the end is bleak. I was very depressed and down in the dumps and I really didn't care whether I lived or died. The usual stuff I guess.

But as soon as I checked myself in, and they made me give them all the contents of my pockets, take off my belt, and give them my shoes...I knew I had made a terrible mistake. As soon as I got mixed into the general population, a punk rock goth freak sat down right next to me and started singing in my ear, "The devil inside, the devil inside...every single one of us, the devil inside" over and over and over again. But that's another story.

-The Rape and the Aftermath

I begged, I pleaded, I screamed, but to no avail. All of my requests fell on deaf ears. I hope that is something you never experience. As he ripped off my clothes and held me down on a couch, he assured me that everything would be all right. He got all of my clothing off in a matter of seconds by ripping and jerking. I was actually cut in multiple places when he pulled off my bra, and that is when I really decided to take action.

Before I could tell him I wanted him to stop, he feverishly thrust himself inside me. The pain was incredibly sobering, and I cried out, "No! No! Stop!!!!" I had never been penetrated before; I had never had sex. His only concern was keeping his hand over my mouth while trying to pump me harder, pump me faster, and stick his dick as far inside me as he possibly could.

I was having trouble breathing. Eventually I couldn't fight him anymore. I was too weak and in too much pain. My struggling was only making it worse. I did not want to fight him anymore. I just wanted the whole ordeal to be over. My entire body, my entire being, went completely numb, and I was staring into blackness with open eyes feeling invisible.

To say he raped me or he hurt me is much too casual of a way of putting it—he violently and forcefully fucked me, and there was nothing I could do except shut down. I know it's not an excuse, but it is the truth. I was a little drunk, but I'm one hundred and nine pounds as well. He's a Marine; does that put it into perspective?

That night, I saw something in his pupils I have never seen before, and I could tell he had no conscience. He was capable of going to a very dark place where he hears no reason. I was afraid he might even hurt me more because he was so strong.

When he was tired; when he was finished with me; he gently kissed me on the forehead, smacked my ass, pulled up his pants, walked into my kitchen opening the refrigerator getting himself a beer for the road. Then he smiled at me and left.

He left me naked, shaking, and alone. I was in a pool of blood, sweat, and God knows what else for hours, unable to move, violated in my own space. I know I will never be the same, but I'm better for it.

He took something away from me that I can never get back, and I really can't explain to you what he took. If it were only my virginity, I'm sure I would have been able to bounce back by now. I should have never invited him back to my apartment for dinner — especially when my roommates weren't home; but that was the whole point. I cooked a romantic dinner — it's all my fault! How was I supposed to know? How could I know?

He was sooo nice. "Who are you talking about Melissa?" I think you know him: John Cazzogratz. Right, the President of Sigma Chi; but when this happened to me he wasn't the President just yet.

I know I don't even need to say this, but I have never discussed this incident before. No one needs to know about it. I am making my peace with the entire situation and now I am in the process of healing. I've seen him since. I actually had relationships with a few of his brothers in Sigma Chi.

Everything is cool now, and it would really upset me if anyone else was to know about this. I have never been able to talk about this before, so please, this conversation goes no further. You're my little sister. I knew I could count on you.

Anyway he said, "I like you," "I care about you," "I'm falling in love with you," I feel completely comfortable with you," "I trust you," "You are everything I ever hoped for in a woman," — and I bought all this shit. I was a freshman just like you are now; I had just become a sister. And let's not forget in high school I was a geek.

He was and still is the big man on campus, he's gorgeous, and he was paying attention to me — I didn't question anything. I just couldn't believe he was paying attention to me. He was fattening me up before the kill; he was manipulating me and I didn't even feel his hands on my shoulders. I suppose that is why he is so legendary.

Thinking about it again, he catered to my every need, just as he caters to all naive idealistic girls needs. I have seen him work since and let me tell you; he sleeps with a lot of women.

And that night, as soon as I deactivated my guard, he knew, and I saw another very real side of him — the monster. I'm a fool. I don't know what's the matter with me! Why did I trust people; why did I assume that everyone is warm hearted? Men are out to conquer; that is why you must conquer them.

I don't have a scar on my body, not even a scratch — but that doesn't mean it didn't happen. That doesn't mean that for a long time I didn't think about it every second of everyday. That doesn't mean I'm one-hundred percent better. I may look all right, but inside my body is crying out. I am still in pain form this experience. I haven't been able to eat anything other than bland foods like bread, salads, and yogurt now for over a year.

I'm not a health nut like everyone thinks — it's just that anything I put inside my body food wise makes me nauseous. Did you know that? See, even though we are sisters, you don't know everything about me. I'm not only your bigger cooler frat sister, I'm telling you this because it can help you; and I definitely never want you anywhere near John.

No, there is nothing to worry about with my diet. At least now, every time I ingest something I don't have to fight myself from throwing it up. I've gotten very good at that — I usually never throw up anymore; but for me being raped affected my eating habits more than anything else. Well, my eating and sleeping habits.

"Everything happens for a reason." Who ever came up with that brilliant phrase must have been really stupid. There is no reason why this should have happened to me. I don't know what I'm supposed to learn from this. I've always tried to find something positive in every tragedy, but there is noting positive about this.

I know I could have gotten a disease, or become pregnant. I am so ashamed and humiliated I can't even walk into a testing facility, but I guess I'm going to have to go sooner or later just to be sure.

Well, maybe the only positive thing is that I can help others. My granddaddy told me we are related to Chaucer, and I've always enjoyed his writings. So in the spirit of Chaucer, and don't think I'm crazy because

I always say this to myself, 'I swear by arms, by blood, and by bones that I will never allow myself to become vulnerable again.'

It took a year and a half of screwing up to come to the conclusion that I will never let my guard down. I can never let my guard down—not for anyone. I'll also never go out with another frat boy again; not that they are all bad, just because from my experience most of them are. I've had enough sex, I've been with enough guys, and a year and a half of that shit is enough for me. I don't want any type of relationship other than a meaningless one.

I'm telling you this not only because you are my little sister, but because you are a lot like me when I first arrived here. I don't want what happened to me, to happen anyone—especially you. Make sure when you go out, if you want to screw a guy and have fun, do that. I would never tell you not to; but try never to allow yourself to be put in a situation where you can be taken advantage of—it just isn't worth it. These frat brothers, if you get drunk enough, a whole bunch of them will try to fuck you at the same time. Some of these guys are animals and have watched too much violent porn.

Have you had sex yet? I think you should have your first sexual experience with a nice guy—maybe a good friend, just so you can ease yourself into everything slowly. It's just food for thought. Get yourself a little cutie freshman.

-Helping Babies to Swallow

You said to me in your e-mail, that I am on the fast track to becoming the person I hate - well if that is the case, then I must be resembling you. I don't think I am — I certainly hope not!

You want to vent? Let's vent.

You took a girl - still hopeful, still loving -- even after all of the shit that she had been through. You took her, you made her trust you, love you, care about you -- and you exploited and manipulated that love for all that it was worth. You made it dirty, based on fear rather than innocence and love.

You told her - you told me - that you would kill yourself if I continued to drink, if I had a baby, if I didn't talk to you, if I disagreed with your plans for us because you are very "fragile" at this time. Is that love?

You think I don't listen, but I do. You pushed me away again and again, when I was giving myself to you to help you. And I couldn't help you. Whether you didn't let me help you, or didn't want me to help you, I guess I'll never know.

And the good times in our relationship - the ones you love to fixate on - I made those moments happen, not you. You simply went along for the ride. Instead of letting me get on with my life, you perseverated on the bad times in my life - you made them yours - you dwelled. Is that love? What happened to me before you had nothing to do with you. Why couldn't you see that?

You don't love me - you love yourself and your tiny world. You want to tell me that I don't help people and you do. You want to know, when is the last time I helped someone? Well dumbass, the other day I told my mom that she was amazing - when did you last do that? Two days ago, I held a two year old until he went to sleep - he was shivering because he had a 102.5 fever.

In a few months, I will be helping preschoolers to communicate with their mothers, and helping babies to swallow. I'm doing what I've been going to school for and what I'm passionate about. So the question becomes, what the hell are you doing?

Please - do well, prosper, get a great job, help people - but don't ever forget that you were the one that fucked up the best thing that you will ever have. The most beautiful thing you will ever have. And ten years from now, I will be successful and happy and have a beautiful family...and you will most likely be dead or alone because you really have become crazy and delusional.

I have no more love for you. -Sleep well- Jessica

-Libreria Cythère Critique

"You know that is a saying that really bothers me, how do you say—it's idiomatic. 'Everything is under control.' What is under control? Such a stupid phrase! Control, such a stupid word!

You know, they say that in France now. Yes, yes, and I'm not a purest, by any means, but I hate that popular American police, and military phrases have infiltrated into our language. Look at my store for Christ's sake! This store specializes in French literature.

Do you remember when America landed on the moon, and somebody said, 'Houston we have a problem;' that phrase as well they use in France. I think we have a big problem in France, they are translating things verbatim, and it just pisses me off.

When I was young, my generation was that of Rock n' Roll, peace and love, the Yardbirds, Simon and Garfunkel, Jimi Hendrix, Janice Joplin.. ...regular people, artists, musicians, coining beautiful phrases that had heart, that had spirit—and when they infiltrated into my language I didn't mind because I knew where they came from, and they weren't just meaningless idioms—they reflected a new renaissance of ideas."

Sometimes you find worldly persons with different accents, different backgrounds, but very similar philosophies. And if you are in Roma, and you are a lover of fine art, or fine literature, or intellectual conversations, there is only one place to go, and that place I guess you would call a bookstore on *Via dei Banchi Nuovi*. I would call it much more than that.

241

My very first friend in all of Italy was a Frenchman. He sits behind his desk all day, smoking cigarettes, occasionally having a coffee, or gelato, playing the most wonderful American music from the sixties, or French music from every decade for that matter, tireless working on his web page, ordering books, fulfilling orders, preparing for his next artistic exhibition, and always happy to drop everything and speak with you about anything with his pompous but genuinely kind and open French attitude.

He treats people like people, and whether or not you are a friend, potential customer, or a person wandering around the streets of Roma in need of directions, he always makes himself available and comes out from behind a mound of work.

I don't think the man sleeps. Perhaps that is why he has one of the best French bookstores; no, one of the best bookstores in all the world period. His passion for collecting and presenting worldly books is unmatched.

I had to change around my entire prejudices. I can say because of this experience, and hanging around meeting all sorts of French folks while here in Italy, that the French really know how to appreciate art, literature, music, food, and good company. They like the best of the best, and my friend is no exception to this rule.

But they are "pussy like"…and do have a way about them. I personally can't take prolonged exposure to large groups of French people. Not only do they disagree with anything one says even when you agree with them; they are better than you, and they know it.

They have a backbone only until push comes to shove. If any intellectual debate ever escalates and gets heated; or if there is any chance they can get into "trouble," or if they sense or see a potential physical altercation brewing; the Frenchman will mysteriously disappear or run away. They are a lot like one of those pets you never know when it's going to turn on you. "Pretty Doberman, good girl...good girl"...then all of the sudden: "SNAP!" The damn dog takes a piece of your finger off.

"We are going to have to kill him sir."

Damn it, don't you think I know that! Thanks for stating the obvious Agent Johnson! I knew we were going to have to terminate him after his last collection of short stories. I just don't know how in the hell or where he's getting his information?

It cannot be. We have no loose ends here whatsoever. Does he have some sort of sixth sense? Some of the things he has written about, we haven't even informed the President of. Where is he getting his information!

"Sir, I am sorry to interrupt, but if we take care of him, won't it seem obvious to the general public? He alluded to the fact the government might try to assassinate him because there are many truths to his 'stories.'"

Am I surrounded by idiots? Are you all a bunch of fucking idiots? First of all watch how you are speaking; and that goes for all of you. We are not the government, we are infinitely more powerful than the government, and do you know why? We don't exist! None of you exist! I don't exist. We aren't even having this conversation right now.

And the conspiracies this bastard is uncovering, they don't exist either—do you understand me? Furthermore accidents happen. The general public will believe whatever we present to them. Our purpose is to assist the government and maintain order and structure in all societies; as well as not forget about the people who pay and fund us.

How do we assist governments? We slowly but surely enable them to gain and retain more and more power, more and more control; and this is for the well being of all the peoples of the world. We have to slowly take away anything of any true value, or anything that may be dangerous.

We cannot have artists like this kicking up so much shit and tainting the minds of our citizens, who are still etherized for the most part. What happens if people really start reading again? Now this bastard is uncovering truths that if they were to be popularly believed by enough people, this could cause catastrophic problems. That piece he did on the Alien craft we found two years ago, that one still blows my mind. The details he had were incredible. No gentlemen, what lies behind closed doors, for very good reasons must remain behind closed doors and not become available to the general public.

Could you imagine what would happen if they knew we created AIDS to help control the population? Or that the cure to all strands of HIV & AIDS is literally sitting on a shelf? Could you imagine what they would do to the governments, how enraged they would be?

Now there really is no way to prove that. And people are naïve enough to really believe that if the cures existed they couldn't be kept a secret from everyone; but what do you think would happen if they knew some of the technology we use everyday was inspired by alien technologies we have studied? What would they do if they knew we are not the only form of intelligent life? What would they do if they found out how we allow drugs into the country, and need individuals to become addicted?

I can go on and on, but we don't have time for this. This son of a bitch must be stopped and never publish, write, or utter another word. He has to know someone. His fictional stories are just too close to the truth, and this has got to stop today. Right here, right now.

Now the first thing that has to happen, is this bastard, let's get a big shot Hollywood director to turn one of his shorts into a movie. The movie will help the short story seem just like that, a glorified fictional grotesque story.

Let this bastard ride a success wave for a while, and let's put him more in the limelight before we completely destroy him. Maybe even support his conspiracy theories, and at his height, he will be the unfortunate victim of a tragic accident. Car accidents always seem to work well; people don't question them all that much.

We can even make the accident his fault, and turn him into an alcoholic and drug addict. Maybe we can have him kill some innocent bystander as well...make it a woman; you know what...make it a woman and a child. And we'll be able to say, not only was he way over the legal drinking limit with drugs in his system, but he took the life of a poor woman and her child. People won't stand for that.

Nobody likes a "drunk driver." People feel very strongly about that, and I don't think his legacy or his work will ever rebound. Once he's dead, he will be seen as just some "crazy" and tortured soul who wrote a lot of crazy shit and pose no more of a threat to us.

Is anybody alive here? Does this sound like a good course of action? Timeline people, timeline! How long do you think this is going to take to pull off from start to completion? I know that look and I know you Johnny; you just want to grab a gun and put a bullet in his head. I'm telling you right now, we can't do that. His stories are already too popular and that will turn him into another Che Guevara. We shoot this son of a bitch now, and people will be wearing T-shirts with his likeness for one hundred years. We don't need that. People really do believe everything he says at this point in time. He has acquired a cult-like status; but don't worry, we're going to get him.

Agent Spensor, that has certainly worked before and I appreciate your suggestion, but let's save that solution for someone else. The pedophile thing is normally a good idea and very easy to implement and frame someone; but in this case we need this guy dead. And we are also trying to kill much more than a man. We are trying to kill his ideas. Being a pedophile would just land him in prison. I'm going to have to say no to that. Let's stick with what we got and start firming up the timeline.

-What My Uncle Told Me

There are black people, and there are fucking niggers. Don't confuse the two, and don't think just because a person has black skin he's a nigger. It's actually a little confusing because in this day and age you have people of every ethnicity, even white people, who are fucking niggers. But I'm just speaking about the blacks right now.

One of the things that makes a black, a nigger, is they are mad at the world. They feel like the entire fucking world owes them something. They feel like the reason they are what they are, or the reason they are where they are, is because of the color of their skin.

They neglect to realize that maybe they haven't worked hard. They neglect to realize that maybe they didn't study as much as they could have in school. They neglect to realize anything because they believe the entire fucking world is against them and trying to keep them down.

And the strength of a nigger's argument always reverts to slavery. Slavery this, and slavery that; and we never got our 40 acres and mule. Never do they mention that the blacks in Africa sold their own people to the whites. No, that clearly never happened in their minds. And you can never try to argue and say, "Well I never owned slaves," or "My grandparents never owned slaves," or "Slavery was a long time ago," because they will hear none of it.

It must be a blessing and a curse to have black skin in this day and age. It's not like one can hide, nor should they want to hide, the color of their skin. But, I mean, what's the first thing you notice when you look

women in the world when it comes to character, when it comes to being excellent mothers, when it comes to working hard. You cannot deny the fact some black women have overcome tremendous adversities—one being they are a woman, and it wasn't until really the 1980's that women were equal; and two, they are black.

If you find a good black woman and love blossoms, the problem you would have, is your little zipper-head offspring. They wouldn't be black, they wouldn't be white, and they'd be ashamed of both of their races. These half n' halves are always all fucked in the head. Unless you have a half Oriental and half white little girl; everyone thinks those are cute. But it's not fair to bring children into this world that already have a few strikes against them.

And if you have a family with a black woman, inevitably her family is going to have a bunch of niggers who are angry at the world; and you're going to have to put up with them. You'll have to associate with a half sister who fucks all of the time and has five or six kids just so she can put their hand out and collect food stamps and welfare. This is what these people want to do. They want to never have to work—and sit on their big fat asses. And if you're successful, then you're really going to have a problem. Her relatives will ALL have their hands out to you asking you for something. I can guarantee that. You are going to be running a bed and breakfast for her deadbeat family members.

Who does that? Have six or seven kids by six or seven different men? I tell you who else does that besides niggers, the fucking spics. Spics are like five different shades of nigger. It's very easy to mistake

I don't know if this is true, but a German told me once that the reason dogs bark at black people in the night is because they can only see in black and white, and it is difficult for the dog to see the niggers other than the whites of their eyes and their teeth. So to a dog they are suspicious looking characters.

Don't let anyone tell you that the word nigger is a bad word. It has been used in bad ways to dehumanize people, but not anymore. And "niggardly" is actually a word as well, look it up. As I said before, niggers or niggardly individuals exist in all races and colors, but most of the time niggers are white trash from the south of just about every country; or angry, lazy, black folks and other people of low class.

And I don't know why we call black people black people, and not brown people. They aren't black at all when you think about it. And I don't know why black people call each other niggers. They say things like, "Whatz up nigga," or "You my nigga." If it is such an offensive term, and if they were really so sensitive to it, they wouldn't use it as every other word out of their mouth. You can't listen to a Rap or Hip-Hop song without hearing the word multiple times. You can't go to a community college or state school without hearing the young adults use the word nigger or nigga all day.

I can also tell you where the term "mother-fucker" came from. The niggers in Harlem; the men used to literally fuck their mothers. They would have sex with their own mothers. That's what kind of animals they were.

This is true. I grew up in New York. I had many black acquaintances as a kid who weren't niggers, and they would tell me this. They would speak of people they knew, even family members jokingly, and laugh about things like "That nigga Ray-Ray is a mother-fucker;" and then they'd go into the story in great detail about how Ray-Ray literally fucked his mother. Back in the day, the niggers were real animals. Imagine what you are capable of doing if you can violate and fuck your own mother? Today "mother-fucker" is just a noun that people casually use, but they fail to think about or remember how this term really came into being.

When I was a kid I would see niggers wearing baggy pants as well; they've been doing that since the forties and fifties. It's nothing new. The reason for the baggy pants was for one: if you went into a store, or a supermarket, you had a lot of room to fit goods into your pants and steal shit. Another reason was the families didn't have a lot of money, because the men would run off, and leave these women to have to raise a litter of kids. Only the women really worked. Only the women kept that culture together.

So the mothers would buy pairs of pants that were very big so everyone in the family could wear and share any pair of pants they had in the home. Just find the cleanest pair and throw them on and roll up the pants-legs a little if need-be.

Only was it many decades later that you had the stupid rich white suburban kids imitating the stupid niggers thinking it was cool, stylish, and fashionable.

Niggers hate white people. There are even a lot of "famous" affluent blacks, who all they do is bitch, and bitch, and do nothing to help their own people. I'm not going to name any names like Cosby or Oprah or Cornel West; but these sons of bitches may appear to like white people, and they must because the whites give them all of their money, but they really hate us. And they hate us only because of our color. It's like a reverse discrimination. They are more prejudiced towards whites, than racist whites are towards blacks. They are just more intelligent about it.

Listen, there must be a very real problem with a race of people who let's make a conservative estimation—they comprise 15% of the population in the US, and when you look at our prisons, 80% of the inmates in prison are black. I'm sick and tired of hearing that shit that blacks aren't afforded the same opportunities and avenues. It's such bullshit!

Let me tell you, in the thirties and forties, the Italians, the Spanish, the Jews; they were all hated and discriminated against as much as the niggers. People still today hate the Jews, and that's only because they are jealous of how strong and wealthy that culture is. These people have been persecuted for thousands of years, and look at them. They are lawyers, doctors, engineers, architects; they are successful professionals who make something of their lives. They all work hard and stick together.

Nowadays you have people from Mexico, the Dominican Republic, and China coming here. You hear people all the time say comments about these individuals, but they are making a life for themselves, they contribute to our society, and they aren't afraid of a little hard work. They aren't afraid to do all the things the quote end quote American folks are no longer willing to do.

The same ghettos the blacks live in now and have lived in for some time, are the same ghettos the

Jews, the Mexicans, the Italians, the Spanish, the Irish, the Germans — and every other at one point minority — these are the same ghettos those people have gotten themselves out of. And the niggers just rather complain and sulk in their own shit, & pray of one day dribbling a basketball for money or getting that big check from somewhere.

Listen, I hope you aren't getting the wrong idea. I'm not telling you to be prejudiced. I'm not saying that, but never say all people are the same by their very nature, and all people are good, because it just isn't true. Don't say the reason someone didn't accomplish something, or made anything of themselves is because of the color of their skin, or the shape of their eyes, or their religious affiliation. These things are just as arbitrary hair color. This is America; and anything is possible for anyone here.

It's really the same thing with fat people. Are you trying to tell me that every fat person has a thyroid problem? Or is big boned? I don't buy it. Fat people are fat because they just can't keep their fucking mouths shut. And I don't feel bad for fat bastards because it is their own damn fault. If you are fat and happy that is one thing, and good for you; good luck not getting diabetes or dying of a heart-attack before you hit fifty. But if you are fat and miserable and angry at the world, then you're a fucking nigger. You see what I'm saying to you?

Yes, it's sad when people are discriminated against. And if you are fat, and you go into a store and need help, or want to return something that let's say was opened or without a tag, you might have more trouble than the slim good looking individual, and that is wrong. But the world isn't fair or just; and if you are looking for fairness or justice, you'll be looking a very long time. But that's beside the point; have you ever noticed there are two types of fat people. There are those who are always on a diet, angry at the world, and just miserable fucks to be around; and then there are those that are the nicest, kindest, most generous individuals who are always the life of the party.

No pun intended, I know you are a young kid, and this is a lot to digest, but let me just leave you with this, because I'm not saying to not have some liberal ideals, but don't embrace them all. When I was younger, and I was in Italy for the first time, I thought just as you did, about how all people are people, and all people are the same. I was a big fan of that John Lennon song, "Imagine."

Now when I think about it, I become sick because it's a fucking awful song. Imagine if there were no countries, or no religions — yes let's just image a world were everyone thinks the same things and everyone is completely the same.

We must learn to appreciate differences, but at the same time recognize that there are good people and bad people, and generalizations exist for a reason. Don't most Italians wear lots of jewelry? Aren't most Jews cheap? Aren't most Japanese intelligent? Aren't most Irish folks functioning alcoholics? Everyone knows about the Polacks.

I'm getting away from my point. When I was in Italy as a young man, they have these people called gypsies everywhere on the streets. Where they come from, who the hell knows, but all Italians hate the gypsies and have little sympathy for them.

I felt bad for these people. I saw some of them disfigured missing hands, and feet, crawling around on the streets, or on the trains, begging for money. Later I found out that they cut each other's hands and feet off just so they can get more sympathy form sympathetic individuals such as myself.

One gypsy in particular and his little son caught my attention. Perhaps his son was four or five, but definitely no older than five years old. I never believed in giving people money. No one ever gave me money, and if I was to give someone money, who the fuck knows what they'll do with it. But I'll never deny someone food. Everyone should have access to food. I think we can agree on that.

So, I asked this guy if he would like me to buy something for him to eat. I went into an expensive sandwich shop with this gentleman and his son, and I let him get whatever he wanted. I spent a lot of money; way more than anyone ever gave him in one shot, I guarantee that.

I proceeded to watch this guy eat just about the entire fucking sandwich except for a little piece of crust, about two inches of crust to be exact, and there definitely wasn't any meat in those two inches. I proceeded to watch this guy drink just about the entire Coca Cola; you know how a plastic bottle of coke has those four little nipples on the bottom — there was only soda left in those little compartments. He gave the two inches of crust, and less than a sip of soda to his son.

Don't tell me that son of a bitch isn't a nigger and is just like everyone else. If it was you, if it was me, we would have given the entire sandwich, and entire soda to our child, and whatever shit fell on the floor, or whatever our child didn't eat or drink, that's what we would have eaten.

And, no; I'm not prejudice towards anyone; until I get to know them and see them for who they are. I would feel comfortable saying this to anyone. Today we have to walk on egg shells with all this political correctness and I hate that. And I want you to at least hear where I am coming from.

Because I know the place you are speaking of, and you should go there. It is full of niggers. You don't have to agree with me, but as you live a little more, you just might begin to say, "My crazy uncle really isn't that crazy after all." You know what; I take back what I just said. Go there, hang out with all the niggers, and observe their behaviors. You'll see, they will add nothing of value or importance to your life. When your mother told you as a little boy, "You are who you're with;" well, you are who you're with.

"And the gospel must first be published," Saint Mark, thirteen, ten. That is what I am trying to do people of Manhattan. That is what I am doing right now! By speaking about, by praising the King of all Kings, I'm publishing the gospel of our Lord and Savior, Jesus Christ.

Saint Matthew, nineteen, twenty-six says, "With God, all things are possible!" Two Chronicles twenty, twenty, tells us to "believe in the Lord your God, so shall ye be established; believe his prophets, so shall ye prosper." That's right! "But thou shalt remember the Lord thy God: for it is he that giveth thee power to get wealth," Deuteronomy, eight, eighteen.

Don't you see how beautiful it is? The Lord, the word of the Lord our God, the Gospel...bothers and sisters, the Gospel is the key to all Life! Amen! The Lord can bring you everything, even great wealth.

Are you a broke ass person? Always down to your last dollar? Are you living on the edge? Stressed out all the time? And have no enjoyment in life. Are you physically and emotionally drained? Is your bank account non-existent? Well, it's probably because you don't have faith. Your faith is not strong enough! The Lord MUST be the most important guiding light in your life!

Your life must revolve around Jesus Christ! It is that simple! Psalm thirty-seven, five says, "Commit thy way unto the Lord; trust also in Him; and He shall bring it to pass." Doesn't that just ring true? Praise the Lord, thank you Jesus! Jesus wants to embrace all of his children, comfort us, and ease our sorrows. Jesus wants you to know, that even if man blows up the earth, that's really not going to matter for you.

Your place is secure at His side in Heaven. Revelation twenty one, four tells us, "He will wipe away every tear from their eyes, and death shall be no more, neither shall there be mourning, nor crying, nor pain anymore, for the former things have passed away."

Philippians one, twenty-one to twenty three says, "For to me to live is Christ, and to die is gain. If I am to live in the flesh, that means fruitful labor for me. Yet which I shall choose I cannot tell. I am hard pressed between the two. My desire is to depart and be with Christ, for that is far better." This world is all we have, but it really doesn't mean all that much. It's a test. It's a test people! Why do you think old people are so joyous when they are nearing death? All of the folks that don't put God first, are failing! They have much to fear, because there is much they don't know. Don't be one of those people!

John four, seven to eight says, "Beloved, let us love one another, for love is from God, and whoever loves has been born of God and knows God. Anyone who does not love does not know God, because God is love." We have all had love before…given love before. And in a sense, we have already felt the power of Jesus.

It's not easy to take that leap of faith for the skeptics, or for those who are afraid, or those who don't believe; there are many people with hardened hearts. They walk around with blinders on their eyes. Deuteronomy thirty one, six tells us, "Be strong and courageous. Do not fear or be in dread of them, for it is the LORD your God who goes with you. He will not leave you or forsake you."

"And we know that all things work together for good to them that love God, to them who are the called according to his purpose;" that's Romans eight, twenty-eight. Manhattan can you feel the energy! Can you feel the excitement! Just do what the Gospel says. Just do what the good book says people, "casting all your care upon him; for he careth for you," Peter, five, seven.

Saint Luke tells us, "For with God nothing shall be impossible," and that is very true. That has never been any truer than today ladies and gentleman. Everything is possible, in addition to the Bible, in addition to the Preachers, the Gospel, the Churches, the Worship Music, and Holy Festivals — in addition to all of that wonderful stuff, God is always around us. And if He's always around us, we can talk to God whenever we want! Whenever we want we can talk to God.

"Hide not thy face from me in the day when I am in trouble; incline thine ear unto me: in the day when I call answer me speedily," Psalm one O two, two. Don't you just love that? If we are in trouble, if we need help, if we are confused, sad, sick, angry, crazy — it doesn't matter! God loves you. God wants to listen to you. God demands that you listen to Him, love Him, respect His word and teachings.

Listen people. I praise the Lord all day. I would praise Jesus Christ and preach His word in my sleep if I could. I'm sure some nights I'm talking in my sleep singing about His glory! If a farmer plants a few seeds, he might get a few crops. If a farmer plants many seeds, and nourishes and takes care of his field, he will reap far more. It's really that simple folks. God doesn't want you to make your life complex. He wants to make it simple and epic. He wants you to be happy. That is why God gave us the Bible. He gave us a roadmap. God gave us everything we need to live this mortal life in peace and harmony. He gave us all the answers.

Two Corinthians says it is up to us to sow the seeds; it is up to God to grow the seeds. We must put God first! Put God first each and everyday, in all that we do. I'm here everyday people. I'm here all day, everyday. Bothers and sisters, now is the time to be saved. Let me help you. God is power, God is light, let God guide your spirit and way, starting tonight!

Right here, right now, if you accept Jesus Christ as your Lord and Savior, you too can have no pain. You too can have clarity and understanding. For perhaps the first time in your life, your life and reason for living will make sense. The world will begin to make sense to you, because God makes sense. And once you feel the Spirit, once you know you have the power of Jesus with you, on your side, I promise you...with God, you can achieve anything. And you will never let it go.

Jesus warms you. Jesus comforts you. He gives you power. He makes you feel alive. Excuse me miss, but don't you just love the Lord! Amen! Jeremiah twenty-nine, eleven says, "For I know the plans I have for you, declares the LORD, plans for welfare and not for evil, to give you a future and a hope." Isaiah forty-one, ten states: "Fear not, for I am with you; be not dismayed, for I am your God; I will strengthen you, I will help you, I will uphold you with my righteous right hand." So you see that...right there God is telling you, I'm going to pick you up. I'm going to help you. Fear NOT!

If you can just open your heart people! Open

your soul and read the good book! Talk to people about the awesomeness that is God. Psalm thirty-two, eight says, "I will instruct you and teach you in the way you should go; I will counsel you with my eye upon you." John five, fourteen, goes on to say, "And this is the confidence that we have toward Him, that if we ask anything according to His will He hears us."

I can go on all day people. I do go on all day. Because I love God. And I know God loves you. And He wants you to know that. He wants you to know, that anytime, anywhere, anyplace; you can accept the Lord Jesus Christ, the King of all Kings, your Savior…into your heart!

Psalm twenty-seven, is so powerful. It's where anyone can begin. "The LORD is my light and my salvation; whom shall I fear? The LORD is the stronghold of my life of whom shall I be afraid?" Just keep saying that to yourself people! The power of Jesus compels you!

-Unleashing Imprisoned Splendor

When two lovers are really open to each other, when they are not afraid of each other and not hiding anything from each other — that is Intimacy. If the lover thinks the other will be offended, then the intimacy is not yet deep enough. Then it is a kind of arrangement, which can be broken by anything. -OSHO

Yes, that is exactly what I was thinking. A dance in beings…a unison of thoughts and spirits. Ever since I saw you when we were very young; ever since I really got to look into your eyes, my life hasn't been the same.

I can't even begin to tell you how many wasted days and sleepless nights I had thinking about you. After our last engagement, I started daydreaming a little, and I could see you in *Castrovillarri*, dressed in blue, having the time of your life.

I see your silhouette against the mountains, against the ocean, against the gardens, on the couch, in the kitchen, in the bedroom — with me — or alone — or entertaining friends and family — enjoying a simple life, with all the amenities. Yes you have evolved, and yes I can see, that you Valerie are a woman I will have in my life in some capacity, now and forever, but I want more than that.

With you I am elevated, I realize I can be me, and achieve anything. Even after years of not communicating, something has brought us together once again, and the words in my mind are beginning to dance. They have always danced when I thought of you, but in your company, it becomes difficult to speak. In a glance, you convey so much too me, and I hope I do the same thing with you. Valerie, there has always been a part of you, that I have never been able to touch, that has never been open to me, and I do know why — the timing wasn't right before.

Now that we are older, will you dance with me? We went to the 9th grade dance, you know I can dance and we had a good time. I'm joking, but seriously: will you give me the opportunity to be your man once and for all. I promise to be as excited and nervous the last time I see you, as I was the first time I saw you. I promise to always be honest with you and share all of my thoughts, realities, and dreams. Dreams are unlived thoughts, unlived desires, unlived longings from the day — I know your dreams and my dreams can become a reality. Let's make our dreams come true! I am tired of dreaming what can be, I am ready to just be. I am ready to know you, understand you, complement you; I mean really Valerie, who are you going to find, who is better for you, than me?

I'm not going to pretend that I didn't always have a crush on you. If I remember correctly, which I do, you actually pursued me first. You chased after me in 9th grade, then you came around again in 11th grade, then the summer after we graduated High School, then two years into college we started talking and always saw each other during breaks. Now we've been working in the business world for sometime and have met up once again.

I know you've always had a crush on me. That's why every couple of years, we've always seemed to find each other and reconnect. And we always have the best time together. Sometimes it's very platonic. Sometimes it's very hot and heavy. But I am tired of only spending brief moments in time together.

And I'm not going to pretend to be a poet, because I am not. But to lay all my cards on the table except one—I'm going to tell you what I think of you. You are a harmonious blend of intellect, sophistication, humor, sex appeal, and compassion. When you have been a part of my life, you consume the vast majority of my thoughts, and the bottom line is, I have always wanted an opportunity to be with you, to discover you—and I know a part of you, has always been intrigued by me.

I believe you are going somewhere, and the possibilities are endless. I believe in myself once again as well, and I know together we can accomplish anything and everything, and have a wonderful time doing so. Every time I close my eyes, every time I blink, I see my thoughts, and they lead directly to you. I see the past, the present, and I see the future. I have so much yet to learn about you, and we have so much yet to experience, and you are already a beautiful novella in my mind.

I can't describe in words the touch of your hand on my skin, the sound of your voice, or the energy you give off, and that is what draws me to you—you are beyond words in many ways, and always have been. You do it for me. What can I say? There is no one I'm more attracted to than you. Right now I am breaking my golden rule, but I must articulate how I feel about you. If I could, I would jump on top of you and rip all your clothing off right now.

Valerie, I am not going to lose you again, no chance, no way in hell. Give me the opportunity to do for you half of what you have done for me, let me be a novella in your mind. Let's do some of those dirty things I know you fanaticized about.

"So if you want it, come and get it, for crying out loud…Let go of your heart, let go of your head, and feel it now." That's a great song, isn't it? Speaking of now, why don't you let yourself go — let me show you one thing I have always been, and you know it. That's right, I am the "World's Greatest Kisser." How did you know I was going to say that? Come here baby! Kiss me!

-The Writer

It's totally amazing when you think about it. Here you are, here I am, and this is our opportunity to spend time together. Entering any book or story, is just like entering into a conversation. Right now, I'm doing most of the talking, but you are here, and I know we're together, and I can't think of a better place to be.

I love to read. I live to write. And I view my life, as an experience. I want to and must be an active participant. There are the folks who watch the parade, and the folks who march in it. I'm neither of those folks. I'd say I'm the kind of person who dreams up the parade for all the folks to watch and march in.

I know I'm not going to live forever. I know you aren't going to live forever either. But in a story, I can live forever, and we can have the opportunity to be together, anytime you like. Anytime you want to escape, anytime you want to be comforted, anytime you want to know that someone out there hears you and understands you, you can pick up one of my books and talk to me.

I might already be dead, like Faulkner, and yet again, here I am...here we are together. So in a sense, just by your very reading of this, there is a little part of me that will spark your interests and live on with you.

Do you want to sing? Are you listening to a song, or is anything stuck in your head at this moment? I just want to make sure I haven't lost you and you aren't thinking about something else with this mushy introduction. Stay with me my friend. Writing is just like anything else.

When I see my writing from a long time ago for

example, sometimes it is so foreign and unfamiliar, that I'm not even sure I wrote it. I can't believe some of the stuff I dig up. I've considered myself to be a "writer" since ninth grade, always taking every opportunity to scribble down notes on any piece of paper available to me at the time; and I save everything; so in other words: I have writing all over the place. My office, file cabinets, desk, and draws, all consist of pieces of paper, notebooks, pads, and receipts. I save receipts for different reasons than most people…all of my receipts have writing on the back. And *Post-it Notes*; don't even get me started on those; what a wonderful invention.

The only way I know with certainty, that I did indeed write the words I find on many pieces of paper is because I know what my handwriting looks like. I can recognize my handwriting from second grade to the present day, from a mile way, no problem. In second grade my handwriting started to have its own unique flare. I even had my own special letters and way of writing things, so only I could understand and in essence "decode" what I had written.

As time progresses, sure, the things you have written or many of the stories and books you have shared and read all seem different in some way. But the truth is; they aren't different at all. You the reader has evolved and changed. You are in a different time, a different place, and a different space.

Think about it? How the hell are the words on this page going to change in ten years from now….in forty years from now…in one hundred years from now? They can't change! They have been safeguarded and secured by good old ink and paper. Only the elements of earth, wind, water, ice, and fire could "change" the works written on this page.

Isn't it cool to experience a book, and then still "have something" tangible? Not only are books an important part of our lives, but books are beautiful. That's what bookcases are for; to display and showcase books. Today people put all sorts of shit in bookcases, that are completely worthless, and it drives me crazy.

You go into someone's home, and they walk you right over to the bookcase and say, "Look at what I got at *Pier One!*" What, the same crap about 100,000 other people in the world bought this week at *Pier One*? Yes, that generically made vase is beautiful and the second you die, one of your children is going to throw it out or sell it at a garage sale for a buck, and it will certainly be worthless in one hundred years from now.

I've actually been to some folks homes, and they don't have any books visible in any rooms of the house. Even worse, some people have flat out said to me, "I don't have any books." And my favorite of the bogus excuses besides one saying, "I really don't read," is of course, "I don't have any books because I just don't have room for them;" or "Books get dusty, and that would just be another thing for me to have to clean." Or they've downloaded a few books off of Amazon dot com and now they think they actually do have a library of books.

People who don't surround themselves with books, art, and living plants scare me. That's another thing that drives me crazy; going into someone's home, and seeing that they have no plants, no flowers, and no artwork of any kind anywhere. Or even worse, they have fake plastic plants with a foot of dust on them that look like absolute shit and a movie poster that some college kid would have in a dorm room. What good is a fake plant? And what good is a $7.00 poster that isn't even framed nicely. At least frame the thing.

But back to books; there are many books in my lifetime that I have fallen in and out of love with, then back in and out of love with once again. Call it a love slash hate relationship I guess. But countless books have helped me become who I am today and enriched my essence.

With many books, I'd say to myself, "I don't know what it is about this novel?" For a few years of my life, some books almost seemed to be a sort of mantra...they gave me new ways of thinking and insights into my everyday life; they made me feel good.

And then for a few years, I'm saying in my head, "I really don't like those books anymore." Who wants to read that depressing shit? Or the characters seem like ungrateful bitches.

And not only do I start knocking the book, but I also start knocking the author. Who the author is as a person, or what light I see them in, also influences the way I enjoy their work. Some authors in time have gone from heroes to jackasses...and others from jackasses to heroes in my mind.

At this point in my life, I don't enjoy reading or writing about anything that has to do with human suffering and misery. I don't like books about war; I don't like horror books, or anything overly grotesque or scary. I don't like books about drug addicts or people with horrible ailments; nothing about prostitutes or crime; and I also don't care to read or write about anything overly romantic and lovely-dovey.

I guess I like things I can relate to and things that give my mind a sense of peace; or I enjoy pure fantasy and escapism. There was a time, when I wanted to read the work of Frederick Douglas, or Karl Marx, or Yeats; learn about Women in 18th Century England, the plight of people in developing nations, or power-through some cumbersome Old English Verse. But that stuff just doesn't interest me anymore. I could give a shit less; especially anything that has to do with human suffering or misery.

And poetry? Don't even get me started on poetry! Let's just say, poetry has never done it for me. Yuck! I don't like poetry and I don't like the people who read and discuss poetry. And unless you're super hot, don't even talk to me if you consider yourself to be a poet. Everyone always wants to share their interpretation of a poem and what it means to them. And the truth is; all poems only have one interpretation, the correct one.

But back to what I was saying a moment ago, and just to give you the perfect example; I don't know too many Jews anxiously anticipating any new Mel Gibson movies, nor do I see them enjoying his old "classics," which came out way before everyone "knew" he hated Jews. And does he even really hate Jews? I don't know? I don't know the man, nor have I really cared to study up too much on the empirical evidence against him.

But that's America for you...we can say he "allegedly" hates Jews, which means that it may or may not be true; and nonetheless we can tarnish his reputation and legacy as an actor; over what may be truth, heresy, a low point in his life where he was full of

272

alcohol and anger; or any combination of other factors, causing him to act in an uncharacteristic fashion. I have a much bigger problem with the once alive Michael Jackson allegedly giving a kid wine in a *Pepsi* can & taking him into a secret room that you have to crawl through a hole in his closet to get to; than Mel Gibson allegedly being anti-Semitic and using racial slurs.

Imagine what it would be like if someone accused you of molesting a cat. Not only were you accused of this, but even worse, a witness or two has said they've actually seen and heard you molesting cats before. One of them even has you on video behind your car in the garage "doing something suspicious."

Even after all the smoke clears; and it is proven that the one person who saw you molesting a cat, really didn't see you doing that at all. What was captured on video was you in your garage, behind your car, unpacking your trunk full of goods from Costco.

And the person who heard you molesting a cat, really heard the radio playing in another room of the house and her boyfriend running on a squeaky treadmill. So even after the witnesses and evidence against you have been discredited, there are always some people who are going to believe and remember, that you are the person who likes to molest cats.

The same thing happened to that poor girl who had the vicious rumor spread around her school that she stuck a hotdog in her vagina. Everyone knows that story. And the attacks and joking around got so bad, that this kid didn't even want to go to school anymore. Her family got up and moved to a new state, and she tried to start again, but within a matter of days, all the kids at the new school new she was the "hot dog girl."

We really aren't all that sensitive towards others. And our minds like to make things concrete. We like to compartmentalize; put things into distinct categories. It is either black or it is white; we don't like to try to process the grays. And our minds are not comfortable with silence or stillness. We like to keep our minds going and busy because yes, things can and do get stale; and this makes us uncomfortable or apathetic.

Seeing the Statue of David is a vivid, life-changing and impressive experience. When you lock eyes with him for the "first time," it absolutely will take your breath away. But I'm sure the people guarding the statue day in and day out don't see it as all that impressive anymore. Their heart no longer skips a beat, and they no longer freeze, saying in their mind, "This statue is beyond words." They're over it. They were probably over it after their first week of work.

And once they retire, you will never ever be able to drag them back to the *Accademia* to see the David. If they never saw that magnificent statue again for the rest of their life, it would probably be too soon.

Like Da Vinci and Michelangelo, I'm very critical of my work. People say, "Why don't you write more?" or "Why don't you share more of your work?" They think because they don't see me cranking out a novel a year, that I'm not writing. Meanwhile, that's all I do all day and that is all I've ever done: write.

"Why don't I share more?" Because when it is written, it is crystallized. As the author, I have to make sure I am ready and confident my work is finished and perfect. I'm not creating a batch of chocolate chip cookies, which we can devour, and after eating them say, "You know, the last batch of cookies was much better than this batch."

Unlike bad cookies which only hang around for a short while, books do tend to hang around forever. When I'm eighty-eight, one of my grandchildren will probably find one of my books and say to me, "Papa, did you write this?" And I'm going to say, "Do you see my name on it? Of course I wrote that book you little bastard." And then, depending on what book it is, I'll tell them at what age they should read it.

That's another thing about great literature. Sometimes we don't know it's great because we are exposed to it at the wrong time during our lives. How can a kid truly understand or relate to Willy Lowman in *Death of a Salesman*? The answer is he or she cannot.

A ninth grader doesn't have a fucking clue about what it is to be Willy Lowman, or Marlow and Kurtz in the *Heart of Darkness*. It's a real shame more thought isn't put into what books are introduced to us at different points in our life. Or there isn't an expert, who one can talk to and say, "This is where I am in my life;" and the expert would say, "These are some books you should look into."

There is a difference between understanding something & knowing something. I will never truly "know" what it is like to be raped, or have an abortion. Can I understand what those experiences might be like; can I sympathize with a person who went through one of those experiences; absolutely. But unless I rob a bank and go to a maximum security federal prison, or some pill is invented that can allow men to become pregnant, and once I'm pregnant I decide all of the sudden that this isn't the right thing for me to do...I'm never going to be raped or have an abortion.

I'm getting off the topic once again. Another of my favorites is, when someone asks me: "What do you write about?" or "What are you writing about?" And when I decide to answer their question and discuss what I'm working on, they don't want to hear it. They rather help me hurry along whatever I'm talking about, so they can throw in their two cents, and tell me what I should "really" write about.

So, here is a person, who never wrote anything in his or her life; their favorite book is some piece of shit shadow written by some schlep for Jay-Z which they read on their *iPhone*; and they are going to give me advice as to what I should write about? Or how I should write?

You can learn a lot about people from what books they've read, and how they are reading them. If you are reading any book written by a reality television star, or celebrity, the chances are, that book is a real piece of shit, or at the very most, somewhat interesting. If you are buying and downloading e-books, it means purchasing a book is of no value to you; and after you look at this download, you'll never pay any mind to it again.

Back to this whole reality of the written word becoming crystallized once a work of literature is "printed" on paper in black and white. I'm not the kind of writer who would ever "go back into" my finished work. I think that's a bunch of bullshit, when a fictional author revises, or adds too, a pervious work.

And what would I consider finished? Isn't that obvious? A book! Once a work is printed and bound, it is complete. And as the author, I must move past it.

It's better for me to not even think about a

finished work to be honest with you. Sure I'll talk about it with someone if they ask me, but I'm not going to analyze it. During the entire process of creation, I analyzed my own work, and now it's time to just let it stand as what it is, on its own. Because I know if I continue to revisit it, after I have finished it, I will always see something I could have, or should have done differently. There comes a point where the writer has to say, "This is now complete." "It is as perfect as I can possibly get it."

And that's one of the reasons I hate fucking e-books. Today anyone can be an author or is an author. Everyone is writing a book or wants to write a book.

When I was in high school and college, we didn't have e-books. I tried to get my creative work published in college, and it really didn't happen for me. I say it really didn't happen for me, because of course I was able to get published in literary magazines or books that were compilations of stories from various authors; but that wasn't my goal and vision.

Every literary agent I went too in my entire life wasn't interested in any of my writing or anything I had to say. I even went to a friend of mine from high school who became some big shot literary agent, and she wouldn't help me in the slightest. Every door I opened was abruptly closed, because "no audience" existed for me according to them.

No audience exists for me? I remember saying in my head, I just showed you twenty different novels I wrote, written in all different styles, spanning every genre imaginable, and there is "no audience" for my work? Or my work uses too much vulgarity. Or my work is too idealistic. Or too difficult to understand and read. Or if "we" could just add "this" and change "that,' then maybe I'd have something. Or my absolute favorite comment about a Science Fiction story I wrote…"It's a little too Sci-Fi -E."

I mean, who are these fucking people? They have been such avid readers and producers of crap, for such a long time, they don't even know what brilliant or genius is. Today, they'd probably tell Dickens his books are a little too "wordy" and Faulkner his books are a little too "difficult" for the average person to understand.

It took me twelve years to break into the world of being a published author. And that is only because, in the world of Social Networks, I am more recognized and powerful than most corporations and celebrities; it really has very little to do with my writing at all, which hasn't changed.

I finally do have a great sense of accomplishment now however. There is nothing like seeing your book on a shelf. There is nothing like seeing someone with your book in their hand, or reading it in a coffee shop. The best is having someone walk up to you and say, "Please sign this for me;" and then they always begin to talk about the part of the book that hit them the most.

Knowing that I now have the opportunity to create as many books as I want, in whatever fashion I desire; that's what I've been working towards my entire life. As a writer, to be able to remain true to your vision is of pinnacle importance.

But when you start working with literary agents and publishers, they don't give a shit about your vision. They care about the bottom line; is this book going to make us money? And they are trying to figure out how they can make the most money with your book, while giving you as little money as they possibly can. They want to keep you hungry to get you to produce more and more for them to choose from.

But yes. Anyone can type a word document, or make a PDF, and write the biggest piece of shit, and turn it into an e-book. And e-books usually cost a few bucks to read, so the pseudo-author can of course make a few dollars as well and say, "I'm a published author."

And the genuine, accomplished author, who blazed a trail with hard covers and paperbacks; even they are no different. They rationalize e-books in the end. Why? Because they can make a shitload of money; that's why. They can reach markets and audiences never before available to them. They say, "Why not regurgitate the same crap in a different format and profit from it?"

And don't think that when real paper books fade away and are sparsely produced, if produced at all, that e-books won't cost just as much or more, as paper books cost today. I image a day, when some e-books are going to cost $29.95, or $70, or even $250 dollar art e-books, which will have to be expensive because they have so many pictures. They're going to figure out how to bang the consumer as hard as possible and maximize profits; that I'm sure of.

I wasn't making that up, about the Jay-Z e-book. The guy who read it on his *iPhone* said it was over 1000 pages, and the great part was many of the chapters linked to videos, and he was able to read a few pages here and there, because he always has his phone on him.

Jay-Z? The guy has a vocabulary of less than 250 words, mediocre music, a shitty clothing line, a hot wife, and more money than God. He must be a wonderful author with a wealth of knowledge and formidable command of the written word.

Who the hell wants to read anything on a screen the size of a pack of cigarettes? I just don't get it. I don't get it, and I'm tired of everyone telling me how I should get into e-books. Or, even better, you should turn your writing into an "interactive application."

That's just what I want; people on their *iPhones* accessing one line of my work, and saying to someone, "Here, just read this quickly." I should turn my work into a bunch of bit-sized fortune cookies, easy to consume and digest? Isn't great writing interactive enough?

I know there is money to be made. I know anyone from three to eighty-eight is reading books in electronic fashions. But I don't care. I want nothing to do with a *Nook*, or a *Kindle Fire*, or an *iPad*. I have no use for that bullshit. They all scare me.

Just look at the *Kindle Fire* for example. Did anyone read *Farenheit 451*? We are destroying books, destroying literature, and destroying the physical process and experience of reading. I certainly don't believe e-books should be used in schools and given to students; and I absolutely don't want any of my writing in any sort of electronic format. It's the one thing I'm not going to compromise.

Back to the process of writing for a moment; there is such a thing as overworking your literary masterpieces. There is a point, when the artist must say, "OK, this painting is finished." And then they frame it, it gets hung on a wall, and from that point forward it is experienced.

You don't hear painters saying, "That painting you bought; I'd like to have it back so I can just touch it up and add a little more to it." And the same is true for a novel, a poem, or short story. Part of the real talent is knowing when your work is complete.

The art of the novel is my true passion. But unfortunately today, people have the attention span of a gnat, and I believe the "good" novel is all but dead. The shitty novel, that's the book that is 220 pages and you blow through it in one day, and say, "That was a great book! Very entertaining!"

To me, that translates to: nothing knocked you off your center. Nothing made you think. Nothing challenged your mind. And, you basically read a brain fart, which is the same thing as watching a "B-" movie. It's fine to read books like that once in a while; but it is better to read books that are capable of throwing you outside your comfort zone, and make you think a little.

On the other hand, and it does make perfect sense to do so in this day and age, perhaps a "great" work of literature, is that which can be digested in its entirety in one sitting. That is what Edgar Allen Poe believed. His stories have a wonderful pace, and they can all certainly be read and enjoyed in one sitting by anyone with half a brain.

I do enjoy great short stories. What's not to love about them? My favorite part about a collection of short stories, and I always feel like somewhat of a rebel, is I decide exactly what order I want to read the stories in. I do not care what order they are presented. First and foremost, I look at the titles of the stories. I see what catches my eye or is of most interest to me at that particular moment. Then I look at the length of the story.

If I have ten minutes to read, I look for a short story that is only a few pages long, and I squeeze it in, while making sure not to rush myself. If I'm not really that tired, and getting ready for bed, then I'll tackle one of the longer short stories; or maybe I'll decide to read a block of the shorter ones.

And after I read a short story, it's the same kind of accomplishment as reading a great novel, except, it isn't an unconscious race, to get to the last page. When you read a book of short stories in any order you want, and you go back and forth to the table of contents, checking off the stories you read…you find yourself looking for the stories you haven't read yet, and counting down to how many stories you have left in the book. If you love to read, you do this with a certain "sadness." It's never a joyful, "Oh, I only have seven stories left to read." A good book of short stories, is one of those books, you never want to end.

When you read a novel, you're saying to yourself, "How many pages do I have left?" You start reading at an even pace, but then you are halfway finished with the book and of course very conscious of this.

When you have exactly fifty percent more to read, you begin to say in your head, "I only have about half this book left." Then, when you have about twenty-five percent of the book left to read, you say, "Holy shit! I already read seventy-five percent of this book!" And then, the end of the book, that last little bit, where all the real magic should happen; that's the part we read at a feverish pace, rather than savor and enjoy.

A novel, even many great novels, they just can't hold it together until the very end. It is almost as if the author was trying to hurry it along as well, and wrap it up. I think even the greatest authors got tired at times, and said, "You know what; I've been working on this long enough and it is now good enough;" or "as good as I'll ever get it."

You don't have to worry about that with short stories. I don't think a short story is long enough to completely fall apart. For the most part, they have a beginning, middle, and end; and if the story is going to suck, it will probably suck from the very beginning.

Is the author presenting a collection of "short stories" in a particular order, and does he or she have more on the way? That's something I ask myself. I'm sure if an author wrote 120 short stories, of course, some are going to be better received than others, but you can't put all the best stories in one book. That would make no sense.

Great bands don't do one album of just their "greatest hits"...even though they most likely know right from the beginning when they release an album which songs are going to be the "hits."

So as a reader, and a writer, I'm a big fan of short stories. If you read a short story and you don't particularly care for it; that was just one short story. At least the entire book wasn't a waste of money or a complete bust.

A novel can start off great, and then just put you to fucking sleep. Or it can end, leaving you with a very unsatisfied feeling. Perhaps the author was trying to get all poetic, or wanted to leave you with a big question mark to seem more intelligent or ground breaking.

That is, for example, the entire reason idiots said the movie *Inception* was so brilliant. "Oh, the ending! The ending was so good." This could have happened, or that could have happened, and you don't really know if he's in the real world, or the dream world... ...I say to the folks who love to analyze shit like that..."shut-up" already! Go read, *The Sound and the Fury*, and analyze that.

Today, we think too highly of too many mediocre people, philosophies, and things. Every child is a little genius. Every musician is talented. Every internet video is super hilarious and cool! Every new product by our favorite companies is a "must have." Everybody in the world has a website. "Here, go to my website!" Those folks make me laugh; they use these free blogging platforms, and they think they have a website.

And now with "Social Networks," people really think others give a shit about what they have to say and what they are doing. Everyone wants to be "in the spotlight;" everyone has a craving to be more than they are and larger than life. They have to be noticed anyway they can be noticed. Let's put up pictures of ourselves scantily clad, or doing something illegal; or let's say very unpopular and controversial things, just to see if we can get a rise out of anyone.

While at the same time, you of course have to be "one of the girls" or "just one of the boys." "I got my hair done;" or "Look at what I'm eating;" "My dog is so cute;" "My kid said the funniest thing today;" "Here's me and the boys fishing;" "My friend just got arrested;"

"I think the President sucks;" "It's about that time for me to have an alcoholic beverage after a long day."

What I say to all of that is: Who the hell are you? Who do you think you are that anyone should give a shit about what you are saying, thinking, or doing? We think we're so important these days. We think that we are "evoking change" or engaging in something meaningful and important.

"Look at the POWER of social networks." I say, look at the idiocy of people. Look at how people are choosing to use their time, and what they are doing with their precious lives here on earth. Look at what Social Networks could be, and look at what they are and have become.

You are going to heat up your dinner in a microwave quickly, so you can go on *Facebook* and bullshit with people about nonsense, as well as play a game like *Farmville* and attend to virtual livestock and crops? You are going to sit next to the one you love, and instead of communicating, use Social Networks, with a television on in the background that nobody is paying attention to and just making noise? After about five minutes, even a child would get bored and say, "Enough of this shit! I want to do something else." And you would hope that something else is, the kid wants to go outside and run around.

Who cares what's on the web? Who cares what's on TV? The world got along just fine without all this shit we deem so necessary today. "Where's my cell phone?" Who cares where it is? Do you really need it? Are you really that important that you must always be available?

The only thing we should care about, are the

Newspapers. The printed newspapers that are created daily; when those die, kiss your ass goodnight. Journalism is already all but dead, and nobody knows what news is anymore; but at least the newspapers are still trying to make an attempt to bring you "information" in a tangible fashion. Something you can hold in your hand; something you can rip out and save a few pages from, to refer to at a later date; that is valuable. News that is printed is news that cannot change over time.

But nobody cares about that. Because newspapers, well, they are made with paper and paper kills trees. That's one of the arguments many morons have discussing why we really should stop making books, magazines, and newspapers. They kill so many trees.

The number of trees cut down because of our printed books and periodicals is extremely negligible. Additionally, technological waste is a much greater problem. All this technology we embrace, changes so quickly, and is obsolete by the time we buy it. A newspaper or book, just throw one in your backyard; you will see it disintegrate into and return to the earth. Your first generation *Kindle* or *iPad* will sit in a landfill, or move around the bottom of the ocean, for a few hundred years.

So we digest our news in the form of "shows" on television, and we watch our favorite reality programs, and we listen to celebrities and comedians tell us "their take" on things, while catching glimpses of infomercials.

The infomercials are the best when you are tired. You'll convince yourself that you are going to start eating more healthy; but you can't until you get a juicer. Or you'll say to yourself, maybe next week I'll try exercising a little each day because, because you see some actors claiming to have gotten "ripped" in thirty days.

An e-book? Now that I mentioned it, I can't get them out of my head. I want people to enjoy my books; fold the corners of pages, have things underlined and highlighted, have thoughts written in margins, and put them in prized locations on bookshelves. Books are meant to be shared; provided you know the person you are lending your book to, is going to give it back to you.

Nothing tweaks my melon more than someone who you lend a book to, and they never give it back. What am I supposed to do now? Just go buy another one; and say "no biggie?"

It is a big deal. I had notes in my copy of that book; I had things underlined, I had corners folded; that was my book and well broken in. I want it back. I just can't buy another one of those books and recreate all I contributed to that piece. It took me a few reads to make it my own, and I can't possibly everything I put in that book.

My books are the most valuable things I own. I imagine, as I near my death, I will begin to part with my books and give the appropriate books to the appropriate people who I know will treasure and value them, just as much as I did. That's going to be difficult. Who in the world is going to deserve my original *Harvard Classics* from 1909 along with the custom bookcase I built special just for them?

People don't care anymore I guess. Or let me rephrase that: People don't care, about anything other than what is of concern to themselves. And what is of concern to them is usually not what they are passionate about, as much as, how they want to be perceived. Nobody wants to look bad, so they will jump on whatever "cause" is popular or whichever topic is "hot" at any particular moment.

We're all circling the drain. All it takes is for a nuclear power plant, or a few bombs to blow up somewhere, contaminating everything, and we will all slowly die. What someone does in one part of the world eventually comes to your doorstep.

We already are all slowly dying. We're killing ourselves with plastic. Microscopic shards of plastic are everywhere, from our food, to our air, to our water; and in case you were wondering, plastic is toxic shit.

Why we wrap perishable items that are going to be consumed in a matter of seconds, with toxic plastic that will be a pollutant on our earth for hundreds of years, is beyond me. You can't get away from seeing and using plastic on everything. And besides the plastic, think about all the chemicals we use, and in some cases we must now use, in and on all of our food.

I don't want to get into that stuff, but I must say: I don't see us turning this ship around; unless of course we revert to a simpler, more caring, and honest way of life. This isn't to say we should sacrifice and abolish all technology and go back to the stone ages. I'm not proposing we live like Native Americans or stop taking long hot showers because it wastes too much water. But we certainly should use the best technologies available to us in any given situation. And we should never sacrifice our world and our well being, for the sake of our global economy. How we are still using fossil fuels and driving around in gas-guzzling cars is another thing that is just beyond the realm of my comprehension.

Most of our technology, and the way technology is progressing, is more than a horrific nightmare. Watch *The Twilight Zone*, read or revisit *1984*; those were just warnings of what we should never become, and that is exactly what we currently are. Some psychopaths today believe we are living in *The Matrix* and none of "this" is real. Well, perhaps we will one day be living in a matrix and be completely unaware of it with no Morpheus to help and guide us. Maybe the crazies aren't that crazy after all.

We must never let our technology become more powerful than the human spirit; we must always remain in control. And technology must never take away any of our freedoms and privacy. But yet, this is exactly what we are doing with all of technology. We're making machines that can think, machines that are replacing people, machines that are "watching and recording us," even machines capable of "fixing themselves." We are not worried about this in the slightest fashion; or we are worried about this, but we say to ourselves, "There is nothing I can do about this."

"We will never have robotic police officers; that's just crazy!" Is it really crazy? I'd argue there will come a time when you won't even be able to "manually" drive your car. All cars that don't "drive themselves" will be deemed too great of a risk to your personal well being and the safety of others if you are to try to operate them. And the robotic police will figure out a way to lock you up indefinitely for being drunk or talking on a cell phone, even though you aren't even technically driving your car anymore.

———

The human element, our natural earth, actual experiences, and all that is tangible; these are the things I believe to be most important. Nobody is ever going to tell me, that there is anything better than a book one can hold in their hands and experience.

Reading books; having good books readily available at your fingertips…along with good food, excellent music, lots of plant and animal life, as well as great company…that is where we should focus in order to begin our journey to try to save this world and all life on this planet.

Forget about "being centered" or "finding peace." How about we ground ourselves and begin to move in positive directions. I'd settle for that story.

You know, the word "story" has negative connotations to it. When someone says, "I have to tell you a story;" there is a part of you that believes, because it is a "story," there is going to be some embellishment. We no longer consider the "story" to be "truth." Does it contain some factual information, or some experiences we can relate to? Sure, but for the most part, it isn't very valuable; nor does it carry much weight.

And I really don't know why this is. I know we don't listen to stories, or remember them accurately. We take "the story" for granted, because we know, we can always ask the person who told us the story, to tell us how it goes again. Or we can refer back to the book, and get the general idea of how the story goes.

I value the "story." I think the story is an art. It is an experience. And it is capable of capturing the truth, more than any other medium of art, or writing style. The story is more than just a tale or occurrence or event or experience; the story is the window into our own souls, where we as the reader have an intimate opportunity to delve deep into and learn about our "true self."

Not only should we continue to tell stories through our very own eyes, but we must make sure we record the stories of our elders and yesteryear. I can't even begin to tell you, all the stories people told me that I don't quite remember; or all the stories I dreamt up, but never recorded, and they are forever lost.

In many cases I'm missing pieces of the stories, or I'm melding them together, or I, for the life of me, just can't remember. And it's upsetting to me, to know, how many incredible stories died with my loved ones; or how many I lost, because I didn't take those few moments to locate a pen and paper and jot a few things down.

People who fought in World War II, or survived the Holocaust; these people aren't going to be alive forever. In fact, I'm pretty sure that only a handful are still alive at this very moment. How easily we forget, that part of the gift we have as human beings, is our ability to preserve and record, the human experience. And we can do this with both tremendous precision and creativity.

"I just poured myself a glass of orange soda." You can see that in your mind. Everyone knows what a glass of orange soda looks like. That short sentence created a picture in your mind, and that picture in your mind was generated by your knowledge and exper- ience. I could have said, "I just poured myself a drink." But now, perhaps what you see in your mind, would be different than what another would see in his or her mind, and entirely different than the truth.

And that's how the music is today. All the music sounds exactly the same. And the same assholes, keep working with each other, pairing up, to perform collaborations, which is nothing more than them sounding exactly the same way they have on every other album they've been a part of.

Pitbull? Who the hell even heard of this guy a few years ago? No-one. Now he's everywhere. How many songs is this guy going to be a part of? How long will he enjoy his time in the sun?

And in every song, Pitbull is Pitbull. That I will give him. If you've heard even one of Pitbull's songs, you've heard them all. You are not going to listen to and hear a song with him in it and say, "I wonder who that is singing?"

I feel sorry for myself and others who go to the bookstore looking for something "new" to read. Of course we know of the thousands of extraordinary classics and books we should read in our lifetime; we're getting around to those. But I agree with you; it's always nice to get something new, something current. When it comes to anything new, I look at the selections of books the stores are presenting and trying to slam down our throats, and I find myself trying to convince myself, that something "might be interesting."

I'm never really excited. I haven't been excited about a "new book" in years. I feel like I'm taking a real chance, and the chances are, the book is probably going to be a piece of shit. Any competent writer can write a good beginning and memorable ending.

Today I was thinking about every woman I have ever known or met named: Gina. And it is amazing, but what I came up with is one thousand percent true. All are very well endowed.

I have never seen a Gina that didn't have anywhere from ample to completely enormous tits. And I don't know what is up with that? But if anyone is having a little girl, and they name her "Gina"...dads should beware. Your little girl is going to grow up with huge knockers!

The first girl I ever had a crush on in seventh grade; her locker was right next to mine, and her name was Gina. She was no exception to this rule. She was the only girl in my class who had "double-D's" at such a young age. I'm pretty sure later in life she had to have a breast reduction, because she was having issues with her back.

...also by Vincenzo Scipioni
...and COMING SOON!

The Last Paperback (the 1st Novel to incorporate Microsoft Tags) ...a story about knowing, attraction, intimacy, estrangement, departure, and new found hopes.

...additional future novels and collections include:

*The Evolution and Digression of Words
*Unseeing Eyes
*When Time Went Back to Zero
*5076: When Children Rule!
*Silent Pages, Loud Thoughts, Short Stories (Volume II)
*What God Doesn't Know
*Existing With Pain, Living in Reality
*Un-authored, Un-titled, Just Found
*Finding Einstein
*Silent Pages, Loud Thoughts, Short Stories (Volume III & IV)
*Only the Dog Knows: A Family's Journey Into Another Universe
*What We Were, Are, Should Be, and Becoming
*Tony
*Love and Unity
*9 Short Stores That Tie Up All the Loose Ends in Life
*Time, Being, and Awareness

(If you enjoyed *Silent Pages, Loud Thoughts, Short Stories* (Volume 1) go to your local bookstore, have them order 2 or 3 copies, buy one for a friend, and leave the other copies. This publication needs your help and exposure in your community and local bookstore.)

-Peer Pressure

Listen to me. Would you just listen to me please? I am your friend. What happened to you is messed up. I don't know why it happened. Shit happens and it's over. It's in the past. So, calm down, stop thinking and worrying, and just listen.

Are you listening now? OK. The most illegal part about what "we" are going to do right now…is the amount of FUN we are going to have. I got this yesterday. It's just a little baggie. And I say, let's do this! Let's run around a little. Yes! That's what I'm talking about! That smile is the first sign of life I've seen out of you all day.

Come here. That's what I'm saying! It's not like we're doing heroin. And everyone today enjoys some drugs every once in a while.

HOPE CHILDREN'S FUND

Like many other African countries, Kenya is grappling with the challenges of modernizing in an era of a rapidly globalizing world. The failure or ruling elite to develop suitable national policies, the prevalent economic corruption, and the mismanagement of public resources, have left the country with inadequate social services and overwhelmed infrastructure. Perennial drought and frequent political instability have only helped to aggravate the situation. Of the country's population estimated to be 40 million, forty-five percent are below 14 years of age. With a GDP of just $800, fifty percent of the population lives below the poverty line. Unemployment is well above forty percent.

To compound the crisis, the AIDS pandemic has ravaged many parts of the country leaving thousands of children to fend for themselves. Consequently, the population of children living in the streets has become a crisis. **HOPE CHILDREN'S FUND**, so far, has taken 79 of these young people off the streets and given them a home. Hope Children's Fund endeavors to equip them with the education and love essential to prepare them for a productive adult life. All the funds raised by Hope Children's Fund support this effort.

Vincenzo Scipioni proudly supports Hope Children's Fund and Co-President Larry Hohler in their quest to help as many young people as they can in a country that clearly needs global support. A portion of the profits from the initial sale of *"Silent Pages, Loud Thoughts, Short Stories"* (Volume 1) will go to the Hope Children's Fund in an effort to sponsor more children. It is Vincenzo Scipioni's hope that his work can continue to support Hope Children's Fund annually; as well as many other humanitarian endeavors.

To find out more information, how to become more involved, or contribute to Hope Children's Fund directly, go to:

http://hopechildrensfund.org

or send your contributions to:

Hope Children's Fund, Ltd.
P.O. Box 387
Setauket, NY 11733

phone number:

(631) 473- 1662

Are you looking…

for some of the *coolest* clothing on the planet by the most recognized faceless icon on Twitter and your favorite author? Be sure to check out:

http://www.unseeingeyes.com

do you want
to hear
What Vincenzo
sounds like?
GO TO:

http://www.youtube.com/UnseeingEyesSpeaks